Aryn's
Desire

Aryn's Desire

AMAZON BESTSELLING AUTHOR

Zoey Derrick

COVER

Cover Model: Christopher John
Photographer: Assad Shalhoub
CJC Photography: http://www.cjc-photography.com
Cover Design: Parajunkee Design www.parajunkee.net

EDITING

Mandy Smith & Lorraine Montuori - Raw Kink Publishing
www.rawkinkpublishing.com

For The Z-Team - For being here for me, for encouraging me and for begging me for more.

For all the latest news on Zoey's Books, please find her on Facebook: https://www.facebook.com/zoey.derrick/, Her Newsletter: http://eepurl.com/bfoZob or her website: http://zoeyderrick.net

Best Selling Erotic, Paranormal and Contemporary Romance author Zoey Derrick comes from Glendale, Arizona. Zoey, was a mortgage underwriter by day and is now a romance and erotica novelist full-time. She writes stories as hot as the desert sun itself. It is this passion that drips off of her work, bringing excitement to anyone who enjoys a good and sensual love story.

Not only does she aim to take her readers on an erotic dance that lasts the night, it allows her to empty her mind of stories we all wish were true. Her stories are hopeful yet true to life, skillfully avoiding melodrama and the unrealistic, bringing her gripping Erotica only closer to the heart of those that dare dipping into it.

The intimacy of her fantasies that she shares with her readers is thrilling and encouraging, climactic yet full of suspense. She is a loving mistress, up for anything, of which any reader is doomed to return to again and again.

The Beginning of the Bold Universe...

Finding Love's Wings
Chasing Love's Wings
Or
The Love's Wings Series Box Set

One Week: 365 Days
Also Available in Audiobook from Audible
Or
The Bold Beginnings Box Set

Claiming Addison
Craving Talon
Redeeming Kyle

Taming Dex
Devouring Raine

Defining US: The Calvin & Eric Story

Her Paranormal Universe:

Give Me Reason
Give Me Hope
Give Me Desire
Give Me Love

BOLD SECURITY

ONE

~ ARYN *~*

I wish I could tell you that the chick slobbering all over my dick was actually doing a good job. Okay, maybe she's not doing a half bad job, but I'll be damned if I'm enjoying it. Sure, it will get me off, eventually, but I'd hardly call it a qualified success.

"That's it, baby," I encourage her. She's blonde and well, easy. I picked her up in a bar not more than an hour ago, and here we are, in the back of my Durango, in some parking lot in the middle of Los Angeles.

Since 69 Bottles came off tour about seven months ago, I haven't had much luck in the chick department. In fact, the last semi-decent experience I had was all the way back in New York, with my charge and best friend Dex and his new wife, Raine. Though that was hardly a success either. Sure, Raine is hot as hell, but the chick had a set of balls on her that drove me mad. Okay, not really balls, but she sure stuck it to Dex. That man was whipped from day one.

I slide my hand into the blonde's hair, guiding and helping her though it seems pointless. I'd had no intention of screwing her, but… "I have an idea," I tell her and I pull a condom from my pocket and hand it to her. Her eyes light up and she doesn't hesitate to rip it open. I fight the urge to roll my eyes. She has the doe-eyed look down pat and I know where this is going. She's going to ask for my number when this is over, but what's sad is I don't remember her name. If she told me, I didn't hear it, or I just don't give a shit.

She rolls the condom over my cock and then sits up, unhooking her bra, though why she's wearing one is kind of beyond me. She's barely big enough to handle one and it's disappointing really. Though I've always considered myself more of an ass man than a boob man, having both is always a perk.

She makes a sad attempt at pressing her tits together around my cock and I let my head fall back. Trying to act interested, though my mind starts to wander elsewhere.

I think back to that night in New York. I'm not entirely sure what went wrong with Raine and Dex that night, why he froze and why she bolted out the door. The reason for my distraction didn't have much to do with Raine or that I was sticking my dick in her, but more to the fact that Dex was naked.

I shake my head, dispelling the thoughts of Dex. No, I'm not gay. I like boobs, I like cunts and the asses that come with them.

She unzips her pants, momentarily distracting me. Oddly enough, a vision comes to mind…what if she had a cock? What if she were…yeah, it's possible. She's not my most feminine of choices. Her jeans slide down, taking her panties with them and I'm met with… I sigh, though to her it probably sounds more like desire as she awkwardly makes her way out of her jeans.

When she's free of the trap of pants, she slides her hand down her stomach and over her hairless mound. Fingering her pussy briefly before bringing her hand to her mouth, licking it and returning it to her slit. She has a nice big clit, one that would be great for sucking on, but I'm definitely not in the mood for that, not tonight.

Her eyes roll up into her head as she pleasures herself. In an effort to keep myself hard, I grab my dick in my hand and start to stroke it gently while watching her. Though I see her, I'm looking through her more than I'm actually paying attention to her. I'm not conceited, okay maybe a little, but I'm a good looking guy. I'm tall, muscular with my own sex appeal and of course the dirty blond hair everyone loves, but this chick has got to be a new low for me. Though I never actually hand over my real name when meeting chicks in clubs, this one in particular got the name I use when I really want nothing more to do with them.

After a few more moans, strokes and flicks of fingers, she finally straddles me. Her pussy comes to rest over the head of my cock. I smell her arousal now and though she doesn't smell awful, it's definitely not a sweet smell, the smell I love so much. She lowers herself onto my shaft. "Mmm," I moan, she doesn't feel half bad. A little snug, this might not be so bad.

Once she's lowered herself onto my cock, she sits up, grabbing hold of the handles that run along the top of the windows in the back of my truck to give herself leverage and I give her points for creativity.

In an attempt to put forth some effort into this excursion, I cup her small tits in my big hands, and roll her tiny nipples between my thumb and forefinger. She moans and her pussy clenches down on my cock. She starts to grind. Her eyes roll up into her head again and she begins moaning louder and louder, to the point of a high pitched squeal.

Her pussy convulses, her hips twitch and she cries out as she orgasms and then stops.

Her hands release the straps and she falls forward onto my chest, snuggling into me. You have got to be kidding me.

I try to slide my cock into her pussy but the angle is awful and she clamps her hips down on me and squeezes me out.

I roll my eyes. A fucking one and done. No wonder why she sucked my cock for so long. If she'd been any good at it, I might have been able to come when she did, but nope.

My cock goes soft. The condom is irritating me. "Up you go." I fight the urge to growl in anger at her.

She groans and snuggles into me.

"Nope, you gotta get up. I gotta take this condom off," I say through clenched teeth and she lazily starts to move, finally rolling off me to sit next to me.

I pull the condom from my dick and tie it off, then stuff it into the trash bag I keep in the back of my truck and I pull my jeans up. "You need to get dressed before I open the door," I tell her and she whines and reluctantly gets up.

She lays her head on my back, wrapping her arms around me. Yup, I should have known she'd be the type. I pat her arm. "I gotta get moving. I have to be to work in an hour," I lie.

"Where do you work?" she says sleepily.

"I'm a bouncer in a bar."

"Oh? What bar?"

"It's exclusive," I grumble.

"Can I come with you?"

I fight the urge to sigh while rolling my eyes. "Not tonight, sweetheart."

"Some other night?"

"Definitely," I lie again.

"Okay, Mike." Oh good, she was paying attention. "I need to get your number," she says as she lets me go and goes fishing for her jeans.

"After you get dressed," I tell her and she scurries into action, pulling her jeans on, then her top. She conveniently forgets her panties. I've seen this routine before; she's going to give them to me as 'something to remember our first night together'.

Once she's sufficiently covered, I pop the back gate and climb out. She follows shortly after, phone in hand, ready to put in my number.

"What's your number, baby?" she coos.

"Nine oh three, five, seven, six, eight," I tell her and she quickly keys it in. I can't help but glance over her shoulder, curious what I got labeled this time. Hottie Mike. I roll my eyes again, she can't even be original.

"Great, I just texted you mine."

"Perfect." There is a chime that rings from the front seat of my car, she hears it and turns toward me. "Got it," I tell her.

She wraps her arms around me. "I wish you didn't have to go so soon."

"I know, I'm sorry." I give her a tentative pat on the back. "But text me," I tell her with a smirk.

"Alright," she says but doesn't release me, instead she tucks something into my back pocket. Her panties.

"What are you doing?" I pull back.

"Oh, just something for you to remember me by."

I smile sweetly at her. The only person in this conversation that knows the smile is fake is me.

I lean down and kiss her quickly on the head and I close the gate of the truck and move around it. She follows and the pleasantries continue for another minute or so before she heads back inside the bar and I pull out. As soon as I round the corner, out of sight, I pull her panties from my pocket and I toss them out the window. I look at my phone.

There's a text from Dex. "You have excellent timing, motherfucker." I smile.

TWO

"I'm driving, what's up?"

"Where are you?" Dex asks. I called him because I needed to put some distance between me and the bar.

"I was out."

"Trolling again? Did you score?"

"Shut it," I snap.

"Wow, what the hell climbed up your cooter?"

"Fuck off," I tell him again.

"No, seriously, what's the deal?"

"Not a conversation to have on the phone. What do you need?" I let the tension and my irritation roll off me the longer Dex is on my phone. Dex and I have been the best of friends since the moment we met a few years ago. Though being a bodyguard should prevent personal relationships, being in close proximity to Dex is something that's required. I quickly learned that he needed me more than he realized and by needing me, it usually meant rescuing him from his revolving door of women or retrieving him from all night drug binges. At least until he got sober. Now I seem to be his voice of reason, well, I was until Raine came along.

No, I'm not bitter about it. She is great to him and even better for him. She and I get along well, despite our history back in New York. I've slept with my best friend's wife. Though I'd hardly call it that and I don't dwell on the fact that it happened. The night was fucked up from the word go and only got worse. I'm not the type to feel guilty about sleeping with a woman, but I did when it came to her. I knew then that she and Dex were meant to be together and I just got in the way.

"Alright, how about Tuesday night, our place?" he asks.

"What time?"

I can tell he pulls away from the phone because when he talks to Raine, he's muffled, but I hear, "He's coming, what time?"

I don't hear Raine's reply and all I want to do is bite back that I haven't said I'd come. Then again, Dex knows me better than that. "Any time after five," he finally answers.

"Yeah, alright. Should I bring anything?"

"A date."

I snort, "Like that's ever gonna happen."

"No, we got it covered," Dex replies, dodging my comment. We seem to be having these conversations more and more lately.

"Anyone else coming?" I ask.

"Nope, just you. Dinner, and a chat."

"About what?" I ask, curiosity getting the better of me as I take the ramp onto the highway, headed toward home. Not that home is really where I want to be, but it's better than being out. At least there I can rub out the orgasm Blondie failed to take from me. I shudder.

"Don't worry about it. We'll have more details on Tuesday and we can go from there."

I roll my eyes for the hundredth time tonight. "Yeah, alright. I'll be there."

"See you then."

"Later," I tell him and hit the end button on my steering wheel.

Tonight is Sunday. I have a meeting with Mills, my boss, and Cami, Mills's boss and owner of Bold International, tomorrow that will likely take up my whole day. It's rare that those downtown trips last less than an hour.

Then…well, fuck, I have nothing else to do until Tuesday.

Arriving home is bittersweet. My apartment is tiny, a mess and well, what would you expect on a bodyguard's salary, at least, when he doesn't work consistently. I am pretty sure that is what tomorrow is all about. Mills rarely calls me into meetings with the Bold bigwigs unless it's something ridiculously important. I've been a bodyguard for Bold International for the last four years. Working for them has led me to work with celebrities, musicians and the like. Which is how I ended up one of a small handful of bodyguards for the 69 Bottles nationwide tour this last spring. If Mills is calling me in, more than likely it has something to do with needing me somewhere else. Which is fine considering the band isn't doing anything for a while.

My apartment is a modest one bedroom in a fourplex building. My apartment is on the bottom right. My neighbor is an older lady who I don't see much, but who has always been nice to me when I've seen her.

The apartment above me is occupied by a family of three. Their son is like four or five, and even though kids are not my favorite humans, this one isn't so bad. He doesn't jump around too much. The apartment upstairs and opposite is vacant and has been for some time. When I knew Raine and Dex were looking, they'd come over and looked at it, but then Addison, 69 Bottles' public relations representative and the wife of 69 Bottles frontman Talon Carver and the band's manager Kyle Black, offered up her condo and I can't say I blamed them for taking that over this little building.

I toss my mail on the counter and go to the fridge, grabbing a beer and throwing my keys in the bowl.

Bringing my beer with me to my bedroom, I unholster my sidearm and lock it in the safe in my closet before shedding my clothes. As soon as I'm naked and looking down, I see my dick sticking to itself, reminding me of the wasted condom. I roll my eyes again.

I've been with a lot of women. I am not going to lie about that, but never have I ever had a one and done like that before. Jesus. You'd think that I would have had it happen before, but she had no regard for me whatsoever, either that or she thought the little grunts I'd given her were me coming and… I shake my head. It's not worth dwelling on. At least not if I plan to stroke one out before getting out of the shower.

Being six-three and a solid two seventy-five has its advantages. The girls love the bigger, muscular guys and while I don't consider myself to be a big guy, they usually do. Not to mention there are not too many guys much bigger than I am. Though Dex has me in the height department by about an inch and his arms are definitely bigger than mine, he's pretty lean throughout the rest of his body. I guess being a drummer has its advantages in the arms department.

I run my hands through my dirty blond hair, it's grown out some since being on tour. I usually keep it military short, but lately I haven't cared much. Since Dex hooked up with Raine while on tour, we haven't gone out much like we used to. Dex was a regular party animal and womanizer, until her.

If you'd asked me what my ideal woman looks like, I'd tell you to shove it. I haven't a fucking clue. I'm thirty-four fucking years old and I've had less than a handful of relationships that have lasted longer than a week. Usually, because I get bored and move on, stop returning phone calls or change my number. I've never once brought a woman home to my apartment, thank god - they don't need to turn stalker.

The strangest part about this is the fact that I've never thought of myself as being a one-woman kind of guy. The idea of monogamy is...I shudder at my own internal thoughts. Basically, I cannot imagine one person I could spend my whole life with.

When Addison hooked up with both Talon and Kyle while 69 Bottles was on tour, I'd started to wonder if that was the type of relationship for me. An open one. I'd never really thought about it before, but I often wonder if I too could handle another guy and a woman.

It's that thought that makes me shiver and my cock harden.

When Dex and Raine hooked up, and for as many times as Dex and I shared women, I wondered if maybe the three of us would end up together. I could tell from the way Raine looked at me that she was attracted to me and the feeling was mutual. But like any other woman in my life, I managed to brush it off as soon as I got off. When Dex started babbling on and on about her, I knew then that he wasn't that type of guy at all. I cannot imagine him sharing his woman with anyone.

The idea of a threesome with Dex and Raine morphed into me with two different women at the same time. One curvy and luscious, the other skinnier but she has an amazing ass. The kind I could sink my fingers into as I drill my cock deep into her pussy while her face is buried in the cunt of the curvy, well-endowed partner laying spread eagle on the bed.

I shiver as I take my cock in my hand and start to stroke. Closing my eyes, I let the fantasy fill me. The sensations of hands, hot cunts, and warm mouths is enough to tip me over the edge and into an orgasm that sends my cum flying all over the shower and forces me to brace myself against the wall so I don't fall over.

I clean up my mess, wash myself off and climb out of the shower, pulling on a pair of pajama pants. I pull my suit from the closet, inspect it, and hang it back on the bar. I'll need it for tomorrow.

Once that's done, I go into the living room, grabbing another beer along the way before hitting the couch and watching TV. Jesus, my life sucks.

THREE

I haven't been up on the top floor of Bold International since before the start of my career with 69 Bottles. Though they are my true priority- well, Dex and Raine are- I often get reassigned for temporary gigs when the band doesn't really need me.

Since the twins were born, Addison, Talon & Kyle's, they haven't had much need for us. Mills usually handles things with them when necessary and then pulls Rusty, another of Bold's security guys and Mills's second in command, into the mix when he needs another set of eyes or hands.

Dex and Raine, though they go out frequently, usually tell me to take a hike, which is fine, but I usually don't go very far. But Dex is the band's drummer and while he's insanely hot, he's not the popular target that Talon is as the band's lead.

Mouse and Peacock, 69 Bottles' guitarists, have Casey, who from my understanding is around them a lot of the time just as friends. Hell, the last I'd heard a couple weeks back was that Casey had moved in with them temporarily. Which I thought was rather odd, given the fact that they just got married about a month ago. Oh well, not my monkey, not my circus.

"Cami is ready for you," Cami's assistant says from behind her desk. I actually kind of miss having Raine up here. But she's doing a damn good job making a name for herself by helping Addison out and taking on more clients.

"Thanks," I mutter as I pass her and knock on the door to Cami's office.

"Come in," Cami says from the other side and I open the door.

Sitting at her desk, Cami is a petite little pocket rocket of a CEO. The girl has no qualms about expressing who she is. Often showing up with multi-colored hair and clothing that makes no secret of the tattoos she wears. When I say she wears them, she wears them and not the other way around. Sitting across from her in one of the two chairs is Mills.

Mills is tall, same height as me, but a little wider in the shoulders. He's ex-military and it shows. Not just in the short buzz cut, but the way he carries himself and his ability to think quickly and efficiently. I guess that may be why we've bonded so well. Though he is ex-Marine and I'm ex-Army, the respect for each other is mutual.

"Thanks for coming in on such short notice," Cami tells me as she stands up. Mills joins her and we exchange handshakes and pleasantries before she gets down to the brass tacks of why I'm here.

"We need your help," Mills tells me.

"I figured as much. What's up?" I ask.

"We have a client. Alyssa Serin, who will be doing a worldwide release tour for an upcoming movie. She needs a small detail team to travel with her."

"Why the detail?" I ask. There usually isn't a need to add a full detail unless there have been issues arising either with her current staff or outside influences.

"She's had a bit of a problem with her current head of security. He's unfocused and frankly, she's concerned that her safety is in jeopardy when it comes to big, public events," Cami answers. Mills hasn't said anything at this point and I start to wonder why he's here.

"Will I have to work with this idiot?" I ask.

"No," Mills states firmly. "We're working to reassign him to someone who is on a much smaller scale than Alyssa. Someone who can afford a distracted guard."

I curl my lip. "Why not just fire him?" I ask. "I mean, it's none of my business, but obviously he's not doing his job very well."

"Well, we're getting there. But often times when we see a distraction, there are other underlying factors and in this case, I'm pretty confident that is the issue," Cami tells me.

"Regardless of that. You'd have a small team of three, including yourself. One spot is already filled with Troy." I nod my approval. Troy joined 69 Bottles' security team about halfway through the tour, after a couple of unfortunate incidents involving Addison. He's good people, and very efficient at what he does. I'm honored to have him as part of any team I am on. "And the other spot is up to you."

"What about Casey?" I ask. Casey is a great choice as a third person. He's efficient enough and he follows directions well. Not to mention that the little shit is quick and has an uncanny ability to sneak up on you. A great tactic when trying to stay incognito.

Mills and Cami both look at each other, before Mills turns back to me and replies, "We'd planned on asking him."

"Good, I think he'd be a good bet," I tell them both. "When does this so-called tour start?" I ask them.

"You're scheduled to return from the album launch on the fifteenth, so that will give you a little over a week. The tour starts here in Los Angeles on the twenty-fourth." She looks to Mills. "We'll have to figure out Dex and Raine's schedule, whether they're going from North Carolina to New York or coming back here then going."

"Dex and Raine are going to North Carolina?" I ask, puzzled. Neither one of them has said anything to me about this trip.

"Yeah, they're leaving later this week." Cami gives me a puzzled look in return.

I raise an eyebrow. "That's news to me."

"Oh," Cami says, surprised. "I'd only heard about it this morning, so…"

"We have plans tomorrow to get together, unless they call me before then."

"Oh, okay, good," Cami says, flustered.

"If you take the new assignment; which we're not giving you much choice," Cami smirks, "When you return from the album launch, we'll need you to get together with Alyssa to start working and figuring out your plans." She hands me a stapled stack of papers. "In there is the itinerary, schedule of events and things of that nature. It is a promo tour, so there are premieres, as well as the radio station and TV events that will fill up your days in the various places. Los Angeles and New York are up first, followed by Nashville, London, Berlin and finally Sydney, Australia. Travel will be intense, hitting many places quickly. Alyssa is the lead, so she is required by the studio to be at all these events. There are several hundred other ones, but she's only taking these main markets."

"That's a hell of a lot of pond hopping. Though I've never been to Berlin or Sydney before," I tell her honestly.

"We've made arrangements with some of our affiliates to step in and help out on the foreign stops. We can't expect you to handle transportation and the likes when you barely know the city itself," Mills tells me, and I nod my understanding and approval.

We continue talking about the finer points that I need to be aware of before I sign my contract and I'm out the door. All the information I need is in my hands. Mills catches up to me after I leave the office. "Thanks for doing this," he says.

"No problem. I'm assuming you've got Dex, Eric and Calvin covered while Casey and I are away?"

"Absolutely. I'm pulling in Leroy, so between Rusty, Tori, Leroy, and myself, it's handled. They don't have anything else on the schedule until well after you're back home."

I nod and give him a smile. "Thanks for giving me my own team," I tell him, and I honestly mean it. Though I've worked with Mills for a few years, I've never tried to step on his toes, which is hard as fuck when you're trying to advance in this business.

"You've earned it, and you deserve it. I've met Alyssa and she's very nice, cooperative, she shouldn't give you too much hassle."

I smile again. "That's good to know, but I'm sure I could handle her if that wasn't the case."

He smiles then and extends his hand. "I know you can." I take his hand and he grabs my shoulder, giving it a squeeze as the elevator arrives. "I'm a phone call away. But I'm sure I'll see you before then. There's that dinner thing on Wednesday this week."

The light bulb goes off. "I'd nearly forgotten. Then I will see you Wednesday."

We part ways when I step into the elevator and descend back to the first floor and to the parking garage.

I text **Dex**: What the hell is in Nashville?
Dex to Beck: How the hell did you find out?
Beck to Dex: Been reassigned…tell you more tomorrow.
Dex to Beck: Fuck that, come over tonight.
Beck to Dex: Yeah, alright, be there in an hour.
Dex to Beck: We're home.
Beck to Dex: Duh, I'm not there…LOL
Dex to Beck: Shut it and hurry up.

I climb into my truck and pull out of the parking garage, turning right instead of left as I head toward Dex and Raine's condo.

FOUR

"What's with the monkey suit?" Dex asks when he opens the door.

"I had to go into Cami's office today." I hold up my duffle bag. "Mind if I change?"

He opens the door for me to come inside. "Not at all, seeing you dressed like that is unnerving. I want to ask you where the funeral is."

I shoulder check him when I pass and he laughs.

"What'd Cami want?"

"Reassignment."

"I knew that. Who? When?"

"Nosy much?" I cock an eyebrow at him.

"Well, I need you to come to North Carolina and Nashville with us, so yeah, you gonna be able to go?"

"What makes you think I want to go?" I snicker.

He rolls his eyes. "Because you're having so much fun here," he says, and he's right. I get bored when I'm stuck in one place too long and Los Angeles is getting on my nerves.

"Yeah, since Cami seemed to know more about it than I do, she would have picked someone else if it would interfere with your trip. So when are we leaving?"

"Friday," Raine says as she comes down the stairs. She's shorter, maybe five-five or five-six with multi-colored hair, everything from blonde, black, red and even some shades of brown about shoulder length. Despite being short, she's confident and well, gorgeous.

"Hi, sweetheart," I tell her and she smiles at me.

"Hey." She smiles as she rounds the banister and comes over to give me a hug.

"You doing alright?" I ask.

"Never better," she smiles up at me. "We're gonna be gone for almost two weeks. That won't be a problem, will it?" she asks honestly.

I shake my head. "Over Christmas and New Year's?" She nods. "No, so long as I have a couple days back home before taking off for New York. Unless we're going straight to New York from there?"

"I hadn't thought about that," Raine adds. "Maybe we should just make arrangements to get up there afterwards, rather than coming back here?" She looks at Dex who shrugs.

"Whatever you guys decide is fine, I just need to know whether I have to pack all my shit for New York too," I add.

"Our friend Derek, the one we're staying with, is sending his plane here to fly us to North Carolina, so whatever luggage you need won't be an issue," Raine tells me. Are private planes flying across the country to pick up these two knuckleheads? Must be nice to have friends in high places.

"Well, you guys decide. I'll let Mills know one way or the other."

"Oh, that won't be a problem," Dex chimes in. "Go change, that suit is making me crazy. Get comfortable. We're ordering in and we have booze," he laughs as he heads into the kitchen with Raine in tow.

Their condo is nice. It's modern, open, with massive eighteen to twenty foot ceilings. Their room is upstairs, a loft. They have a guest room downstairs and another room, but that door is always closed. I don't know what's actually in there, and frankly, I've never asked.

I go into the guest room and toss my bag on the bed and undo my shirt. I'd taken off my jacket before getting in the car, but I threw it back on so I could hang it up when I got inside.

I quickly change into a pair of black button-up flannel pants that look like jeans, but they're fucking comfortable as hell, and a t-shirt. I left my shoes off. Being here at Dex and Raine's is nothing unusual for me. In fact, I've spent many nights here since they moved in. Usually too tired to drive home after a night out. Or on nights like this when we're just chilling, talking, drinking, eating, or having a movie marathon. It might be corny, but being around them is often a relief. I actually feel like I belong somewhere.

The fantasy from last night plays through my mind as I leave the bedroom, and thankfully, I don't get hard from it. That would be a little awkward and impossible to explain, especially in these pants.

"Here you go." Raine hands me a cold beer as I step into the kitchen.

"Thanks," I tell her and I take a seat on the stool at the breakfast bar of the kitchen and watch as she and Dex do normal everyday things.

There is something odd about the way Raine moves around him. This isn't the first time I've noticed this about the two of them, but each time, it becomes a little more pronounced. The fact that it's Raine who hands me my drinks and food doesn't go unnoticed by me anytime we're together, and there is always a sparkle of approval in Dex's eyes when she does things like that.

I've often wanted to ask him about it, but it's never quite the right time, place or circumstances to do so. I toy with the idea of asking now, but instead, I swallow down some beer.

"What's on the menu tonight?" I ask.

"That Chinese place you like so much," Raine says with a smile and I smile back.

"Sounds great," I tell her before taking another sip of my beer. "You sure we're not going anywhere tonight?" I ask before I keep drinking. If I keep it up, I'll be good for nothing.

"Nope, we're staying in," Dex says as he turns around, holding up his own beer and we clink our bottles together.

"So what's in North Carolina and Nashville?"

Raine looks at Dex quickly, but goes back to putting dishes away and he answers, "We're going to see Derek and his wife Dacotah. He's got a ranch house in the mountains and then Nashville has a couple of things we want to go do." His voice holds a hint of mischief and is cryptic even for Dex. I want to pester him for it, but I let it go, for now.

"So why do you need me? Doesn't Derek have his own team?"

"He does," Raine answers as she sets plates down on the breakfast bar. The door buzzer rings and she scurries off to answer it.

"So then, why do you need me there?"

"Just thought you'd like to get out of town," Dex replies before going to the fridge for something.

"I do, but I'd hate to be the fifth wheel for you guys."

He smiles. "Well, I don't see how that would be possible. Besides, we'll be going out frequently and if his team has the detail, well, then you can just relax and hang out."

Raine comes bounding back into the kitchen with two plastic sacks tied up and stuffed full of the best Chinese food I've ever had. She and Dex start unpacking and scattering cartons across the breakfast bar and when they're done, we all dig in.

"So what's wrong with you?" Dex asks.

"What do you mean?" I respond before I finish off my fourth beer, my second since finishing dinner.

"You're just so... I don't know, you seem off. Not getting any?"

I roll my eyes. Leave it to Dex to turn it sexual. "Nothing worth mentioning," I mutter.

"That bad?" he probes.

I shrug. "I don't know. I'm just bored I guess."

"Bars and easy women no longer your thing?"

I stare at him, unsure of how to answer that. Raine delivers another beer and takes my empty. "Thanks, love," Dex says and Raine lights up from his praise.

"You're welcome." Her voice trails off like she was going to say something but then stopped herself.

"Alright, enough of this cryptic crap. What is the deal with you two?"

"What do you mean?" Dex counters.

"Oh, don't play coy with me. I see how you two act around each other, I'm not stupid."

Raine looks at Dex, gives him a small smile and shrugs. "Master," she says and I'm not sure if she's finishing her statement from a moment ago or acknowledging him.

Dex is staring at me intently like I'm supposed to get something, some inside joke.

Master...

I let the word roll around in my brain.

She's always serving me, and Dex. She is always cleaning up, seeking permission...

"Oh, my, god." I look at Dex then Raine and then back to Dex. "For real?" I ask and he nods with a smirk of satisfaction. "Since when?"

"Since the Nashville tour stop."

I give him a quizzical look.

"Do you remember that night, in Nashville, when we went out, without you?"

"Uh, yeah." I nod.

"Well, we went out with Derek and Dacotah. They took us to a club."

I'm pretty sure my face portrays shock, confusion, curiosity and a whole lot more that I can't put my finger on at the moment. "So what, you went to the club and just decided that she was going to be what? Your slave?"

"Not exactly," Dex answers. "But it opened our eyes to something we both already kind of knew we wanted. Derek made himself available to help us. When we were in Vegas-"

"When you got married without telling anyone," I interrupt with a grumble and both of them laugh.

"Yeah, that. We were with Derek and Dacotah that whole week. We spent the week further discussing what we wanted from a relationship and well, a whole lot more."

"I'm pretty sure I don't want to know what that 'whole lot more' is. But why have you never told me this before?" I ask, a little hurt at the fact that I know so much about them, but now I feel like I knew nothing all this time.

"We honestly haven't told anyone," Raine chimes in. "Not that we didn't want to, but...well, the lifestyle, while getting better, isn't widely accepted. Not to mention the fact that things were just getting started between us while we were on tour and we're still working on it." She smiles sweetly at Dex who returns the smile and then he gestures for her to come to him. She does so dutifully and stands next to him. He wraps his arm around her and she melts at his touch.

Watching them now and knowing that they have that kind of dynamic, it all makes perfect sense. The way she blossoms under his praise and even sometimes when he gets a little stern with her, though those times seem rare.

"How did you know you wanted that kind of relationship?" I ask, but the question isn't directed at either one of them, just a general question.

It's Raine who answers, "I've always felt submissive, though I never imagined the dynamic that we have being what I would want."

"What kind of dynamic is that?" I feel like I've put these two in the spotlight, but I am overly curious about it.

"Master and slave," Dex says succinctly.

FIVE

"Every relationship is different. While we have that dynamic, some people are just Dominant and submissive," Dex adds.

"Isn't that the same thing?" I ask.

He smiles before responding, "In some ways, yes. In other ways, no. Raine submits to me in almost all things, all aspects of her life, versus some people who have more of a 'bedroom'," Yes, he used air quotes, "dynamic."

"Wow," I breathe.

Everything they've just told me is a lot to take in, but the idea intrigues me. Enough so that without any prompting from me, touching or otherwise, my cock grows hard.

"It's a bit overwhelming when you first hear about it, or even talk about it, but I'm not sure how I ever lived without it," Dex says as he squeezes Raine's arm gently, reassuring her and me that he is referring to her.

"Since you seem so bored with women, Beck, have you ever considered something like this?" Raine asks and I shake my head.

"Maybe you should," Dex says with a smirk. "It's certainly something to think about."

"I don't know. I'm not necessarily into giving pain or receiving it."

Raine shakes her head. "You don't have to be. BDSM isn't about pain, it's about pleasure and giving yourself over to someone you trust. Whether as a Top or a bottom."

"I could never submit to anyone," I say.

Dex smirks, "You'd be surprised. There are a lot of men and women who have high profile, high powered jobs that enjoy submitting to someone. Then there are some Tops that have the opposite and often find relief by dominating someone. But your job doesn't make you who you are, it's how you feel inside. So unless you've got some type of inclination toward one or the other, you can't really know for sure."

I shudder. "But pain?"

Raine chuckles, "Master?"

It's weird hearing that come from her mouth, but it spills free so naturally that I'm not sure how I could have missed the endearment in the past.

"Yes, my pet?"

"Can we show him?" she asks with a sweet look on her face.

Dex smiles at her and taps her on the nose. "That might be a good idea." He adjusts himself and reaches into his pocket. I'm not exactly sure at first what he pulls out, but then he is at her necklace. He reveals a small key in his hand and uses it to unlock the necklace. A change in Raine overcomes her the instant the locket is unlocked and Dex removes it from around her neck. She becomes somber, almost, lowering her head and her body relaxes. "Play collar, t-shirt and shorts," he says with a commanding tone in his soft voice.

"Yes, Master. Thank you, Master," she says back to him before he releases her with a kiss on the cheek and she disappears.

I look at Dex. "What is that all about?"

Dex smiles at me. "That necklace is her collar, it's complicated to explain, and probably more than you really need to know right now, but she has a different one that she wears when we're playing. Normally though, she'd be naked, but...well, you know." He smirks. "We won't play tonight, but she may want to show you some things, or I might. It might sound weird, but I brought her into the playroom one time without changing her collar." His voice dips as he continues, "Let's just say, it's a mindset thing for her. That night didn't go so well."

I am thoroughly confused by everything that Dex is telling me. It's too much to take in and comprehend in one sitting, but I am curious about what's going to happen as he leads me toward the infamous closed door. I realize that the door isn't only closed, but locked too when Dex produces a key to unlock it. "I need you to remember to keep an open mind about what is beyond this door."

"Oh believe me, my mind is wide open right now," I tell him and he pushes the door open.

Without any prompting, lights flicker within the room and I step across the threshold.

"It looks like a gym," I tell him as I take in a few different pieces of equipment, as well as a chest of drawers. There are a few implements hanging on the walls. Everything from floggers to whips, cuffs and a few more pervertables.

"It does, but I assure you, this is way more fun."

"So it's about sex?" I ask him as I look at many of the objects around the room.

"No, actually it's not really about sex at all. In fact, Raine and I have never had sex in here."

I turn to look at him. "You've got to be kidding? How could you not?"

He smiles. "That's easy. Yes, when we play it turns me on unlike anything I've ever experienced before, but it isn't about burying myself inside her. It's about taking her to a place where she feels free, where I feel free. Believe it or not, we have some pretty vanilla sex, though it is amplified by the heightened sense of arousal we both feel after being in here, but there are many nights where we don't come in here at all."

"I'm not sure I want to know all of this about my best friend's sex life," I tease.

He chuckles. "Well, if it is something that truly interests you, then I suggest you read up on it. Derek can explain things much better than I can since he's been doing this a lot longer. But it would be nice to bring you to the club rather than ditch you in the middle of Nashville all by yourself."

SIX

I guess going to the club with them is better than Dex sneaking out on me. Though he's done it before, it makes me crazy when I find out about it. It also challenges the trust I have in him when he does it. I have no doubt he'd come up with some convincing argument to ditch me in the middle of Nashville and have no remorse about it whatsoever.

Raine comes into the room, and Dex puts his finger to his lips to silence me. I watch as Raine goes to a cushion on the floor in the corner near the door and she kneels on it. "Watch," Dex mouths to me and I watch with rapt attention as he approaches Raine. When he reaches her, his hand slides over her braided hair and she melts into his touch. He bends down, crouching next to her, and she leans against him between his legs. This is obviously a very intimate moment between them and as much as I want to look away, my eyes are super glued on them. "We will not be doing a full scene tonight, pet. We're just going to show Beck a few things, alright?"

"Yes, Master." Her voice is soft, yet confident. Maybe even a little disappointed, but I have no doubt that if I were in her shoes, I would be disappointed too. I imagine being in here is an adrenaline rush that once it starts, it can't be undone easily.

The idea of being in her shoes sends a shiver up my spine, though not in repulsion, but rather desire. It's unnerving to me, but I can't help wondering if it is the scene that is about to happen or if it has something to do with Dex.

That thought pulls me up short and I do what I can to try and shake off the thought. I haven't the faintest clue where all this shit is coming from all of a sudden. It's not like Dex is a new friend. These thoughts have been a little more frequent since Raine came into his life. Everyone around me has been matched up it seems. Mouse and Peacock found each other, Addison ran away with Talon and Kyle, not to mention Rusty and Tori's advancing relationship. They've moved in with each other, by the way.

Dex keeps talking to Raine, but I've tuned out what he is saying to her. He stands, extends his hand to her and she takes it, rising up off the floor and he ushers her over to me. "What would you like to see?" Dex asks me.

I shrug. "I've never seen any of this stuff before. I wouldn't know where to start."

Dex smiles. "Okay then, Raine, can you get the bench out, please?"

"Yes, Master." She turns and goes over toward what looks like an old kneeling bench that you'd find in the front of churches for communion and she slides it across the wood floor, and it glides easily. Whether by wheels or by those furniture pads, I have no idea.

She centers it in the room and then stands next to it, lowering her head. "Thank you, pet," Dex praises her and she lights up under his gentle praise. "Kneel," he orders and she doesn't hesitate for a nanosecond before turning and positioning herself on the lower step of the bench. If I didn't know any better, by the way she places her hands, I'd think she was actually going to pray.

Dex turns to me. "Raine and I have consensual agreements on what will happen here tonight, as well as rules we follow when we're in here alone. She also has a safeword." I give him a quizzical look, silently asking him to explain. "Pet?"

"Yes, Master?"

"Will you explain to Beck your safeword. Why you have it and what happens if you use it?"

"Yes, Master." She doesn't move from her position on the bench and it only takes a moment for me to understand why- he didn't grant her permission to do so. "My safeword is kit-kat, like the candy. I can use it any time Master pushes me too far or he causes me physical or emotional pain that I cannot tolerate. Or sometimes outside of the playroom, if Master has done something or said something that bothers me, hurts me, or otherwise causes emotional distress." I'm beginning to understand, but she clarifies further by saying, "If my safeword is used, it means all activity stops and we discuss what happened to trigger me to use my safeword. If we're in here, I am immediately removed from the situation I'm in and Master removes me from the room. Allowing me a chance to calm down and for us to discuss what happened. At which point, all playing stops for the night."

"Have you ever used your safeword, pet?"

"Yes, Master," she says with a sadness in her voice and Dex comforts her by stroking his hand along her back and she relaxes.

"Safewords are meant to keep all activities safe, sane and consensual. Also, words like no and stop are often used by parties involved without actually wanting the person to stop what they're doing, or because it is a natural reaction. Having a safeword forces the submissive or bottom to make a conscious decision about stopping the scene. Oftentimes, and we've seen it many times, tears are shed and other emotions come out of a submissive during a scene. In fact, there are a couple of people at a club here in Los Angeles that cry their way into subspace."

"What's that?" I ask.

"That is something we can talk about later, but in short, it is a state of mind that a submissive can find within a scene, or by doing everyday things asked of them by their Top. It's kind of like a euphoria, so to speak."

"Uh, okay?" I say with hesitation. Safewords are not something I've heard of before, but then again, I didn't show up here tonight with the intention of coming in here to their private dungeon, though that seems to be the wrong word for it. It's anything but.

As our time in their room progresses, Dex walks me through some of the instruments he uses. He also has no problem showing me how they feel, either on my forearm or my hand, for some of the paddles and such.

I fought hard at first to keep the erection I'd gotten in the kitchen at bay, but there was something highly arousing feeling each implement and watching Dex use them on Raine directly.

It became evident quickly which items were her favorites and which ones were not. Oddly enough, the ones that were not her favorites, Dex gets very little pleasure using them on her and I had a new found respect for him after that. It seemed as though those objects were likely used in a punishment situation and while she didn't object, scoff or safeword out of him using them, her body language spoke volumes and Dex listened to every word it had to say.

When he was done with some of the impact items, he moved on to some of the restraining items, like cuffs, something called a spreader bar (that was very fascinating by the way) and finally rope. When Dex got to that, Raine visibly melted into a puddle. I gathered quickly, before Dex told me, that it was her favorite item out of everything in this room.

When Dex was done, he helped Raine up and scooped her into his arms. "If you give me a couple of minutes, I'll be back down, unless of course you want to go to bed?"

I shake my head, taking in all that I've seen has left my mind reeling in a million different directions. No way could I go to bed right now.

"I'll be back down in a few minutes," he states and leaves the room with Raine in his arms to carry her upstairs.

Once he leaves the room, I can't help but wander around the room looking at the different things he has in here. Aside from the bench, he has an X shaped vertical stand. It is up against the wall, but it is not mounted to the wall. Hanging from the top of the X are cuffs, one on each arm of the X and then down at the bottom, there is the same. I get the vision of Raine cuffed to it, either facing the cross or facing out and seeing that is nearly my undoing.

To have a woman, held helpless and in the palm of your hand sends a thrill through me. This is a path I must follow. Just the idea of new possibilities is enough to have me wanting to go to a club right this minute and find myself my own little submissive girl.

"A penny for your thoughts?" Dex says from behind me and I turn slowly to face him.

"Why didn't we just go tonight?" I ask him. "Why wait for Nashville?" My eagerness is evident.

"Two reasons. One - our favorite club is closed on Mondays," he smirks at me and continues, "And two, walking into a dungeon isn't something you do on a whim. Oftentimes club members who bring in 'unregistered' guests have to make arrangements before they can do just that. Other times, depending on the club, background checks are required before a guest enters the club. Plus, once you get there you have to sign paperwork. Among other reasons, like the fact that walking into a dungeon as vanilla as you were a couple hours ago would have scared the living hell out of you." He snorts.

"I doubt that," I counter.

"Oh, believe me. Going into a dungeon for the first time, even the second and third time, can be quite overwhelming. No two nights are the same. You either have different people all together or you have various different things going on that night. Like edge play or piercing play."

I shiver. "What is edge play?" I ask.

"Knives, sharp instruments, things that can push you to the brink of fearing for your life."

My eyes go wide.

"No, we're not into that. While it intrigues me, I work very hard to not leave permanent marks on Raine. Temporary ones, however, are another story." His eyes light up as he says this.

"You get off on this?" I ask him.

"Come on, let's grab a beer."

I nod absently as he ushers me from the room, and as he is closing the door, the lights go out. Once outside the room, I can finally breathe easier. Though I hadn't realized I was having a hard time before, but seeing all that equipment, was…well, the ultimate rush of desire.

SEVEN

"You asked, do I get off on that?" Dex says as he slides a beer across the breakfast bar to me. I nod. "Not necessarily. Or maybe rather, in a sense, yes. But the high I get from playing with Raine is more about giving her the things I know she wants. For example, Raine likes pain and a lot of it. But also with pain she likes pleasure and sensual things, like rope for example. Seeing her blossom, seeing her float, is the ultimate high, Beck. I mean, I can't describe how it truly feels when I have her in the palm of my hands like that."

He lets me ponder what he said as we both drink our beers.

I understand what he's saying. It's not about her being in pain, or being trapped by rope or some other restraint, it's about the pleasure she gets in the process.

"It's about giving her a chance to let things go. To free her mind of the burdens of her day, to let me take it from her for just a little while. Since Addison had the twins, Raine has been running ragged, between the band's stuff and Addison's too. She absolutely loves it, devours it. She was made to do exactly what she does and she's damn good at it. But one of the things that makes her good, or maybe even better, is her ability to release it all. To walk in the door of our house and know that I will take over from there."

"I'm not sure I quite understand that part," I tell him, and it's true. The bedroom or play room aspect I understand, but the lifestyle is still beyond my comprehension.

"She has very little decisions when it comes to the house. Things like, what's for dinner? I tell her what's for dinner if I don't cook it myself."

I scoff, "You? Cooking?"

"Shut it," he smirks. "Or the bills? I pay them. I maintain our accounts, handle the bills and she doesn't have to stress about it. But having all of that taken care of makes it easier for her to relax at night. Whether we're in the playroom or not. Now that you know, I imagine you'll see it much more from her. I know when we have other people over it's hard for her to let go of our dynamic, and while it is still there, in the background, she has a few less rules to follow, or a better way of putting it is that she has less things she would normally ask permission for."

"But isn't that a bit controlling? To have a hand in everything she does or doesn't do?"

"You'd have to ask her that. I don't see it as such, but I also know she thrives on it. Certain things that I say or do mean a little more to her, like saying thank you to her is a big one. It reminds her that she's appreciated, that what she's done is appreciated. Though that is usually when it comes to me and no one else."

"I noticed it tonight," I tell him. "Little things that you'd say or do would make her blossom in a way that I've never noticed before. She glows under your praise." I press my lips together. "It almost reminds me of a child seeking approval."

He shrugs. "In some ways, I think that's what she's doing, whether she knows it or not, but you also need to know that she has her own reasons for doing things like that. She never got that approval and praise growing up. So I think it would only be natural that she'd want it now." He sighs, "I understand where your concerns stand, believe me, they were mine too in the beginning of all this, but she explained it to me, explained why she wanted or felt she needed it. Again, communication is vital in this type of relationship. Without her telling me that she wanted that kind of thing from me, I'd have never known. Without her telling me when something I do or say doesn't have the impact that it intended to have, I'd never know where to stop."

I run my hand over my head, feeling the prickles of my freshly buzzed head as I do. "I don't think I'm ever going to understand all this."

Dex smiles, "So does that mean you want to try to understand it?"

"The bedroom side of things? That I get. Spicing things up and adding some kinky in the bedroom is all good, but the relationship side of it, I don't know if I'll ever understand that."

He nods. "Good, because I'm still learning and understanding it myself. Things are smoother now. We've managed to work through the majority of our everyday life with what works and what doesn't. So we go a lot longer between incidents of frustration or even irritation. But the bottom line is that it all comes down to communication. We talk about anything and everything. Oftentimes we spend time after dinner discussing her day and mine, things that happened, and she leaves nothing out, with the exception of names because she's held to confidentiality outside of Addison. It's usually at that point where I decide on the best course for the night. Sometimes it's snuggling on the couch watching television or a movie and other times it involves the playroom, and sometimes, depending on whether she's done something wrong or handled something in a way she shouldn't have, punishments."

I shudder. "Why would you want to punish her?"

He gives me a sad smile. "I never want to punish her, but sometimes it's necessary. Like if she's home, and I'm not - though rare - she has a plan for the day, things to do around the house or errands to run and if she doesn't get them done for reasons other than work interference, that usually involves a punishment of some sort."

"What if you give her too much to do?"

He smiles then answers, "Her lists are too small not to finish in the time frame I give her. Because I'm usually the one at home all day, I usually run the errands, clean up the house, so on a rare day when I'm out of the house right now, it's simple things, like cleaning up her office." He shudders. "That is all on her."

I smile and finish off my beer. "I'm sure I'll have a thousand and one more questions about all of this."

"No doubt, but just remember, every relationship is different. Our relationship is the way that it is because it works for us. What works for us might not work for you, or anyone else for that matter. But let me assure you, she's happy, we're extremely happy and there are days that I just have to turn my Dom side off and be with her, just her. No roles, no rules, no punishments, just her and I. Though those sides of us are always on in one fashion or another, it's freeing to let it all go too. But we both get twitchy, for lack of a better definition, if it goes on for too long." He gives me a smile then takes our bottles and puts them in the trash. "Another?"

I shake my head. "I'm good."

"Overwhelmed?" he asks.

"Yeah, a lot."

He snorts. "Don't worry. Like I said, it's different for everyone. You may find a submissive who doesn't like what Raine likes, or maybe doesn't want a lifestyle relationship, but wants to play hard." I nod and stand up as he continues. "Do some more research. Wikipedia is a good place to start." I scoff at him. "Don't knock it. It's one of the rare sites that have a lot of accurate information on the lifestyle. Plus, when you're ready, there are sites out there specifically for meeting others in the lifestyle, maybe even a submissive, or a Top?" He grins at his question.

"Hell no. There is no way I can do what Raine did tonight," I say with conviction.

He looks skeptical as he says, "But you need to know, I got lucky and met Raine and we had a mutual desire for this. If you're going in looking for someone to Top, you're going to need training and lots of it. Depending on who you find, oftentimes you're required to submit first, learn both sides of the dynamic before you're able to move over to the other side."

A shiver slides up my spine at the idea of being a bottom. I don't like it at all.

"Just remember to keep an open mind about all of it. Regardless of what you see, hear or otherwise, just because someone else is into it, doesn't mean you have to be."

He hits the light switch in the kitchen and we walk into the living room and head toward the hallway where his playroom is and my bedroom. "You know I'm never going to look at that door the same way again, right?"

He laughs, "I know, but now you know, and now you have an idea and a decision to make." His laughter fades into a smile. "Good night, man."

"Night."

EIGHT

"Morning," Dex says as he slides me a cup of coffee.

"Mornin'," I yawn.

"Sleep alright?" he asks and I raise my eyebrow at him. "What?" he retorts.

"Since when do you care about how I slept?" I tease him.

"Shut it," he growls and rolls his eyes.

"Yes, I slept fine. Just not long enough." I look around for a clock. "What time is it anyway?"

"Just after ten," he snickers. "Late night?"

I snort and take a sip of my coffee.

When I'd crawled into bed last night, I wasn't really tired and my mind was reeling from all that I learned from Dex. I couldn't get to sleep. So what did I do? I spent almost three hours working my way around Wikipedia and their lifestyle pages on my laptop. With all the information Dex had given me, I couldn't help but research further. It became a mission to read everything I could possibly find on the subject and while I can't say I'm an expert by any means, I was able to learn a lot more.

"Find anything interesting?" Dex asks.

"On what?"

He gives me a 'don't be stupid' look. "I know you well enough to know that when you got back to your room, you cracked open your laptop and tore up the internet."

I give him an exasperated look. "So?"

He bursts out laughing. "I've created a monster…I love it."

I take another sip of coffee before setting it back on the counter. "Did you expect anything less?"

He smiles behind his coffee cup. "No, Aryn, I didn't."

Dex uses my real name for the first time in a very long time. When we were on the road, I'd told him to keep it to Beck and he stuck with it. To this day I don't think Casey or Troy know my real name. "Shit, that reminds me," I mutter as I stand up.

"What's up?"

"Ahh, I gotta call Casey," I tell him as I walk down the hallway and into the guest room. I pull my phone off the nightstand. I click on it, sliding it open and it goes off with a couple different emails. Nothing new in my world. I pull up Casey's number and head back into the kitchen where Dex is messing around on his phone. "Want a laugh?" I ask Dex who gives me an evil smirk. He knows what I'm up to. If I know Casey, he's sound asleep still. Unless the boys dragged him out early.

I put it on speaker, hit send and let it ring.

On the fourth ring a gravely sleepy voice comes on the line. "Helllooo."

"Casey, where the fuck are you?" I bark into the phone.

"Where, what? Who is this?"

"It's Beck, fucker. You were supposed to be here thirty minutes ago."

"Oh shit." All of a sudden the sleepy is gone from his voice and there's a shit ton of shuffling going on as Casey panics, thinking he needs to be somewhere.

Dex and I both crack up laughing.

"You cock-sucking-motherfucker," Casey growls into the phone, then there is a rush of air and a plop that's loud enough to come through the phone. "Asshole," he mutters into the phone.

Dex and I are still laughing as he grumbles his way awake. "What do you want, fucker?"

"I have a job for you."

He groans on the other end of the line. "Yeah, when? What?"

"World Premiere Tour, prep starts on the sixteenth, right after New York. The first stop is here in town on the twenty-fourth."

"Who?" he asks and this is because I know he has an extreme dislike of certain celebutantes, and country singers.

"Alyssa Serin."

"Whoa! No shit?" I picture him sitting up stick straight in bed as he says this.

"Yeah, L.A., New York, Nashville." I wink at Dex who smirks. "London, Berlin and Sydney."

"Jesus Christ, that's a lot of fucking frequent flyer miles. Who's got point?"

"I do."

"No shit? Mills is finally letting you off your leash."

"Fuck off, asswipe. You in or not?"

"Fuck yeah," he says excitedly.

"Nice, now go back to bed."

"I can't now, fucktard," he grumbles.

Dex and I laugh. "I'll be in touch," I tell him and hang up.

"That was fucking cruel as fuck," Dex says.

"But funnier than hell."

We both carry on laughing for a good five minutes before he shoos me off to go get dressed. Raine is at Talon's and Dex wants to go over there, see her, say hi to the guys and visit the twins. I imagine if Dex is going, Mouse and Peacock won't be too far behind. Which means Casey will try and kick my ass in person for his wake up call this morning.

Raine answers the door, holding Logan in a bit of a football hold.

"I could get used to that," Dex teases her and she lights up at his suggestion.

I, on the other hand, look at him from the corner of my eye. He's joking, right? Mr. 'I'll never have kids' wants kids? Jesus, being with the right woman can really change a man.

"Not yet, you can't." She winks at him in some secret kind of way. "Hi, Beck." She smiles sweetly at me and coming down the stairs behind her is Talon holding Emily in a similar fashion.

"Hey guys," he says with a smile. The twins are just over a month old, but they've grown so much since I last saw them about two weeks ago. That was the first time Addison felt like having a house full of people, despite all of us popping in at random times. I'd come over to help Mills out when Rusty wasn't available, but since then, Rusty and Tori have managed it all. Mills did a complete security re-work of the house before they moved in a couple months back and he has an apartment on the property that is attached to the security center.

All of which was much to Talon's dismay, but I guess there have been a couple of times it's come in handy and now Talon praises it. "Where's Kyle and Addison?"

"Kyle ran to the store, Mills is around here somewhere and Addison is sleeping. The twins were up quite a bit last night." He coos at Emily and talks to her sweetly. Definitely not a side I ever expected to see from him.

"Let me have him," Dex says as he takes Logan from Raine and goes to sit down on the couch. I guess his statement shouldn't have come as that much of a surprise. He's become the best non-uncle-uncle ever. I watch Raine as she watches Dex with Logan. There is a sparkle in her eye as she does. I'm assuming there is something brewing here between them with kids, but I haven't a clue what it is. Seeing this just reinforces my loneliness a little more and it is starting to drive me crazy.

"Beck," Mills commands in his own little way and suddenly Casey's leash comment makes sense.

"Yes, sir," I answer. Raine snickers and Dex glares at her. She sobers quickly. I guess since the secret is out, at least with me, Raine couldn't hold it back anymore.

"Want to help me with something?"

"Sure," I say automatically and I follow him out of the back side of the house, through the kitchen. He leads me out on to the grounds, around the pool and into his building. "What's up, boss?" I ask him as we enter his living room.

"I need to reposition a couple of cameras. Mind helping me out?"

"Nah, not at all."

Part of me wonders if Mills is doing this on purpose, pulling me out of the house. While he knows Dex and I are friends, he keeps us separated when possible. I understand his reasoning. When the shit hits the fan, personal ties don't matter anymore. It's all about the safety of those we protect, regardless of who they are and what they are to us.

Sometime later, Dex comes to me and says that he and Raine are leaving. Immediately I understand why he had me drive. He can go home with her, and I can go home from here. "No problem. Let me know what time we're taking off on Friday."

"Why don't you just come stay at the house Thursday night? You can leave your car there, in the garage, instead of on the street at your house. Our flight is leaving Burbank at like, seven Friday morning."

"Alright, I'll let you know when I'm on my way over. Might be kind of late. I have a couple things to do before we leave to get ready for the tour."

"No worries, we'll chat," he tells me as he says goodbye and off they go.

"You got them alright in Nashville alone?" Mills asks.

"Yeah, they're going to Derek's in North Carolina first. He's got his own team in place. I think they asked me to come to placate you and Cami," I tell him with a smirk.

He laughs, "Probably. Regardless of who else is there, they are your responsibility."

"Absolutely. I got this," I tell him with a stoic expression. I don't need to go into details about our plans while we're there.

"Good, call me if you need anything. Now about tomorrow night…"

Mills launched into the details of how tomorrow night was going to go. Talon, Addison, and Kyle are going to some sort of pre-award dinner and party thing and it will be Addison's first night out of the house since the twins were born. I imagine the night will be short-lived, but good for her at the same time. Tori, Rusty, Mills and I are handling the detail this time around. I asked about Casey and Mills told me he had some other things going on with the guys. Despite the tour being over, we're paid and assigned to 69 Bottles, whether we're working or not. When working, our pay goes up exponentially, and with their appearances and whatnot, they keep us busy enough to keep me afloat. Believe me, I make good fucking money and live rather modestly, but still, the pay while on duty makes up for it.

I'll be getting paid the entire time we're in North Carolina and Nashville because I am on 'hazard duty pay.' When I go on tour for Alyssa, I won't be paid from 69 Bottles, but damn if I'm not making more money. There is something to be said for actor and actress protection versus a whole band.

When I get home, I toss my keys in the bowl, put away my gun, and jump in the shower. Different day, same routine. I'm a boring ass motherfucker.

NINE

Dex texted me around noon the next day to let me know that we'd be coming back to Los Angeles before the album launch. That makes things a little easier for me. When we travel with the entire band, I usually take both of my guns with me, among other things, and rather than having to drag them to North Carolina with us, I can just take the usual one.

I'm back in a monkey suit, a black and white one tonight, headed to Addison and the guys' house to escort them to some formal dinner affair.

When I arrive at the house, Dex and Raine are there, apparently they're the twins' babysitters tonight.

"It will be fine," Raine reassures Addison who is obviously having a hard time parting from them. I can't find it in myself to blame her for that. I can't imagine leaving them like this, but Raine is more than capable of handling them. She's been a very valuable asset to them, even before the twins were born.

"There's milk in the fridge, don't forget to heat it up," Addison tells Raine and from the exasperated look on Dex's face, I'm guessing it's not the first time she's said that tonight.

"Come on, baby, they'll be fine." Kyle wraps his arm around Addison and she leans into him, taking the support she wants and needs.

"We need to get going," Mills tells all of us.

"Alright, alright," Addison says as she straightens up.

She tells the twins bye again and again until Talon is practically dragging her out of the house and into the limo where Rusty and Tori are standing by holding doors.

"Beck, Tori - you're in the back tonight. Rusty and I will take the front," Mills commands in the way that works best for him. He is all business tonight. Fifteen years in the military can make you paranoid from time to time, but I cannot imagine what would happen if anyone on his detail got hurt or worse, killed.

When Addison was attacked during the tour, I thought Mills was going to lose his shit. He was nearly impossible to live with in the days that followed, but as we always do, we got past it and so did he. At least until it happened again a couple cities later. Though he never really said anything, I know that incident chewed him up worse than the first time. It did all of us because the one place that was supposed to be safe and sacred for the band was vandalized in ways we never could have imagined.

Addison handled it better than most women ever could. I know Raine's ordeal shook her up worse, but there was a long history there with her attacker. Though I imagine both of them having someone to lean on made it easier for them to handle.

"We're fifth in line," Mills says in my ear and Tori tells the trio, who've been talking quietly since getting in the car. Addison is still visibly upset about leaving the twins behind, but she's finding her public side pretty quickly, which means she'll manage to get through this pretty damn well.

The limo moves up. "Fourth," Mills calls and Tori and I begin a routine scan around the limo, mostly security and staff surrounding us. Fans are lining the streets to catch a glimpse of all those entering the event tonight. The limo lunges forward again.

"I can't do this," Addison cries.

"Yes, you can. Come on, sweetheart. The kids are fine, you're amazing. Just a little while longer," Talon comforts her.

"We will leave as soon as it is socially acceptable for us to do so, I promise."

"I don't want to see all the headlines," she cries harder.

"What headlines?" Kyle asks her.

"They're going to scrutinize me."

"Addison, we've talked about this. You don't look any different than you did eleven months ago. You look amazing and so what if anyone has anything to say about it." Talon continues to comfort her and I look at Tori who shrugs.

"Third," Mills says in our ears again.

The car moves again quickly. "Second." This time it's Rusty, Tori and I who scan the crowd outside the limo.

"On deck, guys," Tori says and Addison manages to right herself pretty quickly. Checking herself in a mirror before stowing it into her purse.

The limo lunges forward. "We're up," I say as the door next to me swings open. Mills climbs out quickly and Rusty slides out after him.

"Showtime," Addison says and I climb out, followed by Tori. I take point, odd. Mills is to my left and Tori to my right. I'm facing the crowd. Scanning, seeing, watching. The crowd is waiting with baited breath to see who steps from the limo. "Kyle's coming out," Mills chimes in my ear and the crowd gets excited. Seeing Kyle means that not far behind him is Talon. "Addison." I tense up a little bit. The crowd gets a little more riled up when she clears the door. My eyes never stop moving, never stop cataloguing what's happening in front of me. Making little notes of those who aren't cheering. Those are the ones you have to watch out for.

I bring my hand to my mouth, "Silent one, ten o'clock." There is a guy just standing there, not doing anything, and then he rolls his eyes at the girl next to him. Though I no longer see him as much of a threat, it doesn't mean he's not.

"Roger. Talon coming out."

That's when the crowd gets a little crazy and Mr. Ten o'clock claps, getting a little more into what's happening around him. I go back to scanning the crowd as the door shuts behind me and the limo moves off.

"Signing line," Mills says, meaning Talon is going to go to the line for a few minutes, snag some pictures and sign some autographs. This is truly the part of the job I hate. It makes it harder to keep tabs on him and keep him safe, but Talon is a stubborn ass and lives for his fans.

Addison joins him and they pose for some pictures. Tori is closer to her than normal, but I don't question it. With Addison's emotional state, it might not take much to upset her.

"Addison, you look amazing." And "Congratulations" are just some of the things being yelled and Addison smiles, blossoming and finding her confidence a little bit more as we make our way to the press line.

Once we're inside the roped-off area, the four of us settle down slightly. There is security staff placed about every five feet along the fan wall, blocking the view of fans but keeping them at bay.

The trio is met with questions, photos, red carpet shots and the like and this lasts for over forty-five minutes. Addison seems to be the main focus of their questions tonight before finally Talon whisks her away from the cameras and questions and we are finally inside the venue.

Addison managed to stay through dinner. Once we got inside and she started talking to people, it became a little easier for her to ignore what was happening in her head.

After dinner though, it was an acceptable time to leave and she was more than ready to do so. I, on the other hand, was having a good time. Not like I was partying or anything, but the visual pleasures were more than enough to keep me entertained.

We snuck the trio out the back, avoiding the fans, the cameras and the hoopla out front so that Addison could go home to the kids.

Raine and Dex were mildly disappointed when they got home so early, but Raine understood Addison's return better than Dex did. The kids were already in bed and Addison made a mad dash up the stairs to check on them. I don't know if I'll ever understand what was going through her head, but Talon and Kyle followed right behind her.

After that, Dex and Raine took off and I followed, shedding my jacket and tie before I got in my truck.

As I headed home, I was thankful that I'd worn an undershirt because I stopped at a bar on the way.

"What do you do?" asks the blonde who found her way to my table within fifteen minutes of me arriving in this hole in the wall bar in Hollywood. It was one of the first places I came across after leaving Talon's. The décor is a bad imitation of early nineteen hundred western saloon meets modern day technology. I've seen the place before but I've never been inside. The tables are made of glass covered wagon wheels. There is a pool table in the back and a jukebox that only plays music from the nineties on it.

The clientele is definitely college age, but more college drop out. In the twenty minutes I've been here, I've watched more than a handful of guys fail at picking up on the group of girls sitting at the bar. They are definitely college girls and far more giddy then what I'm comfortable with. But no less comical.

"I'm an actor." I tell her and her eyes go wide momentarily before looking me up and down.

"I've never seen you before."

I laugh, "That's because I'm not a celebrity."

'Well then, what do you do?" Her voice is whiny and high pitched, almost annoying enough to make me cringe.

"I'm a bodyguard."

"I don't believe you."

I shrug and swallow the last of the scotch in my glass. Coming here was a mistake. There's not very many women in attendance and not a one is going to be any better than the chick from Sunday night. Including this one. I stand up.

"Where are you going?" she asks me, her disappointment is evident.

"Home," I state firmly.

She cuddles up to me. "Want some company?"

I blink at her. "No thanks. I just came for a drink."

I untangle her from around my body as she pouts and I make my escape quickly and confidently. I happen to look back and she's immediately moved on to the next moron, reinforcing the idea that she is easier than riding a bicycle.

I crash through the doors and stomp my way toward my truck.

Giving up on a bad attempt at picking up a woman. It's time to go home.

TEN

I slept like shit. Constant tossing and turning because I couldn't keep my mind off the events of the upcoming weeks. Between North Carolina, Tennessee, then New York and the upcoming premiere tour, I feel like I'm going to start spinning in circles.

I got up early and finished packing, including securing my weapons in their travel cases. We are traveling privately, but there are still laws and requirements that I have to follow. Though it is far easier than flying commercially.

With my packing done and nothing else to do, I go shopping. Yeah, shut up, I know that sounds odd coming from a man's mouth, but I don't know what, if any, time I will have to finish shopping once we're at Derek's. Christmas is only a week away.

"Beck," I snap into the phone. I'm home and not in the mood for conversation. I'm due at Dex's soon.

It's an unknown number. Not something I usually answer, but with the upcoming tour I don't know who might be calling.

"I guess from your tone that you're not happy to hear from me…" There is a pregnant pause on the line before I finally put two and two together.

"Not particularly. What do you want, Alyx?"

"What, I can't call my brother?"

I roll my eyes. "What do you need, Alyx?"

"I guess this means you're not coming home for Christmas," he says sheepishly.

"Why on earth would I do that?"

"Oh I don't know, because we haven't seen you in years."

"For good reason, Alyx. No, I won't be home for Christmas, I'm working."

"You're always working," he says softly into the phone.

"Yeah, I am, so what? Look Alyx, I appreciate the call, but you knew the answer to my question before you called me. So why…"

"Mom's sick."

I sigh. "She's been sick for years, Alyx. This isn't news to me."

"She's dying, Aryn."

"What exactly am I supposed to do about it? You know damn well she doesn't want to see me, so why tell me?"

"Because she's your fucking mother, Aryn," he snaps at me.

I shake my head despite him not being able to see me. "A fact that she conveniently forgot ten years ago."

"I think you should hear her out."

"Alyx, she kicked me out, told me to get out of her house."

"Aryn, you beat the living shit out of dad. What did you expect her to do?"

"No, Alyx, I beat the shit out of dad who… oh never mind. You'll never understand," I tell him and I pull the phone away from my ear to hang up.

"Wait!" he says through the phone and I reluctantly bring it back to my ear.

"What?" I snap.

"I know why you did it. I don't blame you. I'd have done the same thing." I shake my head as he continues, "He deserved what he had coming to him."

"Is that so? You weren't so keen on that fact ten years ago, Alyx. In fact, you stood next to mom as she threw me out of the house. You know as well as I do that she was looking for any excuse she could muster up to kick me out. I gave her what she needed. She threw me out on the street and you just expect me to come crawling back for Christmas dinner?"

He doesn't say anything in response, he doesn't have to.

"Listen, Alyx, I know what you're trying to do and it's not going to work. I've scraped myself off the ground so many times, and I've done it without you or mom. I don't need the reminders and you know as well as I do that the only thing that will come out of my coming home is fighting, arguing and a very un-merry Christmas. So just let it go."

"Alyce misses you."

I hang my head in shame. Being kicked out didn't bother me, ever. I knew all along that I was working my way to being kicked out for years, but Alyce was my one and only regret. I knew that if I left, she'd have no one to protect her. I knew that I couldn't take her with me and I will never forget the day I packed my stuff per my mother's wishes.

The only thing that came out of that whole fiasco was the fact that my stepdad decided against pressing charges against me. Everything else that came out of that day is a complete disaster.

"I know she does. If she wants to see me, she knows how to get a hold of me."

"How do you think I got your number?"

I sigh. "She asked you to call me?" I ask, skeptically.

"Uh, no. Mom did."

"Well, I am not coming home. I have to work."

"Then will you come when you can?"

"No, Alyx, I won't. There is no reason for me to come back, at least not as long as he's around."

Alyx doesn't say anything for a moment. "It stopped that day."

"I know that."

"We've all forgiven him."

"Well, good for you," I snap. "I cannot, and never will, forgive him for what he's done."

"You should," Alyx says simply.

"No, I shouldn't and I won't."

It's with that I disconnect the call. Leaving Alyx wondering what happened. I am immediately transported back to that house…

"What in the fuck are you doing?" I scream at my stepfather Jason.

"Get the fuck away from me," he growls back at me, shoving me into the wall.

"I'm only going to ask you one more time. What. The. Fuck. Are. You. Doing?"

"None of your fucking business," the overweight, middle-aged dirtbag my mother married a few years ago growls at me.

"Oh, yes it is. You. Don't. Fucking. Touch. Her."

"Aryn, don't," Alyce says from the bed.

My furious eyes meet her terrified ones. Seeing the fear in her eyes sends me over the edge and sends Jason flying into Alyce's closet doors. Rattling them and knocking them off their tracks. "Alyce, get out of here, now," I bark.

She scurries off the bed, pulling her comforter with her. Our eyes meet as she passes me. "Thank you," she mouths and that's all the validation I need. I nod toward the door, telling her to get out of her bedroom.

My eyes fall back to Jason's half naked ass as he tries to get up from the heap of doors, clothes and toys on the floor.

"You've messed with the wrong little girl for the last time, you sick mother-fucker." The voice crawling out of my mouth is no longer my own and it's like I'm possessed as I pull him off the heap and throw him against the wall.

From that day forward, once Jason was out of the hospital at least, he never touched Alyce again. What pushed my mom over the edge was the fact that Jason denied what he was doing when I beat him up. He told her that I was pissed off and that I'd said something to him that pissed him off and it went from there. Though how it all happened in Alyce's room never seemed to be a factor for my mother. Regardless of that, my mother decided that it was more important to believe her douchebag of a husband than her own children.

After she threw me out of the house, which she'd wanted to do for a really long time, Alyce and I always found ways to stay in touch. She had a best friend that lived a few houses down from us and she would send me letters from her house and I would reply back to her at that address.

This went on for years until Alyce and I both had email and then our communications became more frequent.

Jason had stopped molesting her and I wished I'd done something sooner. Maybe then Alyce wouldn't have the problems she has now. Because Alyce was a minor, my mother never believed she was telling the truth, or if she did, she decided her douchebag of a husband was more important than her children. When the investigation happened, Jason and my mother denied everything. In an overworked, understaffed situation, they closed the case citing Alyce had a wild imagination. My mother choosing Jason over her own children made her kicking me out just a little more tolerable. It's because of all this that I cannot and will never return home.

Alyce is ten years younger than I am and she is the only reason I went to college while still living at home. I refused to leave her alone, but yet Jason always managed to get his hands on her. Though it only lasted about a year and half before I beat the living shit out of him, she was only twelve when I was kicked out.

After I beat the shit out of him, he stopped with Alyce, but I often wonder if there is someone else who's been on the receiving end of Jason's wrath. After that day, Jason changed his tune with Alyce, changing her environment and altering her perception of him.

Some would call her a spoiled brat, I call it justice.

She moved out as soon as she turned eighteen and I don't know that she's ever looked back since then. She and I have grown distant these last few years and seeing Alyce is literally the only thing that would drive me back to Billings. I can't bring myself to do it.

I shudder, letting the memories of those awful days wash away from me. Bringing myself back to the reality I face daily. The reality of knowing that I left her to fend for herself and the guilt I still feel most days over doing that. In order to stay off the streets, I did what any twenty-two year old would do, I enlisted in the Army.

ELEVEN

It took me awhile to shake off the memories of my childhood home before I could refocus on getting my shit together and my ass over to Dex and Raine's.

I finally rang their bell around nine.

"About time," Dex says as he opens the door.

I shrug it off. "Sorry, got tied up."

Dex snickers, "And they let you go?"

I roll my eyes. "Not like that, fucker." Dex quirks an eyebrow at me as he hears the unfinished, 'I wish' that I don't say.

"You hungry?" he asks as I pull my shit into the apartment. He grabs the last of the stuff behind me and pulls it in. I packed my duffle bag for tonight and clothes for tomorrow.

"I could eat," I tell him and he nods toward the door.

"Come on, we haven't eaten yet either," he says in a way that sounds slightly irritated.

When we step into the kitchen, I see Raine's head over the counter. "Hi Raine," I call, thinking she's cleaning something up off the floor.

She doesn't respond and I look at Dex as I step closer to the island and I see her kneeling on the floor. Her eyes are red and there are streaks of tears down her cheeks. "What the hell?" I ask.

Dex gives me a sad smile and looks toward Raine. "Pet?"

"Yes, Master," she responds quickly, her voice full of remorse and sadness.

"Care to tell Beck why you're crying?"

"No, Master."

I look at Dex, confused, and he jerks his head, indicating for me to come around the island and as I do, my foot crunches on something and Raine jumps slightly. I look down and little white grains are scattered on the floor. The pile grows larger as I draw closer to Raine's kneeling position on the floor.

I raise an eyebrow at Dex. "She was being sassy. She pushed me too far," he tells me.

"So...she's being punished?" I ask him while looking at her.

"Yes, sir," Raine answers.

Dex folds his arms over his chest. "Was he speaking to you, pet?"

"No, Master." The emotion in her voice is stronger now, but she lowers her head. "I'm sorry, Master," she apologizes.

I check out of their conversation, whatever is happening between them is personal and private, and I go back to trying to figure out what she's kneeling on. My eyes wander around the kitchen and while I see various boxes of things, I can't pin point it.

"It's uncooked rice," Dex tells me.

I cock my head.

"When it's dry, and you kneel on it, it hurts like a bitch."

"But I thought she liked pain."

"Pet?"

"I do, sir, but I enjoy pain that brings me pleasure. This brings me no pleasure, sir."

"Ahh," I say, understanding that this is a punishment for what she's done, whatever the case may be, that made Dex mad.

"Can you give me a minute?" Dex asks softly and I nod.

"I'll go put my stuff away."

Dex nods and I leave the kitchen, leaving him to handle Raine in a way that he sees fit. All I hear as I'm leaving is the sound of Dex's shoes on the rice as it crunches under his feet and I shudder. I cannot imagine that would feel very good at all.

When I'm done putting my duffle bag, my laptop and finally my gun bag into the bedroom, I return hesitantly to the kitchen and when I come to stand in the doorway, Dex has his arms wrapped around Raine and she is snuggling into him. If he was mad and punished her, this is a side I do not understand.

After a couple of heartbeats, Dex tilts her chin up and claims her mouth in a chaste, yet ridiculously passionate kiss that I almost turn away from before he releases her. "Thank you, Master," she says and her voice is lighter, the opposite of what it was a few minutes ago while kneeling on the rice.

"Thank you, pet," he tells her with a smile. "Now, can you finish dinner?"

"Yes, Master."

"Say hi to Beck." She turns toward me, a smile spread across her face, almost like she's been replaced with someone happier and more like the Raine I know in a matter of minutes. Almost as though her punishment didn't happen.

"Hi Beck." She smiles a little wider. "How are you?"

I give her a skeptical look. "I'm fine, and you?"

"Perfect." She smiles again before going back to the stove. The rice is cleaned up off the floor as she walks through that part of the kitchen.

I shake my head in disbelief. "Punishment and reward," Dex states matter of factly. "Something was bothering her, which is why she was getting snippy with me. Rather than discuss it with me, she got snippy, which is why she was punished. The idea is to teach her to communicate with me, rather than let things bottle up inside her." He smiles as he watches her at the stove. "We have this discussion about once a week. Though in most cases it doesn't result in rice punishment."

"I don't know how you can do that to her."

He gives me a knowing smile. "I can't. But I know, just like she knows, that communication is very important to both of us and our relationship and when she holds things back from me it can cause more tension than necessary." He leans on the island between us. "In this case, what was bothering her was the packing and making sure we had everything together but rather than sharing that concern with me so that I could help her, she got pissy." Raine slumps in sadness as she works on dinner. "Ordering me around is not something I take very kindly to, is it, pet?"

"No, Master."

"So, she refused to tell me what was bothering her when I gave her the chance to do so, which means that she got punished until she told me. But in this case, she spilled the beans in an attempt to avoid the rice." He snickers at the memory in his head. "But it didn't work, did it, pet?"

"It never does," she mutters.

"What was that?" He pushes up off of the counter. It's almost like watching a spooked cat whose hackles rise on the back of its neck.

"I'm sorry, Master. No, it didn't work, Master."

Dex lets the subject drop and he goes over to help her finish up and plate dinner. It's nothing fancy, spaghetti with meatballs and garlic bread. Comfort food and a common food before we take off on trips. Why is always beyond me, but I think it has more to do with cleaning up the meat in the fridge and making something simple and easy.

As we go through dinner, both Dex and Raine seem to have forgotten what it is that happened before I walked in the door and I envy that type of relationship. The ability to let things slide off your chest and move on with someone.

Fuck envying that kind of relationship, I envy a relationship, period. I do my best to not let that part of me show. I've done a great job of holding it in so far, I don't need to let it out now.

TWELVE

"You must be Beck?" one of the guys meeting us at the airport says as he approaches me. He's dressed in a suit, but it is obvious that he's one of Derek's security guys.

"I am, and you are?"

"I'm Sean. Mr. Hunter's head of security."

"Great to meet you, Sean." Sean is tall, well built, slightly darker skin complexion with pitch black short hair and muscles that rival Mills'. Judging by his stance, he's ex-military too.

"Likewise. Mills speaks very highly of you."

I can't hide the quizzical look I give him as I wonder how he knows Mills. "You know Mills?"

"I do. We've worked together in the past. We were on the same MARSOC team."

"So how'd you end up in this gig?"

He gives me a very poignant look. "Who do you think?"

I snort. "Yeah, he has a way of doing that."

"He does. So, I understand you're on these two?" He points to Dex and Raine as they're getting their luggage loaded into one of the three town cars parked near the plane.

"I am. Dex and Raine."

"Great, if you want to ride with me, I'll go over some of our rules, some of what we do around the house and for Derek and give you a little bit of a rundown of what's happening over the next couple of weeks."

"Sounds great," I tell him and go back to getting my stuff off the plane. When my gun case comes off, I unlock it and strap up.

"Impressive," Sean says as I strap on my ankle holster.

"Thanks," I think.

"These two really that much trouble?" he snickers.

I snort. "God no, though it's never them I worry about."

"Well said. Can I help with your stuff?"

"Absolutely. Thanks."

Sean and I load up my stuff while the other two men I'd seen when I got off the plane load up bags and then get into the car with Dex and Raine, leaving me and Sean alone and climbing into another car. "What's the third car for?"

"Not sure, not ours. We checked it when we got here. It's locked up. I sent the plate back to my guy at the house. He came back with another owner who operates from this airfield, so we let it go.

"Gotcha."

"Hop in," he tells me and I climb into the passenger seat.

He climbs in after me, throwing the running car into drive as we follow Dex's car out of the airfield, through the security gate and on to the open country road.

"The two guys in there with them are the best in the business, fully vetted. You can relax a little, big man," he tells me.

"Sorry, it's habit."

"Never apologize, not around me. I'd be more concerned if you weren't worried."

"Thanks," I mutter.

He starts into some detail about the house. The information he gives me isn't pertinent to just anyone and I remind myself to give Mills a text, to thank him for helping ease Sean into me.

Oftentimes joining forces can be a pissing party between the two teams. Usually resentment from the stationed team having the inconvenience of someone else to look after. I guess Mills made a point to tell him that I could stand on my own two feet.

"We have a series of parties going on at the house. The first one is tomorrow night, though it's a party I've been asked to let you loose on."

"Why's that?"

"Derek has asked you to be a guest, not a statue," he snickers. "It's one of his ultra-private parties, usually meaning security is light and stuck to the outside of the house."

"Ahh," I nod in understanding. I wonder idly if this is a private play party.

I'd done some more research, though I haven't had time for much, and it talked about private play parties among good friends. Usually meaning Doms and subs are invited and well, it turns into a play night.

"Does he host these private parties often?"

"Not that often, but usually only when we're here in town. Have you ever been to one of Derek's parties?"

"No, sir," I tell him, and it's true, I haven't, but I can speculate, based on what Dex and Raine have said Derek's relationship is like with Dacotah.

"They're small, usually only ten to twelve people, and Ms. Miller and Mr. Hunter handle all the catering during the event. Leaving them and their guests in the house."

"Do you know what kind of parties they are?"

He looks at me as he comes to a stoplight. "I do."

"So why aren't you telling me?"

"Because I figured you already knew."

I shrug. "Yeah, I suppose. Though I haven't actually been invited by anyone."

"I imagine Derek will be doing that. He asked that I not steal you away when we get back to the house. Though as of right now, you'll be sleeping in our quarters."

"I'd figured that part."

He nods and the light changes and we make our way through a small town. It reminds me of Montana, small one and two story buildings lining the main street. Trees, though mostly leafless now, line the street on either side and cars are parked along the curbs. It's early afternoon on a Friday so there are plenty of people roaming around with bags in hand as they make their way from one store to the next.

"The next party is Christmas Eve. Mr. Hunter throws a huge extravaganza. Inviting friends and some of his employees to the house. There will be several people staying in the house through Christmas day. One of which is your boss's boss."

"Cami?" I raise an eyebrow at him and he looks at me.

"Yes, she's one of Derek's reps, among other things. Her husband and their son will also be here. It's my understanding that they're staying through Saturday. Then Sunday morning Mr. Hunter, Ms. Miller, Mr. Harris and Ms. Montgomery, along with you, and myself, will be traveling over to Nashville where we will stay through New Year's."

"Perfect." I can't help letting a little excitement into my voice about Nashville. I am just sorry I have to wait that long to get to that point.

He continues on, talking about security procedures in the house, the fact that Christmas has a very tight guest list and no deviations are allowed. That of course is for security purposes and while there are no announced metal detectors, everyone is screened on the way in. I find it odd that a private party like that would cause that kind of search, but I realize that because of the amount of people it is necessary. Sean informs me that there are five-hundred people plus who are scheduled to be in attendance.

I can't help wondering what kind of estate this man has in order to accommodate that many people in his house.

My question is answered not long after that as we drive down a mile long driveway that leads to a massive mansion set in a wide open field. As we draw closer to it, I am completely blown away by the sheer size of the three story residence in front of me. "Good god," I groan and Sean laughs.

"Impressive, isn't it?"

"You can say that again. How many guys do you have on staff?"

"On a normal, vacant day, two. When Mr. Hunter is in residence, we have seven. On party nights, we have up to seventy-five who come in. Many of which belong to Mr. Hunter's guests. It's a coordinated effort. Mr. Hunter often has politicians, celebrities, and the like in his home. So I'm sure you can imagine how that all goes."

"And you lead all of this?"

He snorts. "I do. There are three of us that live on site. Myself, obviously, and one man and one woman, whom you'll meet later. They're my right and left hands. If you can't find me, reach me - though unlikely- they're your go-to."

Sean pulls up in front of the house, right behind the other car as three people dressed in livery suits exit the front door and head over to tackle the luggage. Dex and Raine exit their car and head for the front door "I'll have Sal bring your stuff to your room. Why don't you follow those two in?" Sean says as he hands me a card. "Program that. We communicate with radios, but until I give you one, you can just call me. When you're done with Mr. Hunter, feel free to call me, and I'll come get you."

I nod, unable to speak and overwhelmed by the sheer size of the house and the feeling of inadequacy that is coursing through my veins. Here I thought guarding a rock band was hard work.

I climb out of the car and look up the side of the house and then look right and finally left. Good god.

"This way, Mr. Becker." I start at the use of my full last name. "Mr. Hunter is inside, sir."

THIRTEEN

I find no reprieve to this monstrosity of a house by stepping inside. The entry way is intricately designed with a gorgeous combination of wood and marble. Accented by silver sconces and an amazing dual staircase leading up to the second floor. A car could drive up either side and fit just fine. At the top of the stairs is a wide hallway and another staircase that more than likely leads up to the third floor.

The room surrounding me is absolutely massive. It has to take up at least the entire middle section of the house. I understand now why Derek can host so many people so easily.

Looking around the room only makes me feel smaller as I realize that the ceiling is the entire height of the house. There are various sitting areas throughout the large space, not a television in sight, and at least three double-sided fireplaces. "Good god," I breathe.

"Extravagant, isn't it?" a man says, and it's not Dex.

I turn toward the voice. "Overwhelming would be a better word," I say to the tall, long brown-haired man standing behind me. I've met him only once before. In Phoenix following a dinner party the band had at Cami and Tristan's.

"You must be Mr. Becker."

"Ah, Beck, please. Mr. Hunter, great to see you again."

"Derek, please." He extends his hand. "We have met, haven't we?"

"Yes, sir. In Phoenix, when the band did those recordings," I tell him.

"That's right. Though you guys are great at sticking to the shadows." He smiles. "Please, come in."

He ushers me off to the left side of the door toward a section of couches that are facing each other and on either side are high back chairs. From my right comes Dex and Raine and someone I can only assume is Dacotah.

"Cotah?"

"Yes, Sir," she replies, but Derek gives her a look that is not unlike ones I've seen Dex give Raine. "Master," she corrects herself.

I smile a quick smile and release it fast, not wanting anyone to catch on. "Why don't you take Raine to the kitchen and start lunch?"

"Yes, Master," she says, then giggles before grabbing Raine's hand and running off.

Derek turns toward me. "I apologize. We'd made arrangements for you to work with Sean and his team while you were here. That was until Dex called to tell me of some of your other motives for wanting to come along."

"With all due respect, sir, I am here to work with your team. While I am friends with Dex and Raine, my job comes first and foremost."

He smiles. "I respect that, however, I'd like to offer you better accommodations."

I shake my head. "That won't be necessary. This way I can get up to speed before your party and help Sean."

"You like helping?" His question portrays a deeper question than what's on the surface, like he's indirectly searching for more information about me.

I nod. "When it's needed. As I said, Dex is my first priority, though he'll beg to tell you otherwise, then Raine and finally myself."

"Well, while you're here, I assure you that Sean and his crew can handle anything that gets thrown at us, though I understand he'd like your help Christmas Eve."

"What's Christmas Eve?" Dex asks. So apparently I'm not the only one questioning this massive party.

Derek looks at him and replies, "I have a massive Christmas Eve party. It's friends, co-workers, a few politicians and a few more celebrities. It's quite the shindig."

"Sounds like fun." Dex smiles.

"Oh, it's a blast." Derek lights up a little at telling Dex this news. "It's Cotah's second party and I think I've finally managed to shake her of her nerves. It is black tie."

"Well hell. Why didn't you tell me, I don't travel with suits." Dex scoffs.

Derek laughs and I can't help but snort. "I didn't think you did. I've got it covered. Don't worry."

"I'm not running around in a toga if that's what you're thinking." Dex sits back in his chair and crosses his arms over his chest. The posturing sends Derek into head back laughter that causes both Dex and I to join in.

"I might pay damn good money to see that," Derek says through the laughter, which of course brings an image to mind of Dex in a toga dress and I can't stop myself.

Eventually, realizing his ridiculousness, Dex joins in. "I'm pretty sure the party needs mistletoe," I tease him and of course that eggs everyone on for another minute before we settle down.

"What about tomorrow, sir?" I ask Derek and he gives me a knowing smile.

"I figured you'd ask about that. That is not black tie."

I chuckle. "I figured as much. But what about me attending? Sean said that…"

"Dex?" Derek interjects and indicates for Dex to respond.

Dex sits up a little straighter. "It's one of the reasons we came out here today instead of next week. It's a play party. Derek is inviting some of his friends, many from Nashville.

Everyone will arrive, we will mix, mingle and eat. Eventually Derek will open up his dungeon and well, at that point, all bets are off."

"I thought maybe it would be a better introduction for you than The Box. Though that was Raine's first introduction, it's very overwhelming and people can be a little standoffish with newcomers at the club. Whereas at a private play party, while no one ever really knows everyone, the anonymity remains intact for most people. So it provides a fun, safe environment, though the environment starts the moment that they cross that threshold." He points to the door. "There will be no staff, no security, at least inside the house. The curtains will be drawn and it will transform into something private and personal for our guests. There are two other Doms without submissives who will be coming to the event and I believe one, possibly two, unattached submissives."

My heart pounds with a little more excitement knowing that there is a chance I can meet and talk with someone while they're here.

"Many of Derek's guests will be staying the night here in the house. Though it is not common practice at play parties, Derek certainly has the room for them. The play party ends at four in the morning."

"At which point my staff will return to make breakfast for our guests. However, what happens in the bedrooms, well, I can't stop that from happening." He winks, dropping the subtle hint that he knows all too well what will happen behind those doors.

"How many people?" I ask.

"Counting you, sixteen or seventeen."

I nod.

Derek continues talking about a few more things and he finishes when the girls come and collect us for lunch.

After lunch I called Sean who promptly collected me and brought me to the staff quarters, and while Derek had made it sound like I was going to be staying in a shack, these quarters are still better than my apartment. They're actually quite lavish for staff quarters. I could get used to working for a man like Hunter.

Around five I received a text from Dex asking me to join them for dinner. I declined, telling him that he should hang out with his friends. His reply was simply, "suit yourself".

I ate with Sean and the other two regular guards. Celeste, who is very easy on the eyes, and Cyrus who, well, just don't piss him off.

Celeste made no secret of making flirtatious eye contact with me throughout dinner. I won't lie, she's very attractive. She's well-built, as any respectable bodyguard would be. Tall, maybe five-eight or five-nine. Chestnut colored hair that's long and pulled back into a messy, curly ponytail with bright green eyes and soft full lips. Judging by her comments to all of us at the table, I can tell she knows about the party tomorrow night and that I'm going. That gave her ammunition for a few pointed looks that told me she wouldn't mind being a guest either. Celeste is the type of girl that I would normally pick up at a bar. Not necessarily long term material, at least not in my eyes. It makes me wonder what I would have done if I'd met her randomly in a bar somewhere instead of on a trip. Regardless, she's fun and flirtatious and I certainly don't mind the attention.

When dinner was over, I retired to my room with, yes, I know, nerd alert, a book. I'd changed into my flannel pants and laid down on the bed, putting on my glasses when there's a knock at the door. "Yeah?" I call, turning toward it.

The door creaks open slowly and standing on the other side is Celeste. "Sorry to bother you." Her voice is soft, unsure and I sit up, putting my book down.

I shake my head. "No bother, just reading. Everything alright?"

"Perfect. May I come in?" Her voice is soft, mouselike and polite. My dick stirs in my pants. The sheepish, unsure expression on her face makes her look young and innocent, and very, very submissive.

"Sure," I tell her and she steps inside. It's only now that I realize she's barely wearing any clothes. She has on a skinny tank top with no bra and her D cup tits are less perky than they were at dinner. But her nipples are sure displaying that she's cold.

My eyes slowly rake down her body. She has very tanned and toned thighs. In fact, there isn't much about her that is flabby. My cock grows hard, fast.

I awkwardly try and cover myself. "Close the door," I tell her and she does so quickly.

She climbs up onto the bed and for the first time in a long time, I swallow, hard.

"I've wanted to do this since you got here," she says as she crawls on her hands and knees across the big bed, right toward me.

"Do what?" I whisper.

"This," she says succinctly before slanting her lips over my own. Claiming me in a deep, hard, breath stealing kiss.

FOURTEEN

It takes me a minute to get over the initial shock of what Celeste has bestowed on me. Oddly enough, I'm not sure I want her to stop what she's doing.

Her lips are soft, yet urgent against mine and her hands begin to roam up my chest. I shiver. I do enjoy women who are aggressive enough to go after what they want but I'm not sure this is what I want to happen here. I've only just met her. Shut up, I know I've done this a few times before, but this is different.

I pull back. "Celeste, stop," I say breathless.

She pouts, "Why would I do that?" Her hands slide up my chest a little farther and I take her by her wrists.

"Because this isn't right and you know it."

"Says who?" Her voice is hurt, and the expression on her face tells me that she isn't used to rejection, and frankly, I'm not all that used to dishing it out when it comes to the point of kissing someone.

"Says me. We have to work together."

"So?"

"Jesus, woman, do you sleep with everyone that walks through the door to help you guys?" My voice comes out a little harsher than I intended and I'm immediately torn between apologizing to her and letting it go.

"No, I'm not a slut," she scoffs.

"I didn't say you were. Look, I don't think this is a good idea."

"But it would feel so good," she whines.

She can say that again. She would probably be the best I've had in a long time, but I am so afraid of my own expectations that I cannot bring myself to give into this, not tonight anyway.

The play party comes to mind quickly and I wonder if it might not be a bad idea to have an outlet after that is over. "Let's just take it easy for tonight, alright?" Jesus, what the fuck am I saying? Who the hell am I and what's happened to me?

Her expression changes from shock and rejection to a more passive one. "So you're not saying no?" She presses her lips into a thin line.

"For tonight? Yes, I'm saying no." She pouts again. "But that doesn't mean that I won't say yes another time."

The 'promise' in my voice is enough to pacify her for now. She leans in and gives me a chaste kiss. "Alright," she says before leaving my room.

As soon as the door closes, I throw the covers off and move around the bed to the door, locking it quickly before returning to the bed. Shedding my pajama bottoms as I go.

My cock stands hard as a fucking rock thanks to her. Regardless of rejecting her, he never went down. "What the hell?" I say to my cock before gripping it in my hand and lying back down on the bed.

Images of her fill my mind. Yeah, you're an idiot, Becker.

I passed out shortly after coming all over myself like an idiot. Jesus, it took more than I had to not pull my pajamas back on and go find her and take her for myself. She made it too easy for me and maybe that's part of why I rejected her. Either that or some stupid logical part of my mind took over my mouth and pushed her away because it was the right thing to do. Fuck that. It wasn't the right thing to do, it was selfish. Sleeping with her now, the first night I'm here, with two weeks left to work with her would be torture to both her and myself. I never sleep with the same woman twice. Sleeping with her once and being here for two weeks means I'd have to reject her, hurt her, or worse, put my job in jeopardy.

Sure, I've had women hit on me. It's been that way for years, and sometimes their initiative leads to me taking them someplace private and having my way with them. But more often than not, the girls I take for myself are ones I've intigated and convinced into going into a dark corner with me.

I wake up around one. With the three hour time difference from California to here, I can't say that I'm surprised. Sean had told me that they didn't need me for anything today so it is my day to do as I please.

I text Dex to find out where they are.

Dex to Beck: 'bout time. We've been waiting for you.
Beck to Dex: you could have called, fucker.
Dex to Beck: hardly, get dressed, Raine and I are going into town.

Well, fuck.

Beck to Dex: give me 20.

I take a quick shower, dress and strap up, before walking out of my room with two minutes to spare. I try and find my way back to the main part of the house. Running smack into Celeste.

"Where's the fire?" she teases.

"Uh…" Fuck, I almost slept with this chick last night. And daylight hasn't given me much more perspective on whether or not I want to actually sleep with her. She still looks gorgeous, even dressed in black BTUs and a black t-shirt. Not much different than I am and she too is packing. "Dex wants to leave. I'm trying to find my way back to the house."

She laughs, "This way."

She turns around, leading me back the way she'd just come. "Thanks," I tell her and she nods.

"I was just coming to get you."

"Oh, for?"

"Dex wants to go out," she laughs.

I roll my eyes.

"Here you go," she says as she turns toward me and ushers me down the hallway that leads into the kitchen area of the main floor.

"Thanks."

She gives me a sweet, knowing smile before leaving me to find my way.

I walk down the hall until it opens into the kitchen and now I need to figure out what direction I need to go. The kitchen is bustling with four different people, all dressed in white chef jackets and black pants. I look to my left and see where I need to go and I go there.

Stepping into the great room, everything is… "What the hell?" I turn around, thinking I'm in the wrong place, only to see the front door and the grand staircase and I realize that I'm in the right room. But it is practically empty of all the furniture that was here yesterday.

"Big, huh?"

I look at Dex who's walking toward me from the other side of the staircase from where I'm at.

"You can say that again. Where'd it all go?"

He smiles. "Into the basement. The party will be held in here tonight."

I nod in understanding. "So, where are we going?"

"Just into town. Cotah says that there is a nice little boutique there and Raine wants to look around."

I give him a questioning look. "We're in the middle of nowhere. What could this shop have that Los Angeles doesn't?"

He gives me a knowing smirk. "You'll see."

"We ready?" Raine says as she comes bounding down the stairs, Cotah in tow.

"I am," I tell her.

Derek comes out of a room off the great room. "Afternoon, Beck," Derek says. "Can I talk to you for a minute?"

"Of course," I say, leaving Dex to return to Raine and Cotah.

"Everything alright?" I ask Derek as I approach.

"Absolutely. Cotah would like to go with, do you mind?"

"Not at all. Anything I need to know?"

He shakes his head. "Nah, she'll behave. She wants this play party more than anything, and she knows how to be a good girl." He chuckles slightly. "I know the shop owner and I usually let Celeste stay outside while she's inside, but you might want to investigate the store yourself, you know, for tonight."

"What kind of store is this?"

"To the public? A clothing store. To a select few, well, I'll let you guess on that one. I'd like you to drive." He hands me a set of keys. "The car is gassed and outside. I had them program the GPS, but Cotah knows the way."

"Yes, sir."

My acknowledgement causes him to give a little upturn of his lips. I'm not really sure I understand it, so I let it go.

We pull up in front of a shop in the center of a small town near Derek's estate. I don't know the name of the town, but I imagine there isn't a whole lot to do in this town on a Friday or Saturday night.

"Cotah, this looks like a clothing store," Raine says. "I don't need…"

"Hush, looks can be deceiving," Cotah says with a tease as she opens the door and climbs out.

Irritated that she beat me to it, I climb out of the truck and scan the streets. There are people milling about, but nothing seems suspicious and I escort the three of them into the shop.

"Hello Dacotah," an older woman greets her.

"Hello Mistress Sara," Dacotah responds with a bow of her head.

Mistress?

"Who are your guests?" Mistress Sara asks.

"This is Master Dex and his slave."

I'm not sure I'll ever get used to Dex and Raine being referred to like that, but Mistress Sara comes around the counter and introduces herself to Dex. They shake hands. "May I say hello to your slave, Master Dex?"

"Please do."

Mistress Sara extends her hand to Raine who takes it gently in her own. "It's a pleasure to meet you, pet. Tell me, Master Dex, what is your pet's name?"

"Raine, Mistress."

She smiles at Dex. Obviously whatever this exchange between them is, it's going well. The undeniable mutual respect between Sara and Dex is almost too much to put into words.

"Pleased to meet you, Raine," Mistress Sara says.

"The pleasure is mine, Mistress." Raine lowers her head. In this moment she looks more submissive than ever and I am pleased to see it, for some reason it is awfully becoming on her.

"And who is this, Cotah?" Mistress Sara says to her while looking at me.

"This is Beck, Mistress. He is Master Dex's bodyguard."

Mistress Sara gives me a coy little smile. "This must be a shock to you."

I shake my head. "No, ma'am. I am aware of their relationship."

"Well then, it's a pleasure to meet you. Will I be seeing you tonight?" she asks me and I get the impression that she'd like to make me her little play thing.

"Yes, ma'am."

She perks up. "Excellent." She looks over at Cotah and asks, "Downstairs?"

"Yes please, Mistress."

"Follow me."

There is a definite command to Mistress Sara that I've seen in both Dex and Derek since they've come out of the closet to me and I'm beginning to wonder more about who isn't in the lifestyle versus who is. It seems like everyone is, everyone but me.

As we walk toward the back of the shop, I shudder at the thought of being someone's pet, but yet, my cock stirs.

FIFTEEN

When we entered the basement of Mistress Sara's shop, I immediately understood why they wanted to come here and why this part of the shop is hidden behind a locked door and a staircase. I would imagine people don't randomly wander in here and that the shop upstairs keeps her afloat. Shortly after I closed the door to the basement, there was a chime of the front door opening and I could hear whoever it was upstairs while we all wandered around the room.

It was darker than the shop upstairs with walls painted a dark purple or maybe black, and the lighting was sufficient to see the pervertables that lined the walls. Everything you could possibly think of from vibrators and dildos to floggers, whips, some chains, some cuffs, though probably not the best on the market. There were signs around the store that said custom orders available. I gathered that Mistress Sara has a great supplier and the discreet nature for which she operates her business tells me that she's managed to keep this shop a secret for a very long time.

Though there is nothing illegal down here, the idea that some little boutique in a small town sells this kind of stuff would be the end of her business altogether.

When we walked in, if Cotah hadn't addressed Mistress Sara the way that she had, I would have never put two and two together and I'm curious how Derek found this shop in the first place.

Regardless, the girls dive into the center of the basement where there are all manner of corsets, leather wear, skirts and the like. Raine goes straight for the corsets and she finds one that Dex finds very appealing. I have to agree with him. Though I can't help but wonder what she would wear under it. It would only come to just below her tits.

The girls are having fun and they pull several things off the racks before Raine steps into one of the curtain closed dressing rooms and Dacotah follows her.

After a few minutes, Mistress Sara joins us downstairs. "How are we doing, ladies?" she asks them and they giggle from behind the curtain.

"They're fine," Dex says with a smile.

"Good," Mistress Sara laughs. "How long are you and your pet in town?" she asks Dex.

"Until after Christmas, then we're heading to Nashville for the New Year."

"Oh, nice. Will you guys be at the ball?"

My ears perk up a little bit. "At The Box?" Dex asks.

"Yup."

"As far as I know, it's what's on the agenda."

"Perfect. I will be there as well," she says to Dex but she is watching me as I look through a rack of pants. "Tell me, Beck, are you owned?"

Dex snorts. "Um, no. I'm only just learning about all this. I'm interested in Dominant training," I tell her honestly.

She gives me a quizzical look. "Well then, have you partnered with anyone?"

"No, ma'am."

"Curious," she says, but she gives me a very dismissive look and goes back to talking to Dex. I'm suddenly uncomfortable and I abandon the rack of pants and go to stand by the door as the girls exit the dressing room.

"Did you decide?" Mistress Sara asks Raine and Cotah.

"I've decided, but it is up to my Master," Raine states with a sheepish look in her eyes as she lowers her head.

"Surprise me," Dex tells her and the girls go giggling up the stairs.

I find it odd that she keeps all this stuff down here, but the girls go upstairs to pay for it all. Then it dawns on me that she probably locked the door after the people upstairs left.

I follow the girls up and Mistress Sara and Dex stay downstairs for a couple of minutes before following me up. The girls wait at the register for Mistress Sara while they talk and giggle about something.

It's very obvious to me that these two are good friends and it is nice to see Raine friendly with someone other than Dex. The only time I ever really see her is with Dex and Addison.

No matter, I turn the lock on the door and step outside the boutique and wait for them to finish up with their transaction. While I wait, I watch people as they move about the small town.

The shop is across from a park that appears to be the center of town and given the busy nature of the town on a Saturday, it is no surprise that there are people playing in the park.

The weather here is nice, chillier than California, but not ice cold either.

Finally the door rings behind me and Dex and the girls come out of the shop.

"We ready?" I ask.

"Yup," Dex says and I unlock the truck. The girls climb into the back and Dex joins me up front.

"What was all that about?" I ask him as I back the car out of the parking spot.

"All what?"

"Mistress Sara's dismissal of me."

"Oh, that." Dex avoids answering me.

"Yes, that. Did I do something to offend her?"

He shrugs. "Who knows. Sometimes it is easier to read people, Dominants especially, but I have to say that she's quite the enigma to me. She latched on to me pretty quick."

"Mistress Sara doesn't like unattached Doms," Cotah says from the back.

"Why would she use that against me?" I ask her while looking in the rearview mirror.

"She's not, but you have to understand that this lifestyle is full of predators and assholes. Unattached and especially new Doms, such as yourself, are often scrutinized by other Tops. Until you've proven yourself to them, they tend to shy away from new people."

"I wish I'd known that before," I tell Cotah and the rest of the truck.

"It's really hard to tell. Some people are a little different. I didn't get the same kind of treatment you got from Mistress Sara, but I also started off with Derek as my mentor and Raine as my submissive. I didn't go into the club looking for someone," Dex shares.

"Great, so now my club experience is going to be ruined," I interrupt him.

"I'm not saying that, Beck, relax," Dex tells me, looking at me. "You have to understand, like Dacotah said, this community is used frequently for the predator types. They hide amongst us preying on women and until you're vetted by the club, or vetted to other Tops by Derek, then you may get a little bit of a cold shoulder. But I assure you that Derek intends to do that tonight."

I don't know what to say to that other than, "I'm sorry I got defensive."

He shrugs it off. "Don't be. Believe me, they all have one thing in mind when it comes to outsiders."

"What's that?"

"Keeping the submissives safe." His voice is soft as he says it. He looks over his shoulder toward Raine and I understand immediately what he's saying.

"I wouldn't want it any other way either," I tell him and he nods.

"It's a pain in the ass, but I assure you, it will all work out in the end. Not to mention you look like a fucking beast with that gun strapped to your thigh."

I roll my eyes and turn onto the mile long driveway toward Derek's estate.

When I park, Dex hops out to open the door for Raine and I turn off the engine. Cotah leans forward between the seats and says, "Don't worry about tonight. Derek will vet you to those that are here and when he does that, no one will think any differently. Even Mistress Sara. It's strange the way this community works, and I am still trying to figure it out, but I leave that to Derek to handle."

"Thanks, Cotah."

She leans over and kisses me on the cheek. "No problem. Thanks for taking us."

I smile warmly at her. "You're welcome."

She climbs down out of the truck and I follow her. One of the guys I saw yesterday comes over to the truck. "Will you need it again, sir?" he asks me.

I look at Dex, who shakes his head. "Nope, we're in for the night," I tell him and he takes the keys from me.

"Very well, sir."

I follow the three of them into the house. Cotah made me feel a little bit better about tonight, but I'm more nervous now than I was before. I'd hate to get off on the wrong foot with this group of people. A group that I imagine I will be seeing again, whether here at Derek's or at the club in Nashville.

Derek greets everyone and they start talking about whatever and I start toward my room. I'm about to slide into the kitchen when Derek stops me. "Beck, can I see you for a minute?"

"Sure," I tell him, turning on my heel and heading back in his direction. He ushers me into what I can only guess is his office.

"Take a seat."

"Yes, sir."

I grab a chair on this side of the desk and I think Derek is going to sit down behind it, but he doesn't, he sits in the chair next to me. "I hear Mistress Sara gave you a hard time."

"I wouldn't call it that, but something I said kind of put her off me."

"What did you say?"

"I just told her that I was interested in being a Dominant, though I think I used different words."

He smiles. "Mistress Sara is our resident skeptic. I wouldn't worry about it too much," he tells me as he leans forward, resting his elbows on his knees. "Listen, I want to help clear up that stigma of who you are."

"How?" I ask.

"Well, I put in for your membership with The Box. I hope you don't mind."

I turn more toward him. "How did you do that?" I ask him.

"Well, Sean, as you've maybe guessed by now, is a bit of an information freak. Before you guys came, he'd gotten the information about you that he wanted. Which meant he got your fingerprints, personal information, etcetera."

I shake my head. "I can't say I'm surprised. He and Mills know each other pretty well."

Derek nods. "That they do, and while Mills is often reluctant to give out information, Sean wouldn't take no for an answer. So with that information, I submitted an application for you, along with my recommendation and Dex's."

"I don't, um, thank you, Derek."

He smiles. "You're welcome. Though I don't have the results yet, I was told that they should have them tonight. So along with my personal validation, with any luck, you'll have club approval. All you'll need to do is pay the fee."

"Oh, umm…how much is that?" My eyebrows knit together, running a tally of what's in my checking account at the moment.

"That's private. The Box is an exclusive club, but membership is dependent on several factors. Income is one of them, also your position in the club, top or bottom, attached or unattached. But the fee isn't due until your first attendance. You'll be our guest when we are there over New Year's, so there is no fee, but any time after that, you'll be required to have paid your dues," he tells me.

"Will they tell me when they accept me as a member what my dues are?"

He nods. "You'll be given a packet with all the information you need, which would be great because it outlines the rules of the club, the hours that the club is open, among other things that you'll see when we go."

"Okay then." I smile at him. "Anything else I need to know?"

He shakes his head. "The party starts in just over an hour."

I stand up, excusing myself. "Great, see you then."

He nods but doesn't move and the scene turns a bit awkward. I reach the door and go to turn the knob when he calls, "Oh, one more thing." I turn toward him.

"Anything," I tell him.

"Lose the gun." He grins.

SIXTEEN .

When I walk out of Derek's office, the front door is wide open and there is a group of men walking out. I look around the room and my eyes go wide. The room is slowly starting to look like Dex's playroom.

I escape quickly, ducking into the kitchen which is now empty, but there is a mountain of food on the counter and there are warming ovens off to the side that appear to be full of food. The kitchen smells good and Sean wasn't kidding, no one else will be here tonight. I shake my head and turn down the hallway toward the security team's room. When I round the corner into the common room, Sean is talking with a group of people. He gives me a smile and goes back to discussing the plan for tonight.

Celeste sees me and sends me a coy smile and I give her a small one in return as I duck down the hall toward my room.

I shower again, but this time I take my time. I didn't have time earlier to really take a shower.

When I'm done, I shave and throw some gel into my hair and then go rummaging through my suitcases looking for something to wear tonight. I wish Mistress Sara hadn't put me in her sights at the store because I would have loved to get a pair of leather pants versus wearing a pair of black, loose fitting jeans and my boots. I throw on a black t-shirt and I stow my gun as Derek asked. Though I'd had no intention of wearing it tonight, I'd planned on at least wearing my ankle holster, but I put our fate in the hands of Derek's security team and lock both weapons up before leaving the room.

When I enter the hallway, it is immediately obvious that the group of men and women that were here before are gone. I look at my watch. The party started almost thirty minutes ago, but I didn't want to be the first one there and I haven't gotten any texts from Dex, so I am assuming my late arrival is more than okay.

This time I have no problem finding my way and when I step into the kitchen, there is a group of four girls standing around loading up trays with various food items. One of them is filling champagne glasses in the corner. A couple of them look up, smile wide and make no secret of looking me up and down. I don't blame them. I'm doing the same to them in their scantily clad outfits. My dick stirs in my pants as I step into the great room.

The lights are dimmed and the fires are flickering at a lower flame and there are several different groups of people standing around. But what throws me off guard are the various submissives that are sitting at the feet of their Tops. All silent, all looking almost sad, but there is a strange glow of satisfaction on their faces. One of the Tops gently pats his submissive's head and she nuzzles into his leg. Unfortunately I don't see Derek or Dex and I'm exposed when about a dozen pairs of eyes turn toward me.

I finally spot Derek who smiles and announces, "Uh, ladies and gentlemen, I'd like to introduce you to Aryn Becker." He waves me toward him and somehow I find my feet and walk toward him. "He's a friend of mine and Sir Dex." I find his title for Dex odd, and I wonder why he is addressing him as such, but I don't say anything about it. I vow to ask Dex and I am wishing I had a drink in my hand.

I am met with murmurs of hellos from the Tops around the room.

"I'm happy to report that Aryn is now the newest member of The Box," a gentleman I don't know says and those hellos and murmurs get a little louder, a little more confident. The gentleman who announced my membership steps forward, taking my hand. "I am Master Orik, owner of The Box. It's a pleasure to meet you, Aryn."

I shake his hand. "The pleasure is mine, Master Orik." I give him a smile and he returns one to me.

"Allow us to make some introductions, shall we?" Derek asks Master Orik.

"Certainly." As soon as he says this, there is a silent command and the submissives that were on the floor, rise to stand slightly behind their Tops.

"We don't expect you to remember everyone, but," Derek gestures to Orik.

"This is my partner, Cherry." Master Orik gestures to a vibrant beauty at his side.

"Hello Aryn," she says softly.

"Hello…"

This continues for a few moments, Tops introducing themselves with their respective titles and then their submissive at their side.

Then we come to a cute black-haired female who seeks some type of permission from Master Orik and he nods at her in encouragement. "I'm Diamond. It's a pleasure to meet you, Sir." She gives me a small smile before lowering her head. The gentleman standing next to her gives her a satisfied smile.

"Aryn, I'm Master Caden." He is the first one to step forward, coming to me to shake my hand, but before he manages to reach me, I see a look in his eyes, one that I've seen from Derek, Dex and many of the other Tops I've already met. The same look they have when they address their submissive and I find myself weak in the knees and I don't quite understand it.

"Nice to meet you, Master Caden," I say to him, but I don't feel all that confident and it doesn't go unnoticed by Master Caden. I suddenly feel like I've done something wrong and I cannot explain why I feel that way. Regardless, Master Caden returns to where he was standing, a pleasant smile on his lips but he introduces no one. He's unattached and I find myself curious as to why that is. He's not at all unattractive. In fact, he's bordering on gorgeous, if another man can be gorgeous from a straight man's point of view. If I were a self-conscious person, I would feel inadequate next to him.

The introductions continue around the circle and no, I will not remember all of these names, but that's okay. I'm pretty sure I don't have to. I understand why Master Sara was skeptical of me, but by the time we got to her in the introductions, she was pleasant again. I guess my vetting really made a difference, but what surprised me the most was her submissive. A very cute, short, blonde-haired female sat at her feet and I found that very odd, but only because I didn't see that coming. At least not after she'd busted my balls in her store.

After the introductions were over, I turn toward Derek and Master Orik with a smile on my face.

"How you doing?" Derek asks.

I snort. "I feel like a deer in the headlights."

Master Orik chuckles, "It's a bit overwhelming isn't it?"

I nod. "It is, but I imagine I'll get more comfortable as the night goes on."

"It usually does. Tell me, Aryn, what are your goals, with the club?" Master Orik asks me.

"I'd like to just meet and get to know people, maybe get to know another Top who would be willing to mentor me," I tell him, which is the truth. I know Dex would be willing, but he's being mentored by Derek and I'd hate to have him learning and teaching at the same time.

"I think we can work on that." Master Orik smiles. "I hope you don't mind, but I gave Master Orion," he smiles and clarifies, "Derek, your packet."

I shake my head. "No, that's fine. Is there anything I should know about for tonight?" I ask, honestly not wanting to overstep any boundaries.

Derek shakes his head. "No, I think you've got the basics down."

Almost as if on cue, the four women from earlier enter the great room from the kitchen. They are followed by Cotah and Raine. Raine is dressed in the corset she bought earlier and a very short leather miniskirt. The question I'd had earlier about what she'd wear under it is answered quickly, nothing. I'm pretty sure my eyes bug out of my head briefly when I see her. But I rein myself in and focus more on Cotah. Until I get an unobstructed view and I realize she's not dressed any different than Raine, though she is slightly covered, but barely. The girl is all curves, but she looks sexy as fuck.

The girls are all carrying trays of food and they start making their way around the room, delivering food to the guests and I'm surprised that Dex allows this with Raine. I realize quickly that no one is actually watching them. They take their food and the girls move along. One of the girls from the kitchen comes to me and I take an egg roll type thing from her and she moves off, avoiding eye contact with me.

That's disappointing.

Eventually everyone kind of wanders off and Dex comes to stand with me. "Why did he introduce you as Sir?" I ask him quietly.

He smiles and snorts a little. "Because in most settings, the title of Master is earned. Usually once you've gone through all of the steps and proven your status, then they will acknowledge you as such."

"Do I want to know how many steps there are?" I ask, pretty sure it's not something that can be done in a night.

"I'm not really sure how many, but the first one starts with taking on a submissive role and that, my friend, is something I cannot do."

I shiver, rejection at that idea washes through me. "Me either."

"That's not to say that I cannot be addressed as such in other clubs, but The Box is where we started and it wasn't until later that Raine started calling me Master. So while that dynamic works for us outside of the club, I don't see the necessity of it when it comes to inside the club."

"But Cotah introduced you to Mistress Sara as Master?"

He smiles. "She did and she always will. Her Master has instructed her to do so."

Well, that makes perfect sense. Right? I hold my breath versus the huff of frustration that I'm feeling with all this information. It's impossible to remember everything and eventually, I will screw something up, that I have no doubt.

I'd never thought there would be so much more to this lifestyle than what I'd read on the internet, but I guess like Dex said, every dynamic, every relationship, and I guess every club is different and it is something I'll need to get used to.

SEVENTEEN

The party quickly switches into full swing. Literally.

The subs are directed by their Tops to one apparatus or another. Large duffle bags, suitcases, and various other bags are carried to tables that are set up near the various crosses, benches and tables. Out of those bags comes a wide variety of pervertables, like floggers, cuffs, chains, whips, and stick like things that I've never seen before and quickly decide that whatever they are has to be painful as hell.

There are several occupied stations, but many of them were kind of waiting for someone to take an initiative, and one couple finally does. The first is Master Steven, and his submissive Cassi. She is a gorgeous blonde with a smoking hot body, but she wears too much makeup for my liking.

Master Steven pulls her robe from her shoulders to reveal that she is only wearing the thinnest scrap of underwear and nothing else. Once she is bared to the audience, a glow ignites in her. She enjoys being an exhibitionist. In fact, I would say she thrives on it with no qualms about her appearance. Who can blame her, she's got nothing to be ashamed of. She reminds me of Raine, or rather the impression I have of her after her topless display while serving Derek's guests.

I continue to watch Master Steven carefully. Seeing how he comforts his submissive and how she blossoms under his touch, then he proceeds with little things here and there and in this case, the first thing, is a pair of nipple clamps. She lets out a gentle hiss of pleasure as they are attached to her rose colored nipples.

I shiver and my cock starts to harden.

I continue watching their display and I'm not the only one watching so I don't feel like I'm invading their privacy. But I am completely enraptured when he places a blindfold over her eyes and she visibly melts.

~ CADEN *~*

Ever since I introduced myself to Aryn, I've kept my eyes on him. He has that overwhelmed, deer in the headlights look in his eyes. But that doesn't seem to stop him from watching as couples set up for their scenes. Enraptured is a good fitting word for it.

"So, who is he?" I ask Derek. We've been standing here for the last ten minutes as people start setting up.

"Who's who?" His coy response is laced with knowing, but he wants me to say it for him.

"Aryn?"

He looks at me questioningly. "He's Dex & Raine's bodyguard." His voice holds a hint of curiosity, something Derek is well known for. Though he's usually good about spilling information about people, he doesn't do so freely, he will make you work for what you're after.

"Yet you vouched for him." I turn my head back toward the room, taking a drink of my scotch. Private play parties are good for one thing, alcohol isn't prohibited, and because I'm not here with anyone and have no intention of scening tonight, I'll have a couple.

"So did Dex."

I scrub my hand through my hair, slightly annoyed with Derek's lack of response, but I know better when it comes to him. "Right, but I am pretty sure that Orik wouldn't have delivered the news of his acceptance here tonight if the application didn't come from someone like you. So you vouched for him, Dex backed you up, so either you know him really well or you're following the advice of someone else."

"Or, maybe the fact that he works for Bold, hence his bodyguard status with Dex, he's verified by Sean or he wouldn't be working with him and Sean got his verification from someone I'd trust with my life. And yes, I've met him before, though only briefly."

To anyone outside of this conversation, you'd assume Derek was being snippy with me, but that's hardly the case. Derek is a hard-nosed business man and he doesn't do anything without vetting every aspect. We're also talking about the man who has several Pentagon officials on his speed dial. If Derek is vouching for Aryn, he's legit.

"So what is he after here? What's his deal?" My curiosity is getting the better of me. I can't help asking him what he thinks Aryn's intentions are here and at The Box. Aryn isn't the first person to appear at a play party for the first time. Though the main couples, those quick to the equipment, are our regular playmates. The new ones usually come as unattached subs.

"How so?"

I give him a very pointed look. "What's he really after?"

"A sub."

I snort. "Seriously?"

Derek shrugs his shoulders. "How many of us have walked into a club with the intention of being a Top only to be thwarted, turned down or realize that being on Top isn't what's right for us and we take on a more submissive role?"

"Well, this is true, but you have to be honest with yourself, Derek. How many of those are now Tops?" I counter his claim.

"Sure, most of them are on top now, but they're usually just going through the motions verses actually wanting to stay on the bottom."

"They're all truly a Top, but realize the real direction to being a good Top is to bottom first. I'm pretty sure Aryn has no intention of bottoming. I get the impression he thinks he can just jump right in."

Derek and I both take drinks of the scotch he poured us a few minutes ago. "Well, he's friends with Dex, and he pretty much did exactly that."

I nod in agreement. "Yes, but Dex came prepared with a willing submissive, and a one that I'm sure has no desire to Top him."

He snorts, "I wouldn't say that. She's fiery. I imagine at some point we may find their roles reversed."

I give him an 'are-you-kidding' look and he gives me a sly smile. "I'll believe it when I see it, but Aryn, I don't think he has a dominant bone in him."

Derek snorts again. "No, he doesn't."

I watch Aryn from my perch in front of the bar on the opposite side of the room. I can tell from here that he is engrossed in the scene happening between Steven and Cassi. I can't blame him; they are quite the sight to witness.

"Why so interested in Aryn? What about Kelley?"

I shrug, thinking about my previous submissive and remember why she's not here tonight. "We've run our course. I've done all I can with her. I often wonder if she was bored with me or the lifestyle. We had no long term potential, I offered to train her and I've done that so what happens next for her is up to her."

"That's, well, that kind of sucks. You guys are great together," Derek says to me with a small smile.

I snort. "In the club, absolutely, outside of it, not so much. She always had a hard time following my rules and I always felt like I punished her more then I rewarded her."

"I'm not sure Aryn is what you're looking for then. Besides, he's straight." Hunter states plainly.

I cock an eyebrow at him. "When has that ever stopped me?"

~ ARYN *~*

"Having fun?" a small female's voice asks and I turn toward her. It's Diamond, the unattached submissive I met earlier.

"Uhh, I think so. It's a little…"

"Overwhelming?" She smiles and hands me a beer.

"Thanks," I tell her with a smile as I take it from her. "And yes, very much so."

"You've never been to a party like this before?" she asks. Her voice is soft, comforting and innocent. I find myself drawn to her for some unexplained reason, almost like I can confide in her more than I probably should.

"Yeah, I didn't even know about it until yesterday."

She gives me one of those 'oh-ouch' looks. "Are you staying here, with Master Orion and Dacotah?"

"Master Orion?" My eyebrows knit together.

"Sorry, most of the people here use aliases in a club setting. Derek is his name."

"Oh, yes. I came with Dex and Raine." I can't help but wonder why Dex doesn't use an alias, given who he is and all, but then again, he sits behind the drums, you'd be surprised at how many people don't know who he is.

"Dex is very nice. Raine is sweet. How do you know them?" she asks and I suddenly feel the hair on the back of my neck stand on end and I rub at it, not sure what caused it, but I let it go and Master Caden walks past Diamond and I.

Derek approaches us. "Master Orion," Diamond addresses him and lowers her head.

"As you were, Diamond. Everything alright here?" Derek asks Diamond and I'm surprised by that, then I remember something that Cotah had said about keeping things safe for the subs, always.

"Perfect, just talking with Aryn."

Derek smiles at her. "Good. Can I steal him for a minute?" Derek asks her and she nods and excuses herself.

"Uh…" If I were twelve, I might have actually pouted.

"Sorry, I heard her ask you how you know Dex and Raine and I wanted to give you a couple of pointers about the anonymity that we maintain here. It's the reason we introduced you as Aryn and not Beck." I nod my understanding. "No one here knows who Dex is, or if they do, no one has said anything about it. Master Orik is aware because he doesn't have a filter when it comes to certain people."

"How so?"

Derek laughs, "He's a 69 Bottles fan."

I join him in laughing as well and there are a few heads, including Master Caden's, that turn in our direction. Now why I managed to notice Master Caden out of everyone else in the room is beyond me, but I did. Our eyes lock, but somehow I manage to keep talking to Derek. "That was probably a hard pill for Dex to swallow the first time."

Derek sobers and I am still locked with Caden and I can't understand why. Derek squeezes my shoulder, pulling me out of my stare down with Master Caden and I look at Derek, sheepishly mind you.

There is a knowing smile that spreads across Derek's lips but no explanation of why. "I would just keep things to friends, when it comes to Dex and Raine. But the details you choose to share inside of these walls or the club's walls are your choice. Outside of the club is different."

"I understand."

He smiles then says, "Good. One more thing."

"Anything," I say quickly.

"Did you have any intention of playing tonight?" Derek asks me, and he's serious but, I'm not so sure that he is. I get the impression that if I say yes, he is going to tell me that it isn't a good idea.

"If you mean...no, I don't plan on...yeah, no." I'm suddenly unsure about what it is that I'm really doing here. I haven't a clue how to do any of this stuff and least of all, where to begin with anyone.

"Okay then." He smiles and releases me, turning toward where Diamond had wandered off after he stole me away from her. He jerks his head back toward me and Diamond smiles and starts to approach again. "Watch, enjoy." Derek leans in and whispers, "Though sex isn't off the table."

"I..." I don't know what to say to that, but I let it go and Derek releases my shoulder, stepping back and walking toward Cotah, who kneels before her Master in a way that makes me surprisingly envious.

EIGHTEEN

The night progressed.

Diamond and I talked quite a bit, but eventually she started wandering around, talking to other Tops and then helping with the aftercare of some of her friends. I envied her involvement but oddly enough, I was comfortable watching.

Derek has Dacotah bound in rope against one of the crosses and she seems to be in pure heaven. Dex has Raine on another of the crosses and he is doing all kinds of different things to her. I wander ever closer to them, finding myself more comfortable around them than anyone else.

Some of the scenes have gotten pretty intense and intimate as the night has progressed and while I know they don't mind the audience, I feel like I am intruding.

"Aryn?" Someone calls my name and I turn to see Master Caden commanding my attention.

Somewhere along the night, he hooked up with Diamond and has her strapped to a table toward the middle of the room. I abandon Dex and go over to him.

"Want to see something really fun?" Master Caden asks with a tone of excitement in his voice. He is holding something white, something that resembles that Halloween webbing.

"What is that?" I ask him, true curiosity in my voice.

"It's called flash cotton," he says as his eyes light up. He makes no secret of looking me up and down, but it doesn't bother me, considering he has Diamond laid out on the table. I take it more as a sizing up than anything else.

"Flash cotton?" I ask.

He smiles as he lays it out across her stomach and along her breastbone. Ironically enough, the first thing I notice is the fact that she is strapped down, not the fact that she has shed her corset and is wearing only a pair of black boy shorts. He reaches into his pocket for a lighter and my heart rate increases momentarily when I realize he is going to set whatever this is on fire.

I want to stop him as I'm momentarily panicked by the prospect of what he's about to do. Diamond squirms on the table with a most delicious sound of pleasure coming up her throat. Okay, she's obviously consented to this or had it done to her before, so I let it go.

Master Caden brings the lighter to a raised point in the cotton near her belly button and he rolls his thumb across the lighter and ignites it, also igniting the cotton on her stomach. My breath hitches as the cotton goes up in a quick puff of smoke and Diamond squirms again. Her light pink colored nipples harden and she writhes, silently begging for more.

"Wow," is all I manage to say.

I'm still a little unnerved by what I saw, playing with fire and all, but I am also intrigued by what exactly the purpose of that was. He sets her up for another round. "What's it feel like?" I ask. The words spill out of me before I can catch them.

Master Caden cocks his head at me. "Would you like to try?"

The look in his eyes tells me that he's pushing for more information from me, or he has this unsettling need to get me laid out like Diamond is on this table and it makes my skin crawl.

"No thanks. Was just curious what Diamond thinks about it."

There is displeasure and maybe even disappointment that crosses Master Caden's features at my rejection. For the first time in my life, I feel the overwhelming sludge of disappointment slide over me, along with a desperate need to please him and I cannot wrap my head around why that is.

The thought of pleasing him takes control of my thoughts and the instinct to lower myself to my knees before him becomes almost too much to bear.

Lost in the idea that I've somehow managed to disappoint someone I don't know sends me walking toward the kitchen, down the hallway and as far away from Master Caden as I can get, as fast as I can get there.

~ CADEN *~*

"Well, that didn't go as well as I'd planned," I grumble as I finish with Diamond. We hadn't set any ground rules for playing together. The cotton was something that got brought up in a discussion with someone else and she was itching to try it. And while I was more than willing to take things further, play with her some more, my urge to play walked out the door with Aryn.

What did I say that sent him running for the door?

I shake my head, vowing to let it go.

Derek's words come back to me, "he's straight..." and I inadvertently backed him into a corner.

"You gave him that look," Diamond says.

We have no rules for Top and bottom etiquette because she and I aren't partners. "What look?" I ask her.

"That look, Master Caden. Your Dom face. He wouldn't be the first Dom that has had problems with your Dom face. You have an uncanny ability to make even the strongest Tops weak in the knees. What makes you think he's any different?"

"I do? Huh, I guess I never considered it that way."

She smiles at me before cheekily replying, "It's why subs flock to you."

I help Diamond off the table, unsure of what to say to that. I guess maybe she's right, but I've found so many subs lacking in what I desire. Like I told Derek tonight, I'm ready for someone steadier, more permanent to play with regularly. My eyes wander toward the door Aryn left through. I have an intense need to follow him.

~ ARYN *~*

"Shit," I grumble as I round the corner into the security team's area of the house and smack straight into Celeste.

"Where's the fire?" She smiles at me.

"Uh, nowhere?" I raise an eyebrow at her, but I slide past her, heading toward my room.

Without a second thought, I turn around to look at her and I'm not at all disappointed in what I see. I need to find a way to get rid of this rising storm within me. I turn toward her, pinning her with a gaze that says 'I'm not fucking around anymore' and ask, "Are you off?"

"No," she states simply. "Just roaming through, why?"

Her response is like ice water being poured over my head and it only takes me a second to realize that I need to maintain a professional relationship with her I simply respond with, "Nothing." I turn back around, open my door and close it quickly, though slamming it might be a better description.

I lean against the door and bang my head on it trying to wipe away the memory of Caden's eyes as he stared me down. The eyes that had me uncomfortable and running for the hills. But it's no use. My cock, which grew hard as steel under his gaze, twitches in my jeans and I groan. Pushing off the door and stripping off my shirt, I head into the bathroom.

I turn on the shower, my third for the day, a record, and I strip out of my shoes and jeans.

My cock stands straight out, stiff and desperate for release.

I grip the base as I step into the shower.

I stroke up, hard, tugging on it, wishing it would go away, hoping that I am not about to do what I'm going to do. Jerk off, compliments of a very demanding, overwhelming and sexy as fuck Dom.

I let the water cascade over me, warming me, and I close my eyes, pulling up images of Celeste, and what she looks like under that get up.

Gorgeous tits, suckable nipples, devouring her clit with my mouth, sliding my fingers deep inside her slick sex. The longer I suck on her clit, the harder and fuller it gets...the longer it gets, the more...the minute I explode all over the shower walls, I'm staring hard into the dominating eyes of Master Caden.

NINETEEN

I avoid breakfast the next morning. The advantage of one night stands is the ability to disappear and never have to look at that person again. In this case, I didn't sleep with anyone, but I can't find it in myself to look at Caden. Not only because I got off thinking about him last night, but I ran away from him so abruptly.

I'm still not entirely certain what it was that sent me running for my room, but I'm pretty sure it has something to do with the fact that I'm not entirely sure I'm ready for this lifestyle.

Okay, fine. I am ready for it, but I never expected to feel the way I did last night from a simple look. I've seen similar looks in Dex's eyes when he looks at Raine, though I didn't understand them until this week. They've always been there. It's a typical Dom expression. One meant to have maximum impact of disapproval and it's highly effective.

I text Dex around one, asking if they have plans for the day and he comes back letting me know that Derek's guests have left and they're just going to hang out and watch the game.

Dex isn't much of a football buff, but we've watched games together before. Usually in bars. He asked me to join them and what the hell, Caden is gone, right?

The next two days are filled with various errands, including Christmas shopping in Charlotte with Dex and Raine. I was glad I finished my shopping back in Los Angeles because these two are the only two I'd be buying presents for.

The mall was ridiculously crowded and to my surprise, Dex was recognized twice. He was gracious, for once, and signed some autographs. After that we'd left the mall for another one. With today's social media network, it was only a matter of time before the word was out that we were there. Again, this is Dex and the band's drummer, but most people will take whoever they can get from 69 Bottles. Casey's had the same problem with Mouse and Peacock and Talon has resigned himself to avoiding public shopping at all costs.

The day after was a mess of activity around the house. I spent the entire day with Sean, Cyrus and Celeste learning about the house and the security procedures, should anything happen during the big Christmas Eve party. Because I'm technically a guest of Derek's, Sean insisted that I get an inside post. I argued about it, telling him I'd be suited best where he needs me.

I lost the argument when Derek insisted that I could keep a better eye on Dex and Raine from inside, since they're my responsibility. I shrugged it off at that point. I honestly don't care where I am. I know that because Dex and Raine are guests of Derek's they fall under Sean's responsibility too, so I know I've honestly got nothing to worry about.

Not to mention the fact that we've had a secret service sweep of the property so I'm pretty sure the risks for tonight are very limited.

There is an actual agenda for tonight's event and because of that, I spent the time while eating lunch memorizing the itinerary. The entire event takes place in the main room with limited access to first floor rooms, like the bathroom and a couple of sitting areas (bedrooms that are unused and were converted for tonight). These rooms are for privacy, though there will be a guard posted near each and there are assigned staff to maintain the space.

I've been around wealthy people since I got into this business, but Derek's wealth is very overwhelming. His ability to not only host an event of this size, but to have it in his home is staggering. The more reading of the guest list I do, the more I realize just how many people this man knows and the shear amount of money coming into this house is astronomical.

Knowing I'm the help is an uneasy feeling. Regardless of the fact that I've been around the rich and the famous, it never stops the feeling of inadequacy. I'll never be rich, I'll always be protecting the coat tails of those who are.

I am standing close to the kitchen door and if I'd thought the great room had been cleaned out for the play party, that was nothing compared to this. The room is now one, with no divisions except for the fireplaces that are scattered throughout the room. There are tables that surround a stage and a dance floor. The stage is occupied by an instrumental band that will provide the entertainment for tonight. In the corner opposite of me and the room, is a massive Christmas tree that nearly touches the thirty foot tall ceiling.

There are two additional guards inside that I can see. One standing just off the door and the other is opposite me at the hallway to the bathrooms and the private rooms. There are at least two more guards down the hall. Right before the guests started arriving, myself and Cyrus went through locking all the room doors except the private rooms that are open to anyone.

My eyes scan the room. While it isn't full, there is a steady stream of people flowing through the door. My scanning has me watching the front door as guests come through. Just outside the door there is a tent reception area that checks off the guests as they arrive and then they're screened before coming through the door to the house.

Not that I expected to recognize anyone who arrived at this party, but I'm surprised to see someone coming down the stairs, two someone's actually. Her eyes catch mine and she smiles. Cami has such an infection personality, it's impossible not to smile back at her. I'm a bit surprised to see them; they're usually off in Tahiti or something like that this time of year. But they're not my detail so I don't question it much past that.

Although I do find it odd that Tyson, Tristan's bodyguard, isn't with them, but he could be somewhere else on the property. Sean isn't required to tell me everything, but if he's here, it'd be nice to catch up with him.

Cami and Tristan approach me. "Hello, Beck," Cami greets me and I say hello back. "You remember Tristan?"

"Of course. Good to see you, man." I extend my hand to him. "I didn't know you guys were coming."

Cami smiles. "We got in early today, we're staying until Sunday."

"Oh, awesome." I smile at her.

"How are things going?" she asks and I scan the room instinctively, ever on duty.

"They're good. Been a pretty relaxing week. It's been kind of nice. How about you?"

"We're good," Tristan answers.

"Where's the little man?" I ask them.

Cami lights up. "He's upstairs with our nanny. We never travel without him."

"Speaking of which, don't you guys usually spend Christmas in the Bahamas or something?" I ask candidly.

Tristan frowns. "Tahiti, but I have to work next week, so we couldn't go this year."

Our conversation continues for a few more minutes about mundane things until Dex and Raine come down the stairs followed by Derek and Dacotah. Cami and Tristan leave me to my post and I continue doing what I'm good at. Holding up a wall.

An hour later and the room is filled with men and women wearing extravagant attire enjoying the food and drink. The entrance has settled quite a bit now that the majority of guests have arrived, but there's still a steady trickle as people come and go.

Dacotah and Raine look stunning in black gowns while Dex, in true Dex fashion, is wearing a white dress shirt, no tie, a vest and his sleeves are rolled to the elbows. And judging by the way Raine keeps looking at him, she's thinking about taking it off him. That's one thing about Raine, once you get to know her, it's not hard to pick up on her subtle signals to Dex and it makes me smile.

Derek and Dacotah are playing gracious hosts, stopping to chat with people as they make their way around the room. Derek talks to a few of the attending celebrities and I wonder how someone makes friends like that. I know from Dex that he has his hand in more than a few hotels in Vegas, but other than that, I'm not entirely sure what it is that he does. On Sunday, following the play party, I spent some more time trying to research what it is that Derek does and while his public profile is extensive, a lot of what's there doesn't even begin to explain his exorbitant wealth.

Dex, Raine, Cami, Tristan, Derek and Dacotah are the only ones here that I know directly. Some of the celebrities on hand I know of, but have never met. Regardless, it is a very interesting mix of company and I wonder why it is that Derek would host such an extravagant event without some sort of charity benefit to it. I get having friends, but jeez, this is almost excessive if you ask me.

About twenty minutes into dinner, I'm relieved by one of Sean's guys to take a dinner break. I step into the kitchen where there are a couple of other security guys there, a couple of them have plates in their hands and my stomach growls. One of the staff hands me a plate as I walk past them and I join the others to eat.

Other members of the security team come and go as I finish my plate, and all are offered food as they come in. The kitchen staff operates like a well-oiled machine between feeding us and preparing the next course and dessert, which looks fucking amazing. If my dinner is anything to go by, then it will be delicious.

When I resume my post, dinner is in full swing. Though there are a few people lingering about, most everyone is in their seats and the volume level has reduced to a dull roar and the band is playing gentle music. If it wasn't for the fact that I have no choice but to stay awake, I'd be dozing off.

"Good evening, Aryn." A voice from out of nowhere greets me and I'm taken aback by the name. There are only a handful of people who know that name. I turn to the man standing to my left and my breathing stops altogether. "It's great to see you again."

It takes me a moment to find my voice. I can't help raking my eyes over the man before me dressed spectacularly in a black Armani suit, vest and tie. "Caden," I finally manage to say.

There is a coy smile playing at his lips as he takes in my demeanor. I doubt he missed my reaction to his presence here tonight.

"How are you?" he asks me and I finally manage to find my brain and pull it out of my stomach.

"I'm good, you?"

He smiles then, "I'm great. Having fun tonight?"

"I should ask you that. I, unfortunately, am working."

"I noticed. But you didn't answer my question."

He doesn't unleash the look that sent me running the other night, but the one he does give me is a close second. "I'm having a great time," I tell him. "How about you?"

"Better now." He smirks and turns on his heel, returning back to his seat, which is in the middle of the two tables that have Dex, Derek and Cami in them. He's sitting between Derek and Cami and he picks up a very animated conversation with Cami. Making me wonder if they know each other and that thought sends a million things racing through my mind.

Who is he? Why is he talking to Cami? Do they know each other? Why would Derek invite a club friend to a big Christmas extravaganza? How many other people from the other night are here?

I struggle to pull my eyes away from him and the thoughts keeps me occupied as I scan the room.

TWENTY

~ CADEN *~*

"Are you going on the tour?" Cami asks me.

"I hadn't planned on it. Most of the time I'm just in the way." I chuckle, "No one usually wants to talk to me."

She laughs too, "I doubt that. Without you, that movie wouldn't have been done."

I smirk at her. "You're too kind. I may or may not hit the Nashville premiere. I'll be there at the time." I shrug and take a drink of my scotch.

"You know Beck?"

I can't help but raise an eyebrow at her. "Beck?"

She cocks her head in Aryn's direction. "I saw you talking to him a little while ago?"

My eyes wander over to Aryn and he looks away from me quickly. He's watching me. "Oh, Aryn?" She gives me a brief widening of her eyes. "I met him shortly after they got here, last Saturday I think." No need to mention what it was that we were doing. I imagine Tristan can be quite alpha, but they're hardly into the lifestyle. "Though Derek introduced him as Aryn."

Cami smiles and it reaches her eyes, giving her a very genuine, happy look that you don't see on many Hollywood types. "He's one of 69 Bottles' security team," she tells me. "He's also assigned to Alyssa for the premiere tour."

"Oh reeeallly," I say with a sly smile. "I thought he belonged to Dex." I give a soft snort that goes unnoticed. No - he most certainly does not belong to Dex.

"He does, but we borrow him from time to time. He's one of our top guys."

"Why have I never seen him before?" I ask her, trying to get as much candid information from her while she's talking as I can.

She shrugs her shoulders. "Not sure, but he travels mostly in the musician circles, that could be why."

I nod in agreement and take another sip of my scotch.

Our conversation is cut short when the servers start serving dessert and I let my eyes find Aryn's once more. I am disappointed when I see that he's talking to someone else, someone who's dressed the way that he is, only female. Jealousy slides through me as I take in the girl and the playful smile on Aryn's lips.

~ ARYN *~*

"Sean wants you outside."

I smirk at Celeste. "Why not call me on the radio then?"

"Why when I was coming to the kitchen anyway." She winks at me and moves past me. I shake my head and head toward the front door.

As I do, eyes bore into me and I don't need to look to know it's Caden. The minute he looked up from his dessert while I was talking to Celeste, I not only saw his gaze but felt it along my neck when my hair stood on end. What in the hell am I going to do about him?

I shake my head as I step free of the door and go walking toward Sean's post where they set up the temporary visual equipment for tonight.

Sean showed me the AV room this week and I was blown away when he said he was adding more for the event tonight. He has a three hundred sixty degree view of this entire property with very little blind spots and most of those are usually covered by a guard.

When I enter the hut the guys are laughing at one of the monitors. I follow their gaze and shake my head.

"Some people just can't wait till they get home," I mutter as I watch some woman sprawled out on the bathroom sink with someone up under her dress having her for dessert. The facial expressions she makes has all of us laughing for a good ten minutes before the guy crawls out from under her dress and I'm surprised to see who it is. "Is that who I think it is?"

"Yup," one of the guys says through his laughter. "And that is not his wife."

My eyes widen at the video monitor, getting a good clear look at one Senator Millstone.

I ask Sean what's up, telling him I know he didn't bring me out here to watch that. He laughs and says, "Sure, I did." But he gives me a very pointed look before getting up and escorting me outside.

"What's up?" I ask him when we're clear of the guys, though they're still laughing.

"Don't worry about them, they're all under confidentiality agreements, they can't tell a soul about what they saw. I can't say the same for you."

I snort a laugh, "Believe me, my lips are sealed. I am curious though."

"About what?"

"Will you tell Derek?" I ask him.

He sighs. "Yes, unfortunately I will tell him. He will be pissed beyond words because Sally, the senator's wife, is a very good friend of Derek's and while he couldn't care less for the Senator, he does care about Sally."

I frown. "So, you needed me for something?"

"Not really, thought you could use some fresh air."

I chuckle. "Sure."

"Walk with me?"

I cock my head at him, but follow him through the makeshift parking lot of cars, looking for anyone who may be where they're not supposed to be. There is temporary lighting throughout the makeshift lot and an entire valet team to handle the cars.

We walk for some time before Sean starts talking. We cover the party, the weather and other mundane topics before he says, "I didn't know you knew Caden Matthew."

I shake my head. "Can't honestly say that I do. I met him Saturday night, at the err, the. Is that a problem?"

He shakes his head. "No, not at all."

"What's wrong, Sean?" I ask him as we come to a stop at the far end of the parking lot.

"Nothing, just be careful with him." He turns to look at me.

I cock my head. "I'm not following what you're implying."

"He's not, I don't know, he's not your typical kind of guy."

I want to press him to explain further, but I am not entirely sure I want to know anymore.

"Look, he's just, a friend of mine is one of his ex-subs."

"Whoa, you, how? Wha-what makes you think it's like that with me?"

He gives me a curious look. "I think I find it odd that my assumption wasn't the first response you gave me."

I turn away from him. "I'm not sure I know what you mean," I tell him coyly.

"Your first thought wasn't about you and him, it was curious about what I knew. Very curious," he says with a skeptical tone. I turn back toward him and his eyes are narrowed at me, trying to read me.

"Look, I only physically met him the other night, that's it. And tonight he came by to say hello."

"I'm sorry, I shouldn't have said anything."

"What aren't you telling me?" I ask him sternly.

He sighs. "He has a tendency to find subs, use subs and then move on to someone else."

"Is he really using them or are they not compatible?" I ask, trying to counter his claims about Caden. I have the sudden urge to defend someone who isn't here.

"Honestly? I don't know. I just know that he broke my friend's heart. She was devastated enough to drop out of the lifestyle altogether."

I frown and that's about all I can do. I don't quite know what to say to him about Caden. I'd prefer to make judgments on my own and ironically enough, I can't quite understand why I care about what he's done in his past, why it would matter to me.

"When Caden wants something, he gets it," Sean says out of the blue as he turns and starts walking back toward the hut and the house.

"I'm pretty sure he's not my type," I add on a laugh, letting him know that it isn't something he needs to worry about with me.

"Well, shit," he says. "Why didn't you tell me that?" Embarrassment colors his tone and his cheeks.

"Because I had no idea where you were going with this little speech. I find it admirable that you want to protect your friend and even me, but I assure you, he's not my type, his chest is way too flat." I laugh humorlessly and Sean joins in. I don't find my words convincing to myself, but it's sufficient enough for Sean who does and that's all I care about.

Sean and I walked back to the AV hut and then I left him there to return to my post inside the house.

Once inside, I find that dinner is over and several guests begin leaving the party, while the majority of them take to the dance floor as the band picks up the tempo, livening up the party.

The party finally wraps around one in the morning, though those that remained were staying for the night at Derek's, just a couple stragglers, including Caden.

Sean dismissed me from my post before the end of the friendly gathering, which I'm grateful for. I kept catching Caden watching me throughout the night despite my best efforts to ignore him and do my job. Being able to leave the room made the likelihood of him coming to talk to me diminish.

I escaped back to my room. The living area of the details' quarters is full of guards laughing, chatting, drinking and having a good time as they wind down for the evening. As I pass through, Celeste catches my eye and she holds up a fresh beer for me. I smile at her but shake my head.

For as vulnerable as I feel tonight, drinking with her isn't the best idea in the world and while the distraction would be great to have, if only for tonight, I still have to work with her for the next week or so.

TWENTY~ONE

The next morning I lay in bed, like most days back at home, reading a book I've been working on since I got here. Christmas has never been a cheerful holiday for me and even as an adult, I can take it or leave it. I've spent too many holidays away from family and friends to feel the nostalgia of being around them as a necessity.

Around eleven, my phone rings with a call from Dex, who proceeds to yell at me for hiding in my room. After some half-ass attempts at arguing with him, I throw on a pair of flannel pants and a t-shirt and grab their presents before going into the main part of the house.

I don't run into anyone along the way and it makes me smile when I see Raine and Cotah working in the kitchen versus Derek's kitchen staff. "Merry Christmas," I smile at the two of them who beam back at me with bright excited smiles and a very cheerful Merry Christmas greeting before they go back to finishing what they're doing.

I head into the great room where Derek, Dex, Cami, Tristan and their son Jaden are talking and playing with Jaden's new toys. He's a cute little shit.

They play a little more before the girls emerge from the kitchen carrying trays of food and place it on a table that I overlooked when I came in. It's literally covered with food and I smile.

"We graze for Christmas." Derek smiles at me. "I give my staff the day off."

"Sounds great to me," I tell him with a wide smile back.

We have a small gift exchange, mostly just the presents from friend to friend. It's obvious to me, when I see Raine's new laptop, that they'd all already exchanged their personal presents with each other.

That's fine with me. I would have felt really out of place watching them open their personal presents to each other.

Dex hands me a present and I in turn give them theirs.

When I was struggling to figure out what to get them, I'd remembered the art gallery event we went to a few months back and the painting they'd both fallen in love with. It struck me as odd that neither one of them purchased the painting at the time, so when I saw it, I couldn't resist. I couldn't bring it with me, so I took a picture of it and stuffed it in a card. Yeah, I don't do the whole wrapping thing. In turn they'd given me a new iPad, since I dropped mine at their house a few weeks back, shattering it. While I hadn't replaced it yet, the gesture was a little over the top and more than double what I'd spent on them.

Sometimes having rich friends when you're far from it can be a bit daunting and it makes things seem lopsided. But, like a good little boy, I accepted my gift with gratitude.

After a while, I returned to my room. Dex has always tried to include me, but I can't bring myself to get into it.

The next day, Cami and Tristan took off early in the morning. I didn't see them go, but we followed shortly after in Derek's plane for Nashville.

Derek has a really nice house in Nashville, a third of the size of the estate near Charlotte, and I found it a little odd that he would have a house here. He's barely an hour flight from Nashville. That was until he had to run off to the office and it wasn't in the house. The well-used house seemed a little more personal, at least for Cotah and I get the impression that they actually live here more than they do in Charlotte. It's none of my business so I don't ask a ton of questions about it.

The next couple of days are rather boring for me. Yes, the girls went shopping, and yes, I took Dex and Raine out a couple of nights without Derek and Dacotah, but all in all, it was uneventful and nice to just sit back and relax for a few days.

Tonight, however, is another story. I haven't been this nervous since I was a teenager going on my first date.

Tonight is a fetish ball at The Box and it is also the day before New Year's Eve.

Dex took me shopping, without the girls, earlier this week. He insisted that I needed something else to wear to the club tonight because it is a fetish ball after all. Derek had recommended a couple of different shops in the Nashville area that were more gothic than fetish in their attire and I didn't feel so out of place while inside of them. Granted, I'm a thirty-four year old man shopping in a store geared toward high school gothics not adult fetish wear.

Regardless of the location or the store audience, I was able to find myself a pair of leather pants and for some strange reason, a solid black t-shirt that is about two sizes too small in the chest department.

So that is what I'm wearing tonight. Sans the mask. There's a masquerade element to tonight's party and the girls are wearing them, however, neither Derek nor Dex are planning on wearing one. I take their lead and decide against one too. Unlike Derek and Dex, I'm not famous nor do I feel the need to hide my identity. Especially if I'm planning on sticking around the club after tonight.

Dex, Derek and I are chatting in the living room when the girls come down. Their hair is pulled up and back and they're both wearing the same outfit. Black and red corsets with short tutu like skirts, thigh high red and black striped socks and platform boots.

Both Derek and Dex light up when they see them. They exchange greetings and once again jealousy courses through me. Why am I so jealous all of a sudden?

It's not like I've been dying for a girlfriend or anything. In fact, I am pretty sure I'm better off without one. But then again, I haven't had a solid, steady one since high school and that was more of a relationship of convenience on her part. I was the exact opposite of what her parents would approve of, so I was the fun scapegoat, but whatever. We had fun and took each other's virginity late in our sophomore year. We lasted another two years, only breaking up after I graduated from high school and left her behind to finish her senior year. She used me to gain popularity with the popular cliques in our tiny ass school and once she realized it no longer mattered because I wasn't going to be there anymore, I was tossed aside. It was fine by me.

I shake my head, wiping away the memory of all those years ago just as Derek and Dex hold open coats for the girls.

We pile into Derek's Range Rover and start for the club. We have no security with us, except for me, but I have no weapons on me whatsoever. Club rules.

I had argued about that with Derek, but he said it was the rules of the club for one and for two, it's a member only party and all guests are fully vetted by the club. This is honestly the safest place Dex, Raine and Derek can go without a detail team as there are dungeon monitors and the club's own security team inside at all times.

I watch from the back seat as Derek drives us through town, becoming suspicious of where we're really going when the scenery turns from alternating houses and businesses to industrial sized steel buildings. Loading docks and the occasional eighteen wheeler driving down the road.

We approach an empty area along the street that isn't empty just black as can be. The only identifying marker is the red lights that line the top of the building and Derek turns in.

The building lives up to its name. It literally looks like a big two, two and half story box with no windows and only two doors. One double set and one off to the left of that one. Both doors are lit by overhead lighting, but can easily be missed if those lights are turned off. There is a couple walking toward the double doors and I watch as they open them but I cant see anything inside before the doors close again. No one is going in and out of the other door, but I notice a security pad next to the door. My guess is that it belongs to the offices or maybe the private rooms that Dex had told me about.

At some point over the last few days, I'd broken down and reviewed the package that Master Orik had given me at Derek's during the play party. Derek reminded me about it and that it would be a good idea to brush up on the rules before tonight. So I did. Then went running to him with questions about my dues and what all that money went toward. Ultimately it goes toward maintaining the club as Master Orik does not profit from the club. I have no problem with my dues amount, only it's a lot of money considering I live in Los Angeles making my use of the Nashville club limited to a couple times a year, if that.

The plus side to my dues, I don't have to pay them until after I've come to the club a few times and feel it's really where I want to be.

As we stand in line to check-in, Derek tells me, "All members are required to check-in, this is so that they know who is here for the night and to keep track for capacity rules. There are nights that people are left waiting to get in because it's full. Or they haven't opened up the other side of the dungeon. Tonight is invitation only and responses were required."

"I didn't get an invite," I tell him.

"No, you didn't, but Master Orik is a dear friend of mine and knows that you're my guest tonight, so you're perfectly fine. The responses were required because they used those to determine how many more invites they could send out until they reached about thirty below capacity."

I raise an eyebrow. "Why is capacity so important?"

Derek gives me a pointed look like I should know and understand the answer to my own question but I'm honestly baffled by it.

He sighs. "Sorry, I guess capacity is for two reasons. One, we don't need the police showing up here. Master Orik goes through a great deal to keep this place off the radar. For all the cops really know, this is some type of exclusive bar."

"Oh." I nod for him to go on.

"The second reason is that fetish balls are open to anyone to play as they wish and there are going to be a few demonstrations. If the capacity is reached or exceeded, crowd control can be a problem as well as giving people enough room to work. Tonight, Mistress Aria is going to be doing a whip demo. She needs a lot of room because she wields two single tails simultaneously."

"Good god," Dex and I say together.

"It's quite the sight to see." Derek smiles wide and we move closer toward the podium to get checked in.

Derek and Dex lapse into conversation and the closer we get to the podium the more nervous I get about what's beyond the velvet curtain. The more I stare and try to see beyond it with each person who pushes through it, the more excited I get. Each time someone enters the club, I try to catch glimpses of what's happening inside, but I can't see much more than bodies standing around.

Just as we're about to reach the podium, I catch a good glimpse beyond the curtains of a couple of crosses spotlighted from above. No one is on them and they're imposing and intimidating while being inviting all at the same time.

"Master Orion, Cotah, and guest Aryn," Derek checks us in.

The girl standing behind the podium eyes me up and down before giving me a playful smile. "Welcome to The Box, Aryn." Her voice is sweet and seductive at the same time. She has a mane of tight curly dark brown or black hair. Her skin is pale and she is wearing soft make-up. It's too dark in here to determine her eye color but they sparkle in the low light. My heart pounds a little in my chest.

"Thank you." I give her a teasing smile in return and she blushes slightly as she finishes checking the three of us in.

When she's done, she moves on to Dex and Raine. Once they're checked in, Cotah and Raine check their coats off to the side of the entrance and I catch the girl who checked us in looking at me again and I smile.

If I were anywhere else but here, I'd be pouncing on her so fast, but not here, not tonight. Her demeanor is exactly that of a submissive and I can't help being turned on by the idea that maybe there is someone inside this club for me. Who knows, maybe even her.

"We ready?" Derek asks us before spreading the curtains at the entrance. Cotah steps through with me right behind her. My breathing hitches the moment I step inside The Box.

TWENTY~TWO

Stepping inside The Box is almost indescribable. There are a lot of people hanging around, talking, watching various things going on throughout the room. There are a lot of bottoms sitting at the feet of their Tops and while I see several others not kneeling, they are easy to tell apart.

The room is lit mostly by black lights and then various spotlights over different apparatuses. Everything from St. Andrew's Crosses to spanking benches to something that looks like parallel bars used in gymnastics, only they're much taller and made of solid metal with various rings hanging at different intervals along the bars. I'm not sure what it is, but I imagine it has something to do with suspension.

There is also a high bar looking thing with two chains hanging down. I imagine it's best used like the cross only without the hindrance of wood in front of or behind the person strapped to it. Though none of the equipment is being used at the moment, there are several people standing around a lot of it.

I follow my friends into the club. Derek leads us all to the bar, but there is no liquor behind it. It looks like a juice bar and I listen when Derek orders a coke for him and apple juice for Cotah. Dex does the same only ordering coke for both of them. Derek points to me and I say the same.

Derek proceeds to talk to a couple of people near the bar area and Dex joins in the conversation.Both Cotah and Raine stand in silence, waiting to be addressed and they both blossom when they're introduced to the men Derek and Dex are talking to.

He introduces me and neither of them are people I recognize from the play party a couple weeks ago and while I try to commit their names to memory, it doesn't last.

Eventually, with drinks in hand, we leave the bar. Dex turns to me and says, "Alcohol, while available tonight, is not served in the club. If you want a drink, you're more than welcome to one, but you will be prevented from participating in any events."

"Nah, coke is good."

"Want to get frisky tonight, do you?" he chides.

I snort. "That would imply actually meeting someone." I take a sip of my coke.

"The greeter sure made a visual meal out of you."

I'd nearly forgotten about her until now. I shrug. "She's probably got a Top."

Dex laughs. "Hardly. I can't imagine a single Dom or Domme that would allow that kind of behavior."

I don't know how to respond to that. It's not something I'd thought about, actually. "Do you know who she is?"

Dex shakes his head. "I've not seen her before, though we've only been here a couple times. You could ask Derek."

"I don't want to force anything." I suddenly feel inadequate. Sure, I can talk to her. I can flirt with her. I can do whatever when it comes to her, but she was very obvious about being a submissive and I'm barely capable of calling myself a Top.

Sure, I like rough sex. Sure, I like to take control during sex, and I most definitely enjoy it when a woman's open and willing to do whatever it is that I ask of her, but that hardly qualifies as being a Dominant.

I'm going about this all wrong. Sure, I thought that I could just dive right in, but I have so much to learn about the lifestyle, about behavior, and not to mention I haven't a clue what I want in a submissive. The realization sends me into a tailspin of disappointment that thankfully no one else notices.

~ CADEN *~*

Well, well, well, that's quite the surprise.

I knew Derek was bringing him tomorrow when the dungeon is open, but I had no clue that he would be here tonight and judging by the fact that he looks like a deer in the headlights, I imagine he's not looking for anyone in particular tonight either.

"Who is that?" Cara asks me.

"Who is who?" I ask her back, unsure if she's referring to Aryn or someone else.

"That guy, the one you're looking at. Do you know him from somewhere?"

Shit, I didn't invite Cara to Derek's play party for good reason. I didn't want her there, but how do I explain, I don't. "No clue," I tell her. "He's with Master Orion and Sir Dex; I'd guess he's a friend of theirs."

I lied to her. I wouldn't normally do something like that. After getting back to town from Derek's and then Los Angeles, I'd called Cara and broken off our playing together. The only thing she was upset over was the fact that we'd committed to coming to the ball tonight. I agreed to take her tonight and I agreed to take her under my wing and look over her while she looks for another Dominant. It's the least I can do for her.

She was a great sub, just lacked whatever it is that I'm seeking right now. We hadn't made any commitments to each other and I'd never collared her officially. I did however give her my training collar and that is what I took back from her. At first she expected a full collar as a replacement, but in the end she seemed okay about not getting one.

Aryn disappears from my line of sight and I fight the urge to go after him. The urge is thwarted when Master Orik steps on the stage toward the far end of dungeon two and takes the microphone.

"Good evening ladies, gentlemen, Dominants, Masters, Tops, submissives, slaves and bottoms. Welcome to the third annual Box Fetish Ball." The entire crowd erupts in cheers and clapping. I can't help but join in.

The Box has been a true safe haven to so many people for going on four years now and it is definitely something to be proud of. Orik beams with happiness as the crowd settles down.

"Tonight we celebrate not only the new year, but another year of amazing friends, family, and relationships. I'm proud to say that we welcomed twenty-three new members to the club this year, the latest one just last week." That would be Aryn, I have no doubt. "And I am proud to say that we've been able to kick off some of the much needed renovations compliments of Master Orion, Master Caden, and the many wonderful members of this club, so thank you, Sirs."

~ ARYN *~*

When Master Orik mentions Master Caden's name as one of the top donors for the renovations, my heart sinks. I hadn't expected him to be here tonight for one, and for two, if he can throw money at this club the way that I know Derek is capable of, that puts Caden into a whole new category and it slides me right back down to the bottom of the depression pit.

One of the many things that has kept me to women in bars is the fact that I feel more equal to them. I'm not poor, but I'm not capable of doing a swan dive into a pool full of cash. It's why opening up and spending time with Derek and Dacotah, despite being friends with Dex, has been so hard for me. I've always felt my place is with the help, not with the employers.

Master Orik continues with his speech, thanking a few other people and introducing some of the artisans that are in the building tonight. By the sounds of it, they specialize in either custom fetish wear or pervertables, and I'm curious to check some of these out. He also goes into the schedule for tonight with the various demonstrations being performed throughout the evening.

When he's done, the crowd erupts with more cheers and excitement before dispersing and returning to their previous activities.

That's when I feel it. The hair on the back of my neck stands on end and I know not far away from me is Master Caden.

TWENTY~THREE

~ CADEN *~*

I stay away from Aryn despite my driving need to talk to him. I wonder if he knows I am here. I watch him most of the night as he makes his way around the room talking to people. I felt a huge twinge of disappointment when he met up with Ash, or Ashley, the greeter for tonight's event. They've been chatting a good portion of the evening and she sticks to him like glue.

Ashley is attractive and she is a well-trained sub and would be a great fit with Aryn. That thought doesn't help but drive the disappointment higher. I knew it was a long shot to try and capture Aryn's attention. I know he's not gay, but there was always that hope. You don't have to be gay to be a man with a male Top. I see it all the time. In fact, there are a couple of them in the club currently. But I'm not sure if I could have that kind of submissive.

My disappointment spirals me further down when I watch Aryn and Ash talking by one of the benches. I finally turn to leave the room when Derek and Dex join them and Derek helps Aryn with some things while Ash bends over the bench.

"Where are you going?" Cara asks.

"I need some air," I tell her and walk through the crowd toward one of the side doors.

When Orik bought this building, one of the many reasons he purchased it was because it had this odd kind of courtyard in the center of the building. I'd hardly call it a beautiful site. It's concrete ground and steel walls, with some benches for seating and an awning that covers the "hole" in the building. This area is great because you can step outside in your fetish wear without fear of being seen by cars passing by. I step through the door and pull my smokes from my pocket and light one up. I slide my way past some people that are outside. There are a couple of them sitting on benches making out, some subbies sitting on the ground at the feet of their Masters while they smoke and chat with other Tops. I slide into the far dark corner. Literally dark enough to hide a human being and I lean against the wall.

I stay outside a little too long trying to wrap my head around why I am so drawn to Aryn, why it is that I can't stop thinking about him. I have no clue. The crowd that was out here when I wandered out has dwindled to just a few people when the door opens and out steps Ash, followed immediately by Aryn and I freeze. I am pretty confident he can't see me, but I have a very clear view of him and Ash as they sit on one of the benches. I can't make out much of the conversation but their actions are enough for me.

Aryn sits down on the bench and pats his lap. Ash being the good little sub that she is complies, but she straddles him and a wicked grin spreads across Aryn's face. He takes Ashley's head between his palms and pulls her down toward his lips. He lands a very sensual kiss across her lips. My cock grows hard instantly. Ash's subtle moan resonates through the area. I shiver. I've never been much of a voyeur but this is downright hot as hell.

Ash gets into what's happening and I watch the subtle grind of her hips against Aryn's crotch. His hands roam gently down her arms. I stomp out what's left of my cigarette and the couple closest to me gets up. I fall in behind them as they head for the door. Though I can still see Aryn and Ash from here, they probably can't or haven't seen me.

The couple in front of me reaches for and opens the door and I step up behind them. That's when I can't help but look back at Aryn. His eyes are open, looking at me as Ash moans into his mouth. I try to put on my Master stare, but I can't hide the disappointment I feel as our eyes lock. He freezes and I step inside the club, closing the door.

~ ARYN *~*

"What's wrong?" Ashley asks me when I tense up from looking into the eyes of Master Caden.

"What? Oh, nothing."

"Where'd you go?" she asks. The subtle downturn in her lips portrays her disappointment in my disappearing on her.

"Nowhere," I tell her and pull her back down, locking my lips with hers once again.

She's soft, sexy as hell, smart and simply gorgeous. My hands slide into her mane of chocolate brown curls and I hold her to me. Fighting desperately to clear Caden's disapproving glare from my mind as Ashley's hands roam down my chest.

She pulls back from our kiss and starts kissing down my jaw to the hollow of my ear. I shiver as the warmth of her breath caresses me when she flicks a tongue against my ear lobe.

"Want to get out of here, Sir?" she asks me and having 'Sir' roll off her tongue doesn't quite have the impact I'd hoped it would. If there is going to be any development between Ash and I, bedding her, though willingly, on our first meeting isn't entirely the best way to kick off this adventure.

"I don't think that's a good idea," I tell her. I know it's what I should do, but the tone of my voice does not portray my conviction.

She pouts.

"Listen to me," I tell her and her eyes meet mine. I see her submission in her eyes. It's looking for acceptance or something to take away the sting of rejection. "I like you, a lot," I tell her. There is more conviction in that statement than my telling her that it's not a good idea. "I don't think that the best way to kick off a relationship is by sleeping together when we've only just met."

She nods softly in understanding. I don't need to go into details about my bedding her and leaving. She can obviously see in my eyes that I want more than just a one night stand, which is true. I'd like to have more with her. I'd like to get to know her, see if we'd be compatible in a D/s relationship and then go from there. "Do you have your phone?" I ask her.

She nods and sits up, pulling it from her pocket. She puts in her passcode and then hands me her phone. I am about to do something I've never done. I give her my real number. Once it's saved, I call my number, and awkwardly reach into my pocket to pull out my phone. For some reason I feel the need to show her so I turn my phone to face her, showing that her number is calling me. She smiles and nods. I end the call and hand back her phone. I enter her number into my small contact list.

TWENTY~FOUR

Ash to Beck: Good morning, Sir.

I smile at my phone. I'd asked her to text me when she got home as well as when she woke up this morning, though it's nearly noon.

Beck to Ash: Morning? It's nearly noon.
Ash to Beck: I like to sleep late. Besides, it's New Year's Eve.
Beck to Ash: This is true. Will you be there tonight?

She doesn't respond right away and when she does she sends me a picture. A selfie of her smiling face. It makes me smile too.

The picture is followed up by a text.

Ash to Beck: Of course.

The event at the club starts tonight at six, so Derek, Dex, the girls and I grab a late lunch. Once we're all seated at the table, the conversation picks up. We've all managed to get along these last couple weeks. It's kind of weird to be here and off-duty. To be lead around by other people in security. Well, Sean and Celeste, but I would hardly call that a security following. Watching Celeste since we arrived here, Cotah is truly her main detail. While she doesn't have an issue with anything pertaining to Derek, Cotah is her responsibility. When the girls went shopping earlier today, I tried to go along and was shot down. Celeste could handle it. Though it made me uneasy, I didn't dwell on it too much. If Dex was truly concerned about it, he'd have asked me to go too.

"So, Beck?"

"Yeah." I look toward Derek, who's leaning into me a little, keeping his voice quiet.

"What's going on with Ash?" he asks me with a small smile.

I can't help but smile in return.

"I thought so," he murmurs.

"Should I be worried about something?"

Derek raises an eyebrow at me. "Absolutely not. I was just curious about what you were thinking."

I shrug. "I'm not sure yet. I like her. She's the first woman, outside of a work contact, that I've ever given my real number too."

He snickers, "That's a step."

"Is there something I should know about Ashley?" I ask him again.

He puts his silverware down and looks at me. "Even if I knew anything, which I don't, I wouldn't tell you. One of the biggest steps to a D/s relationship is honesty and communication. I think whatever her history is, she should be the one to tell you. I will tell you that she's been a member of the club for about two years now, while she is a very good submissive, well-trained by her club guardian, she's never had a full time Top. But she's not afraid to play either." His face is sincere as he tells me these things and I can't help but nod my understanding.

"I'm already having anxiety about entering that kind of relationship with her," I tell him candidly.

"Why's that?"

"Uh, because up until your play party, I was vanilla."

He looks at me. "That doesn't mean anything. If you're confident in what you want, there are more than enough ways for you to learn."

"True, but is having an experienced sub the right way to go about that? What if I take too long to learn, what if I can't-"

"I'm going to stop you right there," Dex chimes in.

I deflate a little bit, giving him silent permission to continue. "A D/s relationship is full of learning and learning curves. Anytime anyone hooks up with someone else, there is always a learning period. You can't just jump right into a scene, whether you're an experienced Top or not. You need to take some time to learn your partner, understand what's right and what's wrong, their limits and their dos and don'ts. It wouldn't be any different." Dex's voice is calm and confident as he finishes his speech.

"He's right," Derek says. "There are a lot of things you have to learn, but so much of it involves what it is that you want from the relationship and of course what she wants. The bottom line is if it's something you both really want, you will both figure it out." Derek sighs, "It's not just about what happens in the club, or even at home. The dynamic that you want outside of 'playtime' is something you need to figure out first. Then you go from there. Floggers, cuffs, whips, those are all part of the package. But there are thousands of relationships that are D/s without ever using an instrument."

I nod, understanding what Derek is saying.

"You can have a strictly vanilla sex life but have a D/s relationship. The toys, the club, playrooms, dungeons, those are all perks." Dex smiles a mischievous smile.

"I don't want a relationship without that kind of stuff," I tell them both.

"Then you figure it out. Whether with Ashley or someone else. It doesn't matter. But the point is you can't Top someone without first learning about them. You don't know what she's into; you don't know what any of her limits are. For many submissive types, it's not about sex. It's about the release, the letting go of life, putting the decisions into their partner's hands, whether it is their pleasure, their pain or their life," Derek says and I lower my head.

"I had no idea there was so much to all this," I mumble.

"That's why you're here. This lifestyle isn't for everyone, Beck," Dex says. "And it might not be the right one for you, but this is your chance to figure it out. Ash might be the person that will help you better understand what it is that you want in this lifestyle, or whether or not you want this lifestyle at all."

I don't respond and after a few minutes they pick up their conversations.

I'd been so blinded by what it is that I thought I wanted, I never bothered to step back and think about what it is that I need. Derek and Dex's words are what I needed to hear. Sure, I could take Ashley to bed, but for the first time in my life, I'm not entirely convinced that I could walk away from her.

That thought drives me through the rest of the meal and I rejoin the conversation as we finish up lunch.

When we're done, we head back to the hotel to relax and change before we leave for the club.

TWENTY~FIVE

Walking into the club tonight is way different than it was last night. While there is still similar attire on many of the submissives, the Tops' attire has changed dramatically. Last night there were suits or jeans and t-shirts, tonight there are a lot of leather pants, shit kicker boots. Frankly, many of them look like I do on a regular basis. The submissives in the lobby of The Box are more scantily dressed, many of them wearing corsets that expose their breasts with capes. If there is a top, it's thin and see-through. I swallow hard. I've never seen so many half-naked, naked or nearly naked women in one room. Not even the night of the private party compares to this. So many of them are absolutely gorgeous and the breasts range in size from tiny to huge, and their bodies are the same. Some skinny and many pleasantly plump ones. I'm surprised by the comfort level of the "less than perfect" bodies in the room. Cotah is a good example of this. Though she's not a big girl, she and Raine definitely don't shop in the same stores. But Cotah has one of those perfectly squishy bodies. Big chested and nice wide hips to grab hold of and that is attractive to me.

I'd always assumed that I wanted stick girls, but after seeing Cotah and some of these other women, I find myself drawn to them via their courage and confidence. Until I come face to face with Ash once again.

She's manning the podium again tonight, only this time there is a big Top standing behind her with his arms crossed, looking positively pissed off. Except when Ash says something to him, then his facial features soften and a smile spreads across his lips, changing his demeanor a thousand percent.

"Aryn, this is Teddy." Derek introduces me to the burly man standing watch.

He offers me his hand and I take it. "Pleasure to meet you, Aryn." He smiles, it's warm and oddly inviting.

"Likewise." I smile in return.

He pulls me toward the corner. "Ash is in my charge and I understand you've been talking with her."

A slice of fear rockets through me. "We have. We met last night, I didn't mean to intrude or talk to her without-"

He shakes his head, effectively cutting me off. "No, she is perfectly capable of talking to whomever she pleases. I, however, have a say in private affairs, such as behind closed door conversations and I'd like to get to know you a little more."

I'm confused by his request and Teddy has no problem pegging my confusion.

"What I mean is I don't mind talking, in fact I think that is a great idea, but she is in my charge, which means she is my responsibility. So if you wish to take things beyond talking, like playing together, please clear that with me first and before I allow it, I'd like to get to know you a little more."

It makes sense now. "Of course. I hope I haven't crossed a line."

"No, you haven't. But she has been honest with me, telling me about your conversation. She sees you as someone she'd like to get to know better and possibly even play with, but she won't unless I grant her permission to do so."

"Is she yours?"

"No, she's simply my charge, though I've been the one who's trained her. Single submissives, when they join the club, are given a charge. Someone they know or get to know, someone who is their third party contact. It's a safety measure to ensure they're being treated properly and that they safely seek what it is that they are after or whom. In the case of Ash, she came into the club, much like you have, green and willing. I took her under my wing. I've trained her, and now I take charge in helping her find her person."

"But have you guys been together?"

He barks a laugh. "You see that, sitting in the corner?" He points to the opposite corner, and kneeling on the floor, facing the wall, is a boy, a scrawny one, opposite the one I'm talking to and a thrill runs through me. "That is mine," Teddy declares and it's made clear. Teddy is gay and while he's taken Ash under his wing, there is no sexual attraction there. I smile.

"Well, okay then," I say with a smile and Teddy grabs my shoulder. "Sometime tonight, if you would, give me your number. I'd like to get together with you to discuss your goals with Ash."

Though I haven't decided what it is that I want to do with Ashley, if anything, I hand Teddy my card.

He doesn't take it. "We're an anonymous club."

I smile. "I know that. I've got nothing to hide and no one to hide it from. The closest person in my life just walked into the club with his sub."

"Fair enough." He takes my card and pockets it.

"I don't live here. I live in Los Angeles," I tell him.

He leans in a little closer. "I know," he whispers. I give him a puzzled look. "I'm part of the approval committee." He winks at me and sends me on my way.

I approach Ash, but seek confirmation from Teddy before kissing her on the cheek. "See you inside," I whisper and her breath hitches and her cheeks turn a rosy pink. I smile to myself and walk past her into the club.

Tonight looks empty compared to last night. All the apparatuses are lit up and there are sessions already in progress, but the room is definitely less crowded. I find Dex and Derek, sans Cotah and Raine. "You alright?" Dex asks me.

"Yup, I'm good. Ash is Teddy's charge. She apparently told him about me."

Derek turns toward us. "As she should. That's the point of being a charge. There will be little that transpires between you and her that Teddy will not know. She wears his training collar and until he releases her, she will continue to report to him."

"I'm beginning to gather all that."

"What did he want?" Dex asks.

"Just that he'd like to have a chance to talk to me, discuss my intentions with her and he'd like me to discuss any private, alone time that I want with Ashley with him before doing so."

"Again, as it should be," Derek says with a smile. "Again, relationship dynamics are different, but when under training, the Top has the right to punish the bottom for disobeying orders or for doing something she shouldn't. For example, Ash is probably free to do as she wishes outside of the walls of this club. That includes anyone that she meets, however Teddy likely wants to know where she is going, with whom and a check-in. He cannot stop her from sleeping with anyone, but he can punish her for sleeping with someone from the club."

"Whoa." I don't know what else to say besides, "So had I not turned her down last night, she might have gotten in trouble with Teddy?"

Derek smiles reassuringly. "Teddy was here last night. I have no doubt that at some point in the night she'd already asked him, or she would have before you left."

At some point tonight, I will ask her. Though I didn't tell Teddy about that and he didn't seem too surprised by what she'd whispered to him, he may have already known.

"Where are the girls?" I ask, changing the subject.

Both men smile and look at each other. "Getting ready," Dex says with an excited grin on his face.

"We're gonna be using these two stations. You are more than welcome to watch us, wander around the club, do whatever you want, except Ash." He smirks.

I laugh and I roll my eyes as they set up their tables next to two St. Andrew's Crosses. When they are done and ready, Dex grabs me. "One of the things I know Raine enjoyed most the first time we were here was when Derek brought her back to collect Cotah, giving her a chance to see what it's like from beginning to end. Would you like to watch?"

I hesitate. I don't want to be a part of something that is private and personal. "The girls know you're coming in," Derek adds, countering my conclusion. "You have to remember, this is about communication and I would never bring anyone into the room that Cotah isn't aware of. She may be my slave, but she is also my most precious treasure and I would never violate her that way. I know that Dex wouldn't either. While they both know when we are in the dungeon there is nothing we can do about the onlookers, in my private room here or at home, it's within my control and I would never do anything to make Cotah feel unsafe." He winks and heads for the dark entryway near the bar and Dex follows behind him. I can't help my curiosity, so I follow them both down the hallway.

~ **CADEN** *~*

Looks like I got here just in time. Just in time to see Aryn following Dex and Orion back to Orion's private room. Just in time to catch a glimpse of Aryn's gorgeous backside.

A shiver of anticipation and excitement slides up my spine as I walk deeper into the club.

TWENTY~SIX

** ARYN **

I dutifully follow Dex and Derek toward the room. When they get to the door, Derek unlocks it. I take some strange comfort in the fact that the door is locked and I can't quite understand why that is. It's a rather unassuming door, and there are several doors down the hallway beyond where we are. I follow the men inside and it's not a huge room, but there is a good size bed along the right wall, a book shelf across from it and there are a couple of cuffs hanging from the ceiling. Beyond the bookshelf is a rack of various things, a flogger, and a couple of paddles. The room is big enough that you could play privately inside versus out in the dungeon.

The girls are on opposite sides of the room. Cotah is near the foot of the bed, along one wall, and Raine is near a doorway that looks like it leads to a bathroom and their Tops join them. Derek and Dex both thank their subs for being ready for them, caressing their heads and giving them praise for what they've done to get ready. My chest tightens and the girls blossom under the soft touches of their Tops and I realize that I'm envious. Not of Dex and Derek, no, my envy is directed at the girls.

"Are you ready, pet?" Derek asks Cotah and then Dex asks the same question to Raine.

Both the girls answer, "Yes, Master."

"Then rise up and turn around," Derek says to Cotah.

"Come here, pet. Turn around for me," Dex says and Raine rises, turning to face Dex. Her eyes are downcast and Dex caresses her cheek. "Your wrists." His voice has a soft command and Raine produces her wrists, palms up. Dex wraps first one, then the other, leather cuff around her wrists and secures them. The cuffs are black with a purple lining in them and there are two different sized closed loops on them.

I slowly pull my eyes away from Raine and turn my head to see that Derek has done the same with Cotah and is now securing ankle cuffs to her that have the same look as the ones around her wrist. When he's done, I watch as he gently caresses his hand up her leg, giving her his silent appreciation for what she is giving him now. Her submission.

The girls are dressed only in underwear. Their breasts are exposed and Dex tugs on one of Raine's nipples and her eyes slowly close.

He releases her nipples and I notice that she does not have any piercings in. It puzzles me, but not enough to dwell on it. My eyes wander down and she too has cuffs around her ankles. Dex grabs the ring on her black collar. The same one I've seen before. The one that she wore in their private playroom back in California. He leads her toward me and I sidestep the door, giving them room to move past me. I look at Cotah and Derek as he clips a D-clip to the rings on her cuffs, forcing her hands together and then he leads her from the room. They each have their own way of leading their women out. Cotah needs to be lead because of the blindfold she's wearing.

"You good?" Derek whispers to me and I nod. He smiles and walks past me, leading Cotah from the room. I follow behind them, pulling the door shut. The door locks automatically and I follow them into the dungeon.

I cannot take my eyes off Cotah and while there is nothing sexual about my staring at her, I want to look away when that envious feeling returns. She has given herself over to Derek. Given him her trust by allowing him to lead her from the room. Lead her in a direction she cannot see. Allowing him to guide her to where they've set up in the dungeon.

The trust she has to have in him is awe-inspiring. Making me realize that a submissive truly puts her life in her Top's hands.

It also makes me realize that I should be jealous of Derek and Dex, but I find myself envious of the girls, of the bottoms, the subs.

~ CADEN *~*

Dex and his pet emerge from the hallway, followed shortly after by a blindfolded Cotah with Derek. Following right behind them is Aryn and my heart skips a beat when I see him. Something is bothering him and I'm not entirely sure what it is, but something about his posture tells me that he's stewing on something. In the times that I've seen him until now, he's carried himself like a Top. The little things he says and even some of the reactions he has are more submissive, but if you think about it long and hard, that submissive could be misunderstood easily. His submissive appearance could be nothing more than being confused about what's going on around him or unsure of how he's supposed to act. However, his posture has never been so broken. Aryn appears deflated, defeated even, and my cock hardens wondering if it's not confusion, but really what it seems. Submission.

~ ARYN *~*

I stand back from where Dex and Derek are attaching Cotah and Raine to the crosses and I now understand the cuffs. Derek removed the D-clip that was holding Cotah's hands together, but he hasn't removed the blindfold as he secures her wrists to the cross. After each click of the hooks he caresses Cotah's back to comfort her. While I can't hear his words, he is speaking to her. She shivers and he moves over to the other cuff.

My earlier jealousy rises higher, sending me into a spiral of confusion.

It's like watching a car wreck, you don't want to look away, you want to watch and be a part of what they have going on. But I'm no longer sure that I want to be on the Top anymore and that realization hits me hard.

A few minutes later, voices behind me prompt me to look and I find Ashley talking to another Top and our eyes meet briefly. I give her a smile and I go back to watching Dex and Derek with their girls.

Another minute or so later, Ashley places her hand on my back to get my attention.

"Hi," she says so softly that I can barely hear her.

"Hi, you alright?"

She nods.

"Why do I think you're not?"

Her face falls a little bit. "Teddy granted permission to Sir Alex to play with me tonight."

"Oh, well then, you'd better get going," I tell her, though I'm not sure I actually thought about my answer. Her eyes meet mine.

"Are you sure?" her eyebrows knit together.

I smile. "I'm in no position to tell you otherwise, Ash, and this might sound wrong, but I wouldn't mind watching. If that's okay with Sir Alex, of course."

She blushes slightly. "I will ask him."

I shake my head and smile. "I can handle that."

She nods and hugs me slightly before taking off to wherever she needs to go. Am I bothered by her playing with someone else? Maybe a little, but I'm hardly in a position to tell her otherwise. She goes back to talk to the same person she was talking to before. He has a large bag over his shoulder and he gives her instructions. She nods and lowers her head in the same manner as Raine and Cotah have been doing and she turns toward the changing rooms that are opposite the private rooms. Sir Alex looks at me and I step over to him.

"Aryn, right?" he asks.

I nod. "Sir Alex, nice to meet you."

"Thank you for letting me borrow her." He tells me.

I smile. "She's not mine to loan out. I believe that is on Teddy."

"It is, but she tells me that you two have been talking."

I nod. "We have, but it's been barely twenty-four hours and-" I'm distracted when Teddy walks out of the hallway with what looks like a leash in his hand. Walking slowly behind him is the boy from the corner, his submissive. "She's Teddy's charge," I finish without looking away from Teddy and his boy.

"Of course, but I am not one to step on anyone's toes," Alex tells me. "Ash and I have played before."

I still can't pull my eyes away from Teddy as he approaches a spanking bench. "Oh, yeah, no, we're cool." I finally pull my eyes away as Teddy secures his boy's leash to the spanking bench. Alex turns toward where I'm looking.

"Teddy and Will are quite the sight to watch," he says with a chuckle.

"Yeah, I've just never, never mind. Do you mind if I watch you with Ash?" I ask him and he turns back to me.

"Not at all. We will be over there." He indicates one of the other groups of crosses."

"Awesome, thanks, Sir Alex."

Alex smiles at me and nods as he heads toward the cross he wants to use. My gaze wanders back to Teddy and Will. Teddy has secured Will's legs to the bench and the sight has me enraptured. Will is bent over, and completely naked. I shiver as I watch them.

Well, I watch Will.

TWENTY~SEVEN

~ CADEN *~*

Watching Aryn is more erotic than watching anyone else in this dungeon at the moment.

I've been watching him long enough to realize that he's just as enthralled by Teddy and Will as I am. Though I can't quite tell who has more of his attention. Teddy or Will.

Teddy puts his cane across Will's ass. Aryn jumps when it lands.

I have my answer.

Aryn turns slightly and that's when I see it.

His leather pants leave very little to the imagination. I smile to myself and settle back against the wall.

~ ARYN *~*

Teddy cracks the cane again and I jump. Jesus, that has to hurt, but Will appears to be in heaven. His body is fully relaxed against the bench and with each strike of the cane, he audibly grunts in satisfaction.

Teddy proceeds to bounce the cane against Will's ass and thighs. The cane cracks softly with each little hit. The volume increases as Teddy picks up his pace. I shiver, Will melts further into the bench and Teddy continues with the cane. Then Teddy places his free hand gently against Will's back and my desire to be the boy grows stronger. The desire to be Topped is enough to make me fall to my knees the longer I watch Will.

Teddy increases the strength and decreases the frequency of the hits against his boy's fully exposed, growing redder by the second, ass.

"Ahh," Will cries out and Teddy stops. He slides his hand into Will's hair and lifts up his head.

"I'm here, pet. I have you," he says softly and again his boy melts. Will leans his head in Teddy's direction, taking his affection and gentleness like it's the air he needs to breathe and my chest tightens. The affection in Teddy's eyes as he looks upon his boy is undeniably the hottest thing I've ever seen and my cock jumps in agreement.

I've never wanted affection, never received it, never knew I wanted it, not until this moment.

"Like what you see?"

The voice is a whisper in my ear. Familiar and it makes me jump slightly.

"Maybe," I breathe.

"Oh sweet boy, I don't take maybe as an answer."

Caden's words and inflection are unlike anything I've ever heard before in my life and my knees go weak. But I maintain myself, not giving in to what it is that I know he's pushing me for. "It's not my thing."

"What's that?" Caden whispers in my ear. My resolve waivers slightly. I try and make the next thing that comes out of my mouth sound like a conviction, but I don't feel it.

"Men."

"But they are two willing gay men and you watch them like you need air to breathe."

I try and turn toward Caden, but his back is close to mine and he's unwavering. A brick wall.

"You're not my type," I say, but I feel his chuckle as his breath hits along my neck.

"Then tell me, sweet boy," His voice moves as he switches sides and his warm breath caresses along my neck making me shiver. "If men are not your type," There's a gentle touch against my cock; it slides upward toward the tip. "Why is your cock hard as steel and your eyes haven't left those two since they walked in the room?"

Master Caden backs away from me, leaving me alone and bereft.

I should be disgusted by him touching me, but I'm not. Strangely, it felt too good to reject it.

I return my gaze to Will. Each crack of the cane against his skin makes me jump.

I'm alone standing in the middle of the dungeon. I shiver again. The loss of Caden against my backside makes me feel weak and exposed. I turn around, finally breaking my trance on Teddy and Will, looking desperately for Caden and I catch sight of him as he walks through the curtain into the lobby.

I fight to stop myself from walking after him. I want to ask him what the hell that was all about, why the hell he's stalking me the way that he is, but the realization that I do not want to know the answers to those questions stops me from running after him.

He has something out for me and I'm not entirely sure I understand it. But what bothers me the most is I want to know what it is.

I shake my head, clearing it, vowing to drop it completely and concentrate on why it is that I am so enraptured by the bottoms that I've barely paid any attention to the Tops.

Maybe I should find something else to watch. I go to the bar and get a coke from the gal behind the counter. She doesn't seem to be one for conversation and judging by the sheepish expression on her face, I imagine she's a sub.

With a coke in hand, I survey the dungeon and my eyes land on a very attractive blonde woman. Obviously a Top, but her attire is something I can't take my eyes off of. She's wearing a black leather corset and tight leather mini-skirt with fire engine red thigh-high heels. Her lips are painted with the same bright red and her eyes are surrounded by dark colors. Even from here, her eyes are bright, vibrant against the dark around them. She's gorgeous. If I didn't know better, I'd say she had implants, but judging from the tightness of her corset, she's being held together very nicely.

My eyes slide down to her submissive and my mind starts to wonder about the idea of my being attracted to her. There is a disturbing feeling that overcomes me when I realize that I'm attracted to a Top.

Between what happened in Derek's room, watching Teddy and Will together, and then Caden's very poignant attempt at trying to make me see what I'm missing, I shouldn't be surprised that my mind is wandering down this path. The fact that I'm attracted to a Top is slightly disturbing and after the events of tonight, I guess it should just go with the territory.

Her submissive is male and he's bigger than Will by a long shot. His hair is cut short, military style, and if it weren't for the ball gag in his mouth, his hands tied behind his back, and him being on his knees, I'd have thought he was someone of power. But the blonde Top is making a meal out of him with the flogger in her hand. His chest is red around the harness that he wears.

The blonde comforts him by holding his head to her and judging from the glazed look in his eyes, he's completely smitten.

The envy I felt earlier slides back into place until she walks away from him. There is a twinge of sadness in his eyes as she does.

She walks around him, flogger in hand, and goes back to hitting him across his back. Each hit makes his eyes glaze over a little more.

Lost in the trance of watching them, I unknowingly drift closer to them, hypnotized by what her submissive is experiencing. His Domme is barely a blip on my radar.

With each hit, he grunts a little more, a little louder and longer. When she stops, I'm slightly disappointed. I turn my gaze to the blonde Top and find she's looking at me. She gives me a small smile and then turns her attention back to her submissive and their scene.

The impact play continues until her submissive is barely capable of holding himself up anymore at which point she backs off of him completely, putting down the flogger.

"Carta, comfort him," the blonde bombshell Domme says and a mousy girl appears from the side and crawls across the floor toward the man. The girl crawls to him and wraps her arms around his neck. He rests his head against hers as Carta murmurs to him. "You must be Aryn?" the blonde Domme calls and I give her my attention.

Blue, her eyes are bright blue. "I am. I apologize, I didn't mean to interrupt."

"Mistress," she corrects me.

"I'm sorry, Mistress," I say shyly and she smiles in approval.

"You're fine. Do you like what you see?"

"I did, very much so, Mistress?"

"Mistress Milena. Avalon is a great show, isn't he?"

I nod. "Yes, he is. You're great to watch too," I tell her with a smile.

"Thank you." She smiles. "It's nice to finally meet you. Master Caden speaks very highly of you."

The name jolts me. I didn't expect to hear her mention him. "Does he now?" I ask, though it comes out a little harsher than I'd planned it to.

She laughs a gorgeous, 'make my cock twitch' laugh. "He does, but don't worry, I tried to convince him you weren't his type." She cocks her head toward me. "Or are you?"

I purse my lips but don't answer her.

"That's what I thought," she murmurs. "Well, Aryn, it was a pleasure to meet you." She holds out her hand to me and I take it gently in mine.

"Likewise, Mistress Milena." I give her a smile and she returns back to Avalon and Carta. She grabs Carta by her ponytail, pulls her head back and kisses her with fervor. Mistress Milena's eyes meet mine, taunting me, and my cock twitches again.

I can't keep watching them. At this rate, I'm going to explode in my pants like a teenager. As I leave them to their scene, Derek approaches with Cotah in his arms. She's covered and snuggling her face against his neck.

"You alright?" he asks me and I give him a small nod. "I'm going to take Cotah back, Dex is right behind me." He jingles his key. "Help me?"

I nod again, still feeling very lost in my skin as I take the key from him and I fall in line behind him until he stops in front of his doorway. I unlock it for him and push it open. He steps in with Cotah and lays her down on the bed. I don't follow him in, wanting to give him the privacy I know he needs. Dex comes down the hallway carrying Raine. She's playing with his necklace. She's more animated than Dacotah was when she came down off the cross and Dex smiles at me.

Dex steps inside the room and lays Raine down on the other side of the bed with Cotah. As soon as she is down, Cotah gravitates toward her and Raine wraps her arms around her. Despite the fact that Cotah has yet to open her eyes, she moans as Raine's hands slide around her stomach. Raine looks up at Derek and Dex and asks, "May I please have permission to comfort Cotah, Sirs?"

"You may, fingers only," Derek says and Raine lights up. Her hand slides along Cotah's stomach, toward her panty line. Cotah moans. My cock twitches, reminding me that I am not gay and that I love women. Especially open women.

I follow Dex and Derek out into the corridor and over to where they scened. I'm disappointed. I wanted to watch Raine and Cotah. I'm a man, what do you expect? "You just leave them in there like that?" I ask, curious.

Dex chuckles, "Cotah is floating."

"Floating?" I ask.

Derek turns back and smiles. "She's in subspace. I learned early on that Cotah needs affection following a scene, especially one that puts her over the edge. Normally, that would be me in there, but-" He shrugs it off with a slightly wider smile.

"I had no idea Raine was so open." I look at Dex.

He chuckles, "Yeah, she's my kinky kitten, but Cotah is the only girl I know she's played with. They have a good bond together and Derek and I trust them both to stay within the limits of what we allow. Tonight Derek said fingers only. Which will drive Raine nuts, but she'll stick to it."

I shake my head, unable to wrap my head around it. Around the idea that the two of them allow the girls to play like that.

"It's only after a scene where we'd consider leaving them alone like that. If they were both floating, we wouldn't have left them and I know exactly what will happen," Derek says as he starts to pack up his stuff. "Raine will get Cotah off, allow her to float for a little longer, then give her something sweet, chocolate in this case, and some water. Then they'll both just lie there until we return." I catch movement in the corner of my eye. Teddy is releasing Will from his restraints. His big hands and big body are five times the size of Will, but the affection is undeniable as he carefully scoops Will off the bench and carries him down the hallway. When they disappear, I turn back toward the guys. Dex is cleaning up, but Derek is watching me. He smiles slightly and goes back to cleaning up.

Why do I get the feeling that he knows what's going on inside my head right now?

TWENTY~EIGHT

The ride back to Derek's Nashville home was quiet. The girls rested, Derek drove. He and Dex were up front. I crawled into the back row of his SUV to give the girls a chance to cuddle with each other. Dacotah was still pretty glossy-eyed when they came out to leave, but she seemed okay. I wasn't really sure what to expect to see from her when she emerged. I guess maybe I figured she'd be her normal, bubbly self. Instead she was quiet and calm and for lack of a better term, centered.

When we got home, Derek and Dex helped their girls inside and we all said goodnight. I didn't expect to have the night carry on, both the ladies seemed rather desperate for some alone time with their men.

I made my way into the kitchen for a bottle of water and something to nibble on.

No matter what I did, I couldn't seem to quiet my mind of all I witnessed tonight.

Dex and Raine, Derek and Cotah, Teddy with Will, and then finally Mistress Milena with her submissives, Avalon and Carta. At least judging from that kiss, she has two.

What a challenge that must be. I don't fully understand the dynamic Mistress Milena has with Avalon and Carta, I imagine it would be rather interesting to hear about.

"You alright?" Derek's voice breaks into my stewing over what happened tonight.

"Yeah, I think so."

He goes to the fridge and pulls something out, but I don't pay much attention to him until he's sitting right in front of me and sliding another bottle of water my way. "I saw you with Caden tonight. You want to talk about it?"

I shake my head. "Nothing happened." Well, accept he touched my cock and it didn't piss me off. "He was whispering some stuff in my ear. He wanted to know why I was watching Teddy and Will and not you or Dex." That's not at all he said, but it's not entirely untrue. Just twisted a bit.

"Why were you, you know, watching them?" he says as he pops something into his mouth.

I shrug. "Not sure. I guess I was just caught up in what Teddy was doing to him. Trying to absorb as much as I could. Make sure it's what I really want."

He doesn't say much for a few minutes, just keeps munching on whatever is in his hand. "Have you decided anything?" he asks me bluntly.

"Yes and no."

"I'm not trying to force you to talk, but maybe I can help you sort out what it is that's bothering you so much."

I sigh. He's probably my best bet. I know I can talk to Dex but I'm not entirely sure how to tell him or how he would handle what I have to say. "I was so confident, before tonight, that Ashley was what I wanted. If she was willing to give me a chance to learn my role."

"And now?"

I finally look up at him. His features are soft, understanding. It compels me to keep talking. "Now I'm trying to figure out which side of the coin I need to be on."

"In other words, you're starting to see what many of us have seen all along."

"What's that exactly?"

He stands and the chair scrapes along the floor. My eyes follow his as I wait for an answer. "When you figure it out, let me know." He steps away from the table toward the door. "Sometimes the path we think we want isn't the path we need. I'll see you tomorrow." He gives me a wide smile and disappears, going back to his room and back to Dacotah.

What do they see? What do I want?

Once in my room, I strip and hit the shower. I can still smell the club, the sex, the furniture polish, the smell of Caden and I'm desperate to wash it away in hopes of cleaning my mind enough so that I can sleep.

When I climb into the shower, the hot water hits my body, I shiver and my cock gets hard as Mistress Milena slides into my mind. Wondering what she looks like under all those clothes, what it would be like to bend her over a table and pound into her from behind.

The fantasy morphs into bending Mistress Milena over a bed or table and her face is buried deep in Ashley's cunt. Their joint moans and screams of pleasure spur my hand faster along my cock. Imagining myself taking control and sliding into her. Watching as each of my forward thrusts pushes her deeper into Ashley's pussy. Ashley's hands cup her breasts, tweaking her nipples as Milena works her over.

My orgasm builds, my balls tighten up, the pleasure races through my veins.

"Come for me, my sweet boy," says the fantasy in my head and I explode. But it wasn't Milena who ordered my orgasm. No, it was a man. Master Caden.

I spend another ten minutes in the shower scrubbing myself clean and raw.

Despite everything I try to do to wash away the idea that Caden ordered me, from inside my mind, I can't shake the raging hard-on I have despite my previous orgasm.

I towel off and manage to corral my dick into a pair of pajama bottoms and crawl into bed.

I lie there staring at the ceiling with Derek's words bouncing around inside my head. "You're starting to see what many of us have seen all along." "Sometimes the path we think we want isn't the path we need." What does that mean exactly?

As my eyes grow heavy, it hits me…submissive. I'm not a Top or a Dominant…I'm a submissive.

Maybe I'm meant to be a sub to someone. Mistress Milena, Sara, someone else I've yet to meet. Mistress Milena made no secret that she found me easy on the eyes. She didn't seem to shy away from taunting me. Maybe that's what I need. Maybe I'm going about this all wrong.

But I want to be on top.

I'd love to have Ashley beneath me. I'd love to learn, for her. I shake my head. Sure, I'd love to learn, but she is the only one I'd love to learn for. Maybe I'm not supposed to learn for her, but from her?

It's with thoughts of being Avalon, splayed out for Mistress Milena that I doze off to sleep…

I'm awake, but yet I can't see.

I'm bound but by something unknown, something I can't see.

My mouth is held open. My arms are tired and strained, pulled tight behind my back.

I feel fingers along my cheek. They're soft, yet I can feel the light scratch of nails as there is a tug against something and my mouth is free again. But only for a minute before soft, sensual lips land on mine.

My body comes alive. My heart starts pounding, and my breathing is heavy. The taste of sweetness and lipstick stays on my lips and tongue when she pulls away. She doesn't say anything and she doesn't return the gag back to my mouth.

Instead, a new presence, an unknown presence somewhere in the room. I can't see anything, but I sense it. I feel it walking a circle around me.

I shiver as the air stirs and hits my rock hard cock. I can't see it, but I feel it jump, I feel it straining for a release.

I groan.

There are no voices, only breathing. My breathing. The sound mixes with the blood rushing in my ears.

Then something taps the tip of my cock, gentle enough to not hurt, but solid enough to make me jump.

The tap moves off my cock to the inside of first one thigh, then the other. Unsure of what to do, I relax. Spreading my legs wider.

Then I feel something, hard, yet forgiving tapping gently against my balls. There is a sharp prick of pain with each tap.

The tapping increases in frequency. The pain grows, and my breathing slows as I process the pain.

The thing smacking me moves. Capturing the inside of my thigh, then the other, repeatedly. I cannot spread my legs any further. My hands are bound behind my back, and the gag rests against my neck.

"More," I moan out.

There is a sharp smack against my ass.

"More please, Mistress," I moan and there is an even harder smack. This time against the other cheek and I jump. Unsure of what it is she wants from me, I groan. Dropping my request.

A rough hand slides into my hair, pulling my head back.

The smell in my nose is very distinctly male and familiar.

Lips, soft, but the kiss is rough. The prickle of a five o'clock shadow rubs against my lips.

The kiss stops, and my lips left wet and cold in the chill of the room.

"My sweet boy."

The blindfold comes off and my eyes meet his.

"You're mine, my sweet dirty boy."

"Yes, Master. All yours."

I bolt upright in bed. Dripping in sweat, my balls on fire with a desperate need to come.

Unable to stop myself, I grab my cock in my hand and pull once, twice, and I come all over myself with one person on my mind.

Caden.

TWENTY~NINE

Why Caden? Why not Mistress Milena, or any other Mistress or Domme?

I swear to god the dream started off with Mistress Milena, but I can't shake the feeling that I'd manifested that, that the person I was really kissing was Caden.

The thought makes me shiver with annoyance. Sure, Caden is a good looking, well-built man who's bigger than I am, but I am certainly not gay, so why the sudden fantasies of him?

I've never been shy about men. I've shared plenty of women with another guy. And okay fine, I've thought about what it would be like to play with the man, but the only one I would have crossed that line with has been Dex, and that is probably only because he and I have shared our fair share of women since I started working for the band. But why now?

My thoughts keep me busy the rest of the night. When I can't take lying still anymore, I get up and head for the kitchen.

When I do, I realize that I'm probably the only one awake and that brings me a little bit of comfort, until I step into the kitchen and find Derek sitting there drinking coffee and reading a paper.

"Morning," I grumble as I clear the island and head for the coffee pot.

"Morning. You look like you didn't sleep much."

I grunt.

"That bad?" he asks as he sets the paper down and turns toward me. I look at him and just give him a look that says 'take a wild guess'. "Want to talk about it?"

I snort. "The last time I did that, I ended up staying up most of the night."

"True, but I'm guessing that what kept you awake was what I brought up to you last night?"

I nod and add some sugar to my coffee. "Is it really that obvious?" I ask, my voice is soft, contrite almost.

"Is what obvious?"

I purse my lips and turn toward him, looking at his expectant expression. "That I'm not a Dominant." He raises an eyebrow, not saying anything, but I get the impression he expects me to say it out loud. "That I'm probably more submissive than dominant."

The corners of Derek's lips twitch as he fights a smile. "Yes, it is that obvious."

"But how?" I slouch a little, defeated. I have this small blossom of hope pooling in my chest. Maybe he'll refute my realization.

"How did I know?" I just nod. "Call it a Master's intuition."

I cock my head at him. "Do you all have that or something because I am pretty sure you're not the only one who's seen it?"

"No, we don't all have it, but no, I'm not the only one who's noticed," he says almost regrettably. "Sometimes you can just tell. Sometimes it is just a matter of perception or how people see you."

"Mistress Sara figured it out in her store. I think that's why she looked down her nose at me."

Derek snorts, "No, Mistress Sara is, well, she's a horse of another color. She doesn't see anyone as a dominant until they've proven themselves to her. She's old school and skeptical of everyone. I wouldn't take it personally. In fact, if I remember correctly, she did the same thing to Dex when they first met."

"So then there is still hope?" I raise an eyebrow at him, expectant and maybe a little more hopeful than I should be.

"There is always hope, Beck. But I think your dominance will stem from training as a submissive before turning the tables. As much as I know you'd love to have a submissive under you, I'm not sure you'd be doing yourself any justice in that department." He stands up, grabbing his cup and coming toward me and the coffee pot. I slide out of his way and take a sip. "Come, let's talk in my office."

Though the order is there, it's softened by the add of going to his office, and despite the fact that I'm doing my hardest to deny the fact that I'm starting to believe he's right, I can't help but dutifully follow him.

Once inside his office, he gestures toward one of the two couches and closes the door. "So, Ash for example, sure, you like her, but does your like extend into Topping her or simply bringing her to bed with you?" He takes a seat opposite me and I drink more coffee before finding the answer that's real and not just what I think he wants to hear.

"Sex, mostly. Though I wouldn't mind other stuff, I'm not sure there is a relationship there besides sex."

"But you gave her your number?" Again with the eyebrow going up.

"I did, but I also gave it to her at a time where I truly thought that I was meant to be on top."

"So you're going to stop talking to her?"

I look down at the coffee cup in my hands and don't reply for a moment. His question brings me right back to where I've been, wishing I hadn't given her my number, but in the same token, I'm not entirely sure I want to give her up either. "No, I don't think so. I think we have more in common than I'd originally realized."

"Submission," Derek states simply.

"Yeah, maybe, I don't know." I rub my hand on my thigh, fidgeting a little bit, looking around his office, doing anything but looking at him.

"Let me ask you something?" I shrug and he doesn't miss a beat. "Did it ever occur to you that maybe the reason you're struggling with this so much is because your introduction into this lifestyle has been from a Dominant's perspective?"

My eyes finally meet his. "How was it supposed to be different?"

"It wasn't." He looks at me, reading me. "Just that maybe rather than listening to Dex or myself, maybe you should start talking to Cotah and Raine."

"I don't know about that. I don't know that I can." My voice is barely a whisper before I finish talking.

"I think you can, and I think maybe you should."

I set my coffee cup down and stand up and start to pace around the room. Admitting to myself that I may not be dominant is one thing, but admitting to two girls, two women that I have the upmost respect for, hardly seems like the appropriate way of dealing with my submission. "I don't want to seem weak."

"Stop right there." His voice is stern, his dominance evident, and I stop pacing and turn to look at him. His eyes are hard, his features tight. "Submission is not weakness, Aryn. In fact, it is the opposite of that. Weak and submissive are two words that do not and should never go together. What makes you think that they would receive you as weak?"

His words, his tone, have made me feel very small, scolded almost, and I don't answer him right away. "Because I'm a man."

Derek snorts. "And that has what to do with the price of tea in China?" He shakes his head in exasperation. "There are plenty of male submissives. In fact, there are almost as many, if not more men who submit than there are women. Submission isn't about your gender, it isn't about what you have between your legs. Submission is about who you are as a person, about the need to willingly surrender yourself to someone, to let them take control and give you the power to let it all go. Submission is about an unwavering desire to please and to be pleased. It is so much more than who you are physically, it's what you are mentally."

His words sink in, sliding through me like the blood pumping in my veins.

"It takes a very strong person to submit to someone else. Whether it is for sexual pleasure or lifestyle gratification. Regardless, willingly surrendering yourself to someone takes more balls than being the one to cradle and cherish the gift being offered." He stands up, placing his hands in his pockets as he too starts to pace. "I don't get very personal with people about my relationships, but one of the reasons that Cotah and I are a Master/slave couple is because I am unwilling and incapable of handing my submission to someone. Incapable of letting someone else hold the reins of my life. There are many submissive men. You met Mistress Milena last night. Did you meet Avalon?"

I shake my head. "She was working him over."

He nods goes back to pacing. "Avalon is a perfect example of men, like me, giving up their power. Avalon, when not in the club, is one of the richest men I know." He gives me a very pointed look. "And believe me, I rival his income, but he's a lot like me. He owns multiple companies across different continents and he is constantly on the move, working his ass off for his companies and his release-"

"Is his submission," I finish.

He looks at me with a smile on his face. "He has the ability to let it all go, to hand it all over to his Mistress when he walks in the door of The Box. Not many people are capable of doing that and I'm one of them. I am incapable of doing it which is why I made the worst possible submissive ever."

"You were a submissive?"

He smiles at me. "I was. You don't get a publicly respected Master title without first completing the training. Well," he snorts, "It's not like karate or anything, but most Masters have earned their titles, have trained, have properly stepped through the stages of a BDSM lifestyle. Now that doesn't mean that you couldn't walk into a different club as Master, but most veterans will call your bluff pretty quickly. Also, clubs vet their clientele. Often times that vetting includes discussing you with other clubs before admission." He shakes his head. "Sorry, we got off track, but you get the idea. Willing to submit does not make you weak. It does not make you any less of a man, in fact, in my eyes, it would make you more of a man."

"How do I change that perception?"

He looks at me, expectant. "What perception?"

"Um, mine. It's been put out there that I was a Top."

Derek stops his pacing and levels me with a stare. "You just change, you find someone willing to take you under their wing, and train you, teach you. You find other subs to befriend and talk to. No one at the club, especially at the club, is going to judge you for switching. In fact, you'd be surprised how many people do. When Dex first talked to you about coming out here, he didn't really know how else to explain things to you, so all he had to give you was from a Dominant's perspective. What you saw last night, what we've talked about, that has given you the chance to see it from the other side. There is nothing wrong with switching sides."

"Is that what Caden sees in me?"

He snorts. "Caden is," he takes a deep breath, "Caden is someone who sees a challenge, and when he sees it, he wants it, and when he wants it he will stop at nothing to have it."

"So he has his sights on me?"

He rocks on his feet from heel to toe and back again. "You could say that."

"But I'm not gay," I say sternly.

Derek snorts again. "Neither is he."

"So then why…" I don't bother to finish the question. Derek already answered it. Caden sees me as a challenge, something to conquer, something to have bowed down before him and I'm definitely not that kind of guy. "What about Mistress Milena?"

Derek smiles at me. "She is a handful, but she's good at what she does."

"She was eyeballing me pretty good last night. I guess that also plays into your theory too, doesn't it?" It all makes perfect sense now. If Derek can see it, Mistress Milena can too.

Derek just nods.

THIRTY

After my talk with Derek, I spend a good portion of the day arguing with him in my head. Despite all the obvious signs that I appear to be a submissive, something about the idea just doesn't sit right with me. Sure, it turns me on, but I cannot imagine myself kneeling before a woman. I've never been one to take much from them, except for the things that I want, but to 'bow' to one is just something I can't seem to wrap my head around.

A little later in the day, the girls wanted to go shopping and Derek insisted that I be the one to take them. I argued with him about it because he seemed to think spending time with the two of them would give me a chance to discuss the newly discovered information, but I didn't feel comfortable doing so. It's one thing to admit it to myself, but to two women whom I respect immensely and who I fear will see me as weak is a huge, impossible, pill to swallow.

So I did my duty, watched them, watched out for them and let them have their fun while I hung back in the background and they did their thing.

The next day was worse. I was so exhausted from my lack of sleep the night before that all I managed to do was plop down in bed and pass out. At least that gave me some peace from the turmoil roaming around inside of me. But it was short-lived when I started to once again dream about Caden topping me and it shot me awake.

Luckily though, it was later in the morning and I'd managed to get a decent night's sleep anyway.

My peace was short-lived when I found out from Dex that they would be returning to the club tonight and he thought I should come along.

I don't want to put myself back in that vulnerable position of being there, but then again I want to be there to disprove Derek's theory that I am a submissive and more importantly, that Caden is interested in me.

After a long back and forth battle with myself, I get dressed and go with them.

We enter the club in the same manner as before, but tonight Ash isn't manning the check-in podium and I'm disappointed.

We haven't talked much since the last time I was here. Not without effort, though. Either she was working or I was working and we just didn't connect. I'll admit that I wondered a couple times if my lack of interest has anything to do with what Derek said about me.

Tonight I am determined not to let it get to me. I am determined more than anything to just simply pay attention to Derek and Dex while they work Cotah and Raine.

My determination is blown to bits when Caden escorts Ashley over to one of the crosses. I don't know that I would have paid much attention to it except for the fact that Ash has her hands bound in front over her. She is topless and gorgeous as sin in her black boy shorts.

Caden is shirtless, wearing only a pair of leather pants and black boots, much like my own.

Seeing him topless is something to behold. His chest is chiseled, defined and he puts me to shame in the working out department. Shirtless he looks like a menace not to be messed with. He's tall and appears totally in control.

He secures Ashley's hands to the cuffs on the cross. Caden is gentle with her. His fingers trace down each arm in a gentle, comforting caress and Ashley's cheeks turn a soft pink.

Caden repeats the process with the other arm and when he reaches her side, the other hand joins him as he slides them down over her hips, down her thighs and then he coaxes her to open her legs for him and she does. His gentle touch continues as he secures her ankles to the cross with the same softness.

Once she is secure, he glides his hands back up her body and she shivers. Caden presses his back against hers, giving her the comfort of knowing he's there and she melts into him. He is whispering in her ear and while I can't hear what he is saying, it has a very visible calming effect on her.

Jealousy slices through me like razorblades in my blood. Cutting me open, exposing me.

Sensing this, in some uncanny way, Caden turns toward me, pinning me with a glare that has my knees shaking and weak, ready to buckle under my weight. I take a step back in an attempt to balance myself and a wicked little smirk spreads over Caden's lips and I shiver.

He whispers something to Ashley and she nods.

Caden raises his hand and gestures for me to approach. I close my eyes, attempting to dispel the compulsion to do as he has asked. Realizing that I can't stop myself, I take a step forward, a step toward them, and I open my eyes. Caden's smile has returned, but the look in his eyes is commanding me forward, making me move in a way I hadn't expected. Solidifying everything that Derek has been saying.

I. Am. A. Submissive.

What would happen next would alter me forever. Alter me in a way that I could have never imagined possible.

I approach him, but I cannot find it in myself to acknowledge him. Despite the fact that I know I could royally piss him off, I simply cannot give him that satisfaction. Not today.

"Would you like to help Ash?" Caden's voice has a soft, seductive tone to it that sends my blood racing through my veins.

I nod.

Caden's smile grows impossibly larger as he steps back from Ashley's body and she shivers at the loss of contact. "Go around to the other side of the cross, facing her. Comfort her."

I nod my understanding and I sidestep Caden and walk around the cross. Ash's eyes are on me and she smiles. Her smile is so sweet and welcoming that I can't help but smile back at her.

"Kiss him." Caden's voice is dripping with pure command and she raises her chin toward me and I smile because the restraints have her in a position that even though she's been ordered to do it, she can't obey, not without my help. My eyes dart to Caden who chuckles silently but nods.

I lean down and kiss Ash hard. Her breathing hitches and she moans as my tongue slides in along hers. Her eyes close and my eyes go to Caden who is standing there watching us. For the briefest of moments, his dominance falls as he enjoys the sight before him. I close my eyes and deepen the kiss with Ash and she moans again.

Then her breathing turns from steady to short bursts and the sound of leather on skin fills my ears. I pull back.

"I didn't tell you to stop," Caden admonishes with his eyes pinned on me and I shiver as I catch sight of the flogger he is wielding along her backside. She groans with each hit. I lick my lips and take her mouth with mine once again but I can't help watching Caden. I am doing my best attempt to make him jealous and failing miserably.

My cock grows hard with each flick of her tongue, each lick of the flogger, and groan that escapes Ashley's mouth.

The flogger cracks hard against her backside and she pulls back, screaming and breathing through the pain Caden has inflicted on her.

Caden's eyes grow angry because she's stopped kissing me and in an attempt to help calm her, I slide my fingers into her hair. Reminding her that I too am here to help hold her and she settles into my touch. Caden resumes his flogging of her backside and every fifth or sixth strike, Ashley rattles her bindings and I hold her tighter to my lips. If she really wanted to pull away, she could. Her cries of pain are swallowed by my kisses and quickly turn to moans.

The smell of polish on the cross quickly fades and the sweet scent of her arousal begins to assault my nose. I inhale deeply and I open my eyes to find Caden's eyes are on me. Realizing what I'm smelling, he stops his flogging and steps forward, pressing his backside to Ash and grabbing a hold of her hair. He pulls her head back and away from my lips.

"You sweet little slut," he growls as he takes over her lips with his and my cock jumps as he possesses her in a way that drives the jealousy right back through my veins. "What would you rather have? My whip or his cock?" Caden asks Ash and she shivers violently.

"Your cock and his." I suck in a quick deep breath.

"Ahh, my sweet slut, that is not an option. My whip or his cock?"

He tugs her hair a little harder and she moans, "His cock, Sir."

There is a tremor that visibly runs through Caden as his eyes meet mine and he cocks an eyebrow at me. "Which would you rather have, my sweet boy, her pussy or my whip?"

The name 'sweet boy' sends a thrill through me unlike anything I've ever felt before and I can't explain it. "Your whip." The words tumble out before I can stop them. I wanted to say her pussy but those words were just too hard to say at this moment.

Ashley's head snaps in my direction and for some reason I expected disappointment, but instead I am met with a reassuring smile.

"Well then, since it is my choice, I am going to give you her pussy." His voice is dark, brooding and commanding in a way that I am not sure what I really expected him to say. While I said whip, I'm pretty sure that he wouldn't tie me up to the cross and start whipping me. If I remember anything about this lifestyle, negotiations have to come first and we've discussed nothing.

"Please, Master," Ash begs him, "Please."

"Untie her," Caden orders me and I move around the cross, kneeling to undo her ankles first. Her legs are fucking gorgeous. Toned, tanned and sexy as fuck. I can't help running my hands up them as I stand to undue her hands. First one, then the other, as I press myself against her, holding her to the cross while she catches her footing. "Carry her," Caden orders and I do as he's asked of me, scooping her up in my arms and turning toward him. His bag is slung over his shoulder and he nods in the direction of the private rooms. I dutifully follow him with Ash in my arms.

THIRTY~ONE

Ashley snuggles into my hold and places her face in my neck. "Are you sure you're okay with this?"

"Are you?" I counter in a whisper.

"Absolutely," she breathes.

"Then yes," I tell her quickly, not wanting Caden to hear us talking. I don't want to anger him, after what I've just seen in his eyes, I imagine making him angry isn't a hard thing to do.

I follow him down the hallway past the unmarked doors of the private rooms. We pass Derek's room and stop one down and opposite his door. Caden unlocks the door and holds it open for us to enter. His eyes meet mine in a strange, reassuring kind of way that makes me smile.

We step inside and the room is only slightly bigger than Derek's. I briefly wonder if all the rooms are like this before I remember the speech from the fetish ball and conclude that because of their contributions, Derek and Caden have priority rooms.

A four-poster bed sits in the center of the room with six inch thick posts. There are cuffs attached to each one of them. "Lay her down," Caden orders and I do as he's asked and I step back.

Caden puts his bag down on the floor near the door and then he climbs on the bed with Ashley.

"Pet?" he says to her softly.

"Yes, Sir?"

Then he leans in and whispers something in her ear and again the jealousy slides over me. She nods and then Caden climbs off and comes to stand next to me. "Do you agree to do as I say?"

"Yes," I tell him easily.

"It's about fun, no limits really being pushed, but I'd like to know if you'd have a problem being tied to the bed?" Ashley climbs off the bed.

"No," I answer with confidence. For some strange reason, I'm intrigued by what is about to happen with Ashley and me and what role Caden is going to play in it.

"Take your clothes off," he orders and I have no problem following his commands.

I quickly shed my clothes and wait for the next command.

"Suck him," Caden orders Ash.

The look in his eyes is full of lust and desire as he gazes at my body. I shiver and Ashley kneels before me with a big Cheshire grin on her face as she takes in my cock. Caden steps back and sits in a chair positioned at the end of the bed. His eyes never leave mine as Ashley takes my cock into her mouth.

I groan and I fight to keep my eyes open with the sensation. Her mouth is hot and wet as her lips wrap tightly around me and she swallows me down. The muscles in her tongue caress my cock and I shiver. This time I can't fight the roll of my eyes as she works me with her mouth. If she keeps this up, I will be coming down her throat in a matter of seconds. I groan.

"Enough," Caden orders and Ashley dutifully stops. "Lie down, Aryn," he adds and I step around Ashley who is still on the floor. I climb onto the bed and lay on my back in the middle.

Caden comes to the other side of the bed, grabs my arm and secures it into one of the headboard cuffs. I shiver when the gentle caress of his fingers reaches my arm as he wraps the soft lined cuff around my wrist. He has a wide smile on his lips when he rounds the bed and repeats the process with my other arm. Once I'm secured to the bed, he turns to Ash and grabs the button on his pants and my cock jumps when he rips them open.

He stands there and Ashley takes her cue. She puts her fingers in his waistband and tugs down his pants and his cock springs free. A drop of pre-cum slides down my shaft as Ashley takes him into her mouth.

Jealousy slides over me again when he slides his hands into her hair, holding her to him, forcing himself inside of her mouth. She tenses as he pushes into the back of her throat. His cock is larger than mine in the girth department, but watching Ashley suck him is a sight to witness. He releases her hair and she gasps slightly for breath before taking him back into her mouth.

Caden's eyes never leave mine.

After a couple more sucks and strokes, Caden releases Ashley and steps back. His cock stands hard and ready and neither Ashley's nor my eyes leave it. Not until he commands Ash onto the bed with me, shedding her boy shorts as she does. Her perfectly shaved pussy comes into view and she has the most delicious, suckable clit. Her nipples are hard as diamonds and taut. My tongue slides over my lips in anticipation. I turn my full focus to her as she climbs on top of me, but she does doesn't go near my cock. Instead she slides up, placing her delicious nipple at my lips, rubbing it, teasing me.

I stick out my tongue, desperate for a taste of her sweetness and she gives it to me. I slide my tongue up along her nipple. She lets out a moan of pleasure and she presses her nipple into my mouth. I latch onto it like I need it to breathe and our eyes meet. Desire and lust are reflected back at me and I flick my tongue. Her eyes roll up and I do it again, sucking harder on her nipple and using my teeth to nibble slightly.

The pain sends a thrill through her and she groans above me before popping her nipple free of my mouth. My disappointment is brief when she slides the other one along my lips and I suck it into my mouth. Giving this one the same treatment as I did the other one.

My cock is so hard it is starting to hurt and I want to grip it into my hand and fuck myself senseless, but alas, I'm tied to the bed and the frustration sends a new wave of desire through me. I nibble a little on the hard nipple in my mouth. She frees herself from me and I move my head down her stomach, licking and kissing until I can go no further. My message becomes clear and she climbs up my body further, placing her slit just out of reach of my mouth.

I arch up, breathing in her sweet aroma as I stick out my tongue and lightly lick her folds. My heart beats a little faster as her sweetness coats my tongue. Quite possibly the best pussy I've ever tasted is only inches from me and I desperately want to bury my face in it. I tease her with a few more licks in hopes of coaxing her to lower herself. She moans and her legs start to tremble as she moves down enough to give me what I want. Her eyes glisten with desperate need as I finally suck her clit into my mouth.

Her eyes roll up and I flick my tongue against the tight nub and she grinds her hips against my face, urging me to suck harder and faster.

She moans again and my eyes close.

Then everything changes as I feel a hand on one of my legs pushing it out further, only to be embraced by a soft cuff. I shiver and moan into her cunt and she responds equally as loud.

My other leg is brought over and the same warm touch caresses along my leg on its way to the cuff that is quickly secured around my ankle.

I am completely exposed, completely vulnerable, and there are two things I want to happen. One, I want Ashley to come all over my tongue and two, I need to have hands, a mouth, something on my cock. Then, the bed dips and I jump slightly when a pair of warm hands start to caress along my thighs and higher.

I should stop this, I could stop this, but I can't find it in me to do anything about it. The touch, his touch, wipes out any will I have to make it stop because I know in the back of my mind that I can't stop this because I don't want it to end. Ashley's moans grow louder and her thrusts against my face increase as I eat her pussy. She's getting closer and I am one step closer to my goal.

My cock throbs, desperate to be touched. Natural instinct tells me that I want Ashley to reach back and grab it, but Caden is so much closer.

I cry out around Ashley's pussy when my cock slides into Caden's hot mouth. "Fuck," I groan. Every nerve ending in my body ignites, sending goosebumps across my skin. My nipples harden and Ashley grinds her cunt against my mouth. I suck her in, hard. Nibbling and sucking, licking and stroking my tongue along her clit and slipping into her opening.

Caden's mouth slides down my cock and his hands grip onto my balls, sending waves of pain mixed with undeniable pleasure through my body. On the verge of exploding down Caden's throat, I attempt to take a deep breath, concentrate on Ashley's pussy on my face, licking and sucking. Her moans grow louder with each passing second and I can't stop. She's close, she is going to come and that is what I want more than anything. I scrape my teeth against the sensitive nub once and on the second pass she explodes. Her body trembles above me as she rides out her orgasm. Her cries echo off the walls around us.

Caden's hand tightens around my balls and he swallows my length down his throat. He repeats these actions, over and over, until it's all too much and I explode down his throat in the most intense orgasm I've ever felt in my life.

I gasp for breath after coming and pull my head away from Ashley's pussy. Caden doesn't stop sucking and when he flicks his tongue across the underside of my cock, I squirm and my cock hardens again.

Ashley slides off my chest and to the side. Caden grabs her by the back of her neck and quickly takes her mouth with his. She moans when his tongue slides along hers.

I catch my breath and my bearings while they devour each other's mouths. Caden kisses along Ashley's jaw, down her neck before drawing one nipple into his mouth. He sucks and pulls on it with gusto before moving to other one. My cock jumps when Caden tugs on her nipple, stretching the skin taut. Ashley has mercy on my neglected cock and begins to stroke me with her hand while Caden works her over with his mouth.

His other hand comes into view to reveal a set of clamps. He releases her nipples from his hand and mouth then takes the wet one between two fingers, pulling hard and then clamping the alligator clip onto it. Her eyes flutter and her body shivers. Her breathing hitches then lengthens as she processes the pain of the clamp against her nipple. Caden repeats the process with her other nipple and Ashley hisses as her eyes glaze over and she gives in to the sensations.

Caden produces a foil packet and rips it open with his teeth before pushing Ashley's hand away from my erection. He slides the condom down my shaft with a few unnecessary strokes, keeping me hard and wanting. His eyes meet mine and the same lust I saw in Ashley's eyes as she climbed on top of me is now reflected back in Caden's. I can't help but wonder what he plans to do to me, but then he tugs on Ashley's chain, the one hanging between her nipples and she cries out in the most delicious, desperate moan I've ever heard.

"Fuck him, pet. Fuck him hard."

"Yes, Sir," she moans as she straddles me. She reaches between us, grabs hold of my cock and strokes it a couple times before rubbing it along her hot pussy. I shiver as she slides me inside. Caden hasn't moved from between my legs.

"Ahh, fuck," I groan and squirm in my restraints. Being completely at her mercy and the mercy of Caden is a very heady combination. I am ready to explode the moment she bottoms out on me.

Ashley repositions herself, gaining more leverage over me. She tucks her feet under my thighs and her hands on my stomach. She leans forward, giving me a line of sight on Caden whose eyes are looking down at where we're coming together. He's watching us and it sends a wave of pleasure through me that's amplified harder when she grinds her pussy against me, rubbing her clit on my pelvic bone.

Her eyes roll up and she slides up my shaft. Her pussy is soaking wet and hot as hell against my cock as she starts to slowly slide up and down. That's when Caden comes up behind her, wrapping his hands around her stomach, sliding up toward the swell of her breasts and he pulls on the chain attached to the nipple clamps and she cries out. Her pussy clenches tight around me and I groan.

He releases the chain and cups her breasts in his meaty hands. His lips kiss along her neck, and her rhythm increases against my cock as she soars to find her release.

My cock is buried to the hilt inside her when Caden puts pressure on her shoulders to keep her where she is. She grinds down on me and he releases her.

He continues licking and kissing along her neck and shoulders, but his hands disappear as he grabs another foil packet and he rips it open.

Ashley doesn't move, but I purposefully twitch my cock inside of her, reminding her that I'm here, she shivers and licks her lips as our eyes meet.

Then Caden presses her down toward me and the coldness of the chain presses against my chest causing my nipples to harden and she takes advantage. Running a fat wet tongue over one nipple, then the other before kissing her way to my lips. Just before her lips land on mine, Caden pulls her head back with a forceful hand in her hair. Her pussy clenches around me and she cries out. "Do you have permission to kiss him?" Caden growls at her in a low, husky voice.

"No, Sir. I'm sorry, Sir," Ashley whimpers.

He leans in and claims her mouth with his. Disappointment rolls through me as he steals my kiss. Then jealousy returns. But I'm not jealous of him. I'm jealous of her.

THIRTY~TWO

~ CADEN *~*

I brush the tip of my condom covered cock against Ashley's back entrance and she gives me a subtle nod.

I release her hair and lay her back onto Aryn's chest. "Kiss him," I order her and she complies. I'm momentarily frozen when her lips take his in a ravenous kiss. I took a huge risk sucking him off. That could have gone in so many wrong directions but he never told me to stop and more importantly, he grew harder and had no problem coming down my throat. I shiver as I remember the salty sweet taste of his cum as it slid across my tongue. He's definitely not the first man I've sucked off, but I'm almost certain I'm the first for him.

Having lubed the condom while kissing Ashley, I waste no time pressing my dick against her back entrance. I slide in easily as Ashley relaxes to accommodate two hard cocks filling her up.

Aryn's cock jumps inside of Ash as I slide further inside her and she moans into his mouth. His eyes meet mine and I know the lust I am feeling in this moment is directed at Aryn a thousand times over. I pray he sees that in my eyes. When he shivers, I know he is seeing what I'm feeling.

When I caught him watching us in the dungeon, I knew that Derek was right. He is truly a submissive and despite his reticence over the idea, which is obvious, he's very open to exploring. I am sure he'd rather have a woman to tower over him, but I am not going to let that happen.

Once I'm fully inside of Ashley, I reach back and undo Aryn's leg restraints and help him lift his knees, giving him some leverage and control. "Untie his hands," I order Ashley and she quickly releases first the left, then his right hand. Aryn exercises his freedom by grabbing Ashley by the back of her neck and cupping one of her tits. He devours her mouth as he continues his assault on her chest. I push back inside Ashley's ass and Aryn uses his new leverage to do the same before pulling back out. I slide in, and he copies my movement.

The see-saw action is exactly what we needed in order to make this work and he's caught on quickly. I slide in and pull out, he slides in and out in opposite strokes and Ash melts like butter between us. Aryn continues with her breasts and when she cries out, I know he's tugged on the chain between her nipples.

Wanting to help him out, I reach around and our hands touch. A zap transfers between us and I know he feels it too, his eyes meet mine. I give him a warm smile as we both continue sliding in and out of Ashley's snug holes. "When I take it off, suck it into your mouth, hard." I tell him as I indicate to the clamps on her nipples.

"No, no, no," Ashley moans.

"What's wrong, pet?"

"Nothing, Sir," she says breathlessly. I grab the end of one of the clamps and release it. Aryn pulls her nipple into his mouth and she cries out in a mix of pain and pleasure and her body locks down as she explodes all over his cock.

"That's a good little slut." I caress along her back, providing her with some comfort and Aryn releases her nipple with a gentle pop.

Knowing she'll likely come again and not knowing how much longer Aryn can hold out, I leave the other nipple be while he and I continue pumping in and out of her. His speed increases and he groans, "I'm gonna explode." I match his rhythm, and my balls tighten with my own need to come. My imagination runs with the thought of being buried inside Aryn, and not Ashley, driving my orgasm to nearly unmanageable levels.

Her moans increase, Aryn starts to grunt and I reach around for the other clamp. Aryn's eyes meet mine and he nods. I pull the clamp from her nipple and Aryn quickly sucks it into his mouth and once again, Ashley finds her release. "Fuck! Fuck! Fuck!" Aryn cries out. Knowing Aryn is coming sends me over the edge and I slam into Ashley one final time, exploding into the latex barrier.

It takes us a few minutes to catch our breath before I slowly extract myself from Ashley. My cock has fallen soft and I'm disappointed in that, but the sight I see as I back off the bed is one to behold. Aryn, buried in her pussy and still hard as a rock. I shiver and my cock tries to harden again in the condom. I leave the room and go into the bathroom, pulling the condom off as I go. I grab a towel and clean myself up. Washing away the latex feel with the warm cloth has me hard again by the time I leave the bathroom.

When I return, Aryn has flipped Ashley over, giving me a glorious view of his backside and I can't help but stare at it.

He is in amazing shape. I guess that's the product of lots of time on your hands and having a job that's quite physical at times. His body rivals my own. I guess our bodies are both a product of our work.

Aryn's hips and ass flex as he pumps inside Ash. She breathes in little pants with each thrust.

This is what I wanted to watch the whole time, but I couldn't help myself. I needed to be a part of it. I slide into my chair in the corner with my cock in my hand as I watch Aryn fuck Ashley.

His mouth is wrapped around one of her nipples, her hand is in his hair, though I can't see his eyes from where I'm sitting, I have a pretty clear picture of what's happening and I like it.

His thrusts increase inside of her and her body hums with her need to come again but she's fighting it. She doesn't want it to end and I can't say I blame her. I'm not sure I want it to end either. Aryn increases his pace, pulling himself up onto his hands as he pushes into her harder and faster. Her legs wrap around his hips, attempting to hold him to her, but he doesn't slow his pace and before I know it, her back arches as she explodes with her fourth or fifth orgasm. I've lost count at this point.

As she comes down, Aryn slows his pace and she relaxes. I shift in my chair and capture his attention. His eyes land on mine and they roam down to my hand on my cock and he shivers.

There is a glaze of lust in his eyes as he watches me pump my cock, watches me as I watch him with her.

He gently pulls out of her and she curls up, spent.

I cock my finger at him, gesturing for him to come to me and he does without hesitation, reinforcing Derek's working theory that Aryn isn't a Dominant but rather a submissive and I want nothing more than for him to be my submissive.

He comes to stand over me, his cock still covered in a condom. "Remove it," I tell him and he does so. He is still rock hard. "Return the favor?" I smile sweetly at him and he kneels before me. But he shakes his head. "Do you want an order, my sweet boy?"

He nods.

"I won't ask you to do something you don't want to do, that's not how this works, Aryn."

"I didn't say I didn't want to," he breathes and his eyes meet mine. The lust remains there, unshaken by our exchange.

"Suck it, now," I command him and he slides closer to me on his knees before taking my cock in his hand.

"I've never…"

I can't hide the surprise on my face. I hadn't expected that. "You hide it well." I caress his cheek and he melts into my touch, into my comfort of him. He has no business trusting me and yet he's here. I've given no reason for him to trust me, to feel the comfort he feels when he leans into my touch, but yet here he is. Accepting my touch like he needs it more than air. Taking my comfort like it gives him life and hope. I tilt my head as my resolve waivers. I'd had no intention of turning this into anything more than a club relationship, but seeing him vulnerable wakes up something inside of me that I haven't felt in a long time.

There is so much more than what is on the surface with him. I can see a glimpse of all the pain he is hiding from everyone. It all makes sense to me now, why he runs from women, why he enjoys the one night stands, and why he can't give into his deepest desires. He needs more.

THIRTY~THREE

I want nothing more than his mouth on my cock, but I can no longer ask that of him. Forcing him to do this isn't what I wanted to happen. His willingness to do so shows that my order was enough to make him do it, but without talking to him about what he wants, what his limits are, I'm feeling as though I am pushing him into something he isn't ready for.

"Now isn't the time," I say softly.

His eyes open slowly, only to lower them and his hand runs through his hair. Confusion and disappointment radiate off him. "Why?" he breathes and I stroke my thumb along his cheek and his eyes flutter closed.

"Because, I don't feel it's right to ask something of you that you're unwilling to do without being ordered."

His eyes come back to me. "But I want…"

"Shhh," I breathe. "It's alright. I'm not going to push this with you, not here, not tonight."

With my hand still cupping his cheek, he leans into my touch a little bit more. His mouth twists as he struggles with what I've told him. Gone is the peaceful comfort my touch provided him a few moments ago, but yet he doesn't pull away from me.

Nothing more is said until Ashley starts to stir on the bed. She climbs out of it and heads for the bathroom, but before she disappears, her eyes meet mine and she gives me a reassuring smile. I nod and she closes the door.

I remove my hand from Aryn's cheek and his eyes slowly open.

A number of things happen quickly. The lusty veil on his eyes clears quickly and he's returned back to the Aryn I've come to know these last few days. His shoulders tighten and he looks around the room as though he's been in a fog this whole time. I cover myself and he stands up and gathers his clothes. "I have to go," he says in an urgent tone.

"I can take you back to Derek's house," I tell him, confused by his urgency.

"They don't even know where I am." He pulls his pants up his legs, taking away the view he gave me of his backside and a flutter of disappointment courses through me. I was enjoying that view.

"It's fine, Aryn, they saw us come back here. They won't leave without you."

He sits down on the bed and pulls his socks on. Jesus, even his feet are sexy as hell. Is there anything about this man that isn't completely sex on legs? I doubt it.

Ashley comes out of the bathroom, as naked as she was when she went in. She too goes to her clothes and starts to put them on. "Where's the fire, you two?" I ask, trying to sound light, and it comes out all wrong. Ashley freezes and looks at me.

"Sorry, Sir."

I give her a small smile and nod. "It's alright," I tell her and she smiles back at me before getting dressed. Before she even has her panties on, Aryn is dressed and heading for the door.

Without a word, he opens it, looks left then right and takes off out the door.

"Fuck," I growl as I get off the chair I'm sitting in.

"Let him go, Caden." I turn to her quickly, wanting desperately to be pissed off at her for addressing me by my name, but I can't find it in me. "You can't stop him."

I nod, defeated.

By the time I got dressed and checked Ashley over before dismissing her and returned to the dungeon, Aryn was gone. I asked around and no one remembers seeing him since before we'd gone back into the room. I head toward Derek's room and knock on his door.

Dex answers the door. "Hey Caden, everything alright?" he asks as he opens the door.

I shake my head. "Yeah, I think so. Is Aryn in there?"

Dex's eyebrows knit together. "I thought he was with you?"

I shake my head. "He was, until about twenty minutes ago, then he took off."

"I'm sure he's just outside, probably near the truck."

I nod and turn back toward the dungeon and Dex grabs my arm. "Be careful with him. He's having a hard time with all this."

"I know, that's why I need to find him."

Dex nods and releases my arm and I head back into the dungeon and straight through the velvet curtains and the double doors. When I get into the parking lot, there are only a few cars left and Derek's SUV is one of them but Aryn is nowhere to be found.

I run around the parking lot checking between cars before climbing into my car and taking off out of the parking lot. The road that the club is on is quiet this time of night. The area is industrial which makes it the perfect location for the club. Little to no activity at night and on weekends. This allows for some major anonymity for the club and the reason why Orik, Derek and I chose the location.

While on the main street, I drive slowly, hoping to find Aryn walking along the sidewalk, or in a worst case scenario, hiding between the buildings, but I come up empty.

Once I realize that he may have gotten lucky and managed to hail a cab, I head for Derek's house.

While at a light, I text Derek.

Caden to Derek: I can't find A. Headed to your house. If you see him, let me know.

I don't get a response, I didn't expect one. Not if they are in his room back at the club.

During the drive to Derek's house, I can't help thinking about what I did. I have no doubt that I pushed him too far, but if that's the case, I need the chance to apologize to him, to talk to him.

When I arrive at Derek's, there isn't anyone there, at least outside of the security staff. Celeste is quick to tell me that he's not there and while I don't believe her, I don't have much choice.

My options at this point are to let it go, wait it out, or at the very least, text Derek.

I climb back into my car and my phone chimes with a text.

Derek to Caden: Don't know where he is, is he at the house? We're on our way home now. Cotah is floating pretty hard; I need to be with her tonight.

Caden to Derek: No, not at the house, Celeste said he's not here. Can you please give him my number? Not going to make this worse than I already have.

Derek to Caden: I'll talk to him in the morning.

Caden to Derek: Thanks.

I pull out of his driveway and I'm about two miles down the road when Derek approaches from the opposite direction. I flash my high beams and slow down. Derek slows next to me and we roll down our windows.

"You alright?" Derek asks through the window.

I shake my head. "I pushed him too far."

"I wouldn't worry about it," Dex says from the passenger seat. "He'll show up. When I see him, I'll let you know how he's doing."

"Thanks, Dex. I appreciate it."

Both men smile at me and Derek nods before rolling up the window and heading off toward the house. It takes me a moment to move my foot from the break to the gas pedal and to make the short drive home.

~ The Next Day *~*

Derek to Caden: He's back in Los Angeles.

Caden to Derek: What do you mean? Dex is still here isn't he?

Derek to Caden: Yes, he arranged it with Sean, said he had to head back for something urgent. We know otherwise. Dex & Raine leave for New York tomorrow; he'll be meeting them there. Dex says when he sees him, he'll talk to him.

Caden to Derek: Thanks, I appreciate it. You guys coming over tonight?

Derek to Caden: Wouldn't miss it.

THIRTY~FOUR

~ ARYN *~*

"I don't need a fucking lecture, Dex," I bark into the phone.

"Who's lecturing you?"

I sigh into the phone. "I freaked out."

"Well hello, Captain Obvious, welcome to the party."

"Fuck you."

He sighs into the phone, and I know his disappointment must rival mine over running away from Nashville.

"Look, I'm sorry. I just wish you'd talk about it."

I take a deep breath. "There is nothing to talk about."

"Obviously there is, you ran away."

"I just, I'm fucking confused," I admit as I start to pace my apartment.

"About what? Caden?"

"No," I snap.

"Yeah, alright. Listen, Caden is concerned about you. I'm going to text you his number. Please call him, or text him. Tell him you're alright?"

"Fine."

"You know what, jackass? Despite what you think, there are people in this world that fucking care about you. Caden is torn up over whatever it is that happened that night and he needs to know you're at least physically okay. It doesn't have to be any more than that."

"Alright," I relent. "I'll text him."

"Good. See you in a couple hours." He hangs up.

We arrived in New York a couple hours ago with Talon, Eric, Calvin, plus the security team, sans Tori who stayed behind with Addison and Kyle. The twins are too young for traveling right now so Talon came alone. He's a mess. He's talked to them at least three times since we left the house in Los Angeles. I've never seen him so lost and confused, but if I know Talon when the shit starts moving and he's on the spot, he'll be right as rain.

We're only missing Dex and Raine who will arrive soon. Tonight the band has their first appearance on one of the late night shows. This starts the week of album promo that will have us running around like madmen crisscrossing the city.

When Caden's number came over, it took everything I have to talk to him. Rather than texting him, giving him an outlet to reach me, I blocked my number and called him. Hoping like hell he'd be busy and not answer his phone. Private numbers usually turn people off from answering their lines.

There was no answer and no direct send to voicemail which means I truly did catch him while he was busy and I left him a message.

"It's Aryn, I'm perfectly fine. I, uh, I'm sorry I ran out on you the other night, but uh, yeah, I'm alright." I hung up the phone and did my best to push all things Caden from my mind.

A task that is proving to be impossible.

He's all I've thought about since that night. He's all I see when I close my eyes. That night was something else altogether and I'm not sure I'm capable of explaining it to myself anymore. All I know is that Caden rejected me with the sweetest, kindest, warmest touch I've ever experienced before in my life. That rejection was confusing since I know he wanted me, he was hard as a rock, and yet he reacted the way that he did. Who does that?

But what makes me the craziest? The fact that his touch completely obliterated all my concerns, my fears. It made me feel safe, wanted, protected and most importantly, it made me feel like I really mattered. He touched me like that and rejected me in the same breath.

That is what I don't understand. What I can't wrap my head around.

A knock on my door, pulls me out of my thoughts about Caden, despite the fact that he remains there, in the back of my mind regardless of what I'm doing.

I open the door and Mills greets me by saying, "Time to roll." I nod, grab all of my gear and head out.

THIRTY~FIVE

~ CADEN *~*

"Why is this so important to you?" Derek asks me through the phone.

"It just is."

"He's fine, Caden."

"I just wish he'd call me again," I tell him.

"Why don't you call him back?"

"I would if he hadn't blocked his number and believe me, I've already tried to crack his encryption."

He snorts into the phone. "Good luck with that. Those boys have some of the wildest technology, even you'd be jealous of it."

I frown. "And you still won't give me his number?"

"No, I won't. He hasn't given Dex or me permission to do so. Why does this mean so much to you?"

I sigh. "I've never felt like this about anyone."

"Do you really think he wants to be a submissive?" he counters.

"No, I don't. I don't think he wants to be, but I think he's coming to the reality that it just might be who he is. He had no problem following my commands that night, let alone the fact that he wanted permission from me before he'd consider giving me head. I'm pretty sure his realization of that fact is what sent him running. You know as well as I do that it happens all the time."

He snorts again. "You think his confession is what sent him running? What about the fact that he may not be gay."

"I'm not gay either."

He chuckles, "You tell yourself that, but Caden, do you honestly think you'd be as attracted to him as you are if you weren't at least bi?"

"Bi I can accept, but I'm not gay. I enjoy women just as much as you do. I enjoy them more when they are at my feet, but that's beside the point."

"Is it really?" Derek counters. "Think about it, Caden. Is Aryn really what you want or is the challenge of turning him, molding him, what's really driving all this? You, more than anyone else I know, love this kind of challenge. It's what keeps you motivated and more importantly, it's what keeps you single. When you have a submissive at your side, you're content until they're trained, until they stop putting up a fight. The minute that they become compliant, you want to dump them for someone else."

"Hardly," I argue.

"Regardless, he's a challenge, but what if he doesn't want you, what if he'd prefer someone else? A woman?"

I shake my head despite the fact that he can't see me through the phone. "I don't think that's the case."

"But you don't know," he argues and I can't dispute that because honestly, he's right. I don't know.

"That's why I want to talk to him," I tell Derek softly. "I can't know until I hear it from him. You, above anyone else, should understand that."

"What are you talking about?" he asks.

"Oh, I don't know, you aren't exactly the poster child for rational thought here my friend." He knows exactly what I'm talking about, his own insane decisions make mine look like a cake walk at a school carnival.

"Fair enough," he tells me. "But that doesn't mean I'm handing over his number. But-" he hesitates, "You plan on going to any of your premieres?"

It's my turn to snort. "No. You know I don't do those damn things anymore."

"Well, you might want to."

"What are you talking about?" I ask him.

"You might want to reconsider." He muffles the phone then comes back on, "I have to run."

"Derek, what do you mean?"

"Just consider it. I have to run."

He hangs up the phone, leaving me hanging, wondering why the upcoming Lost Hope premiere is suddenly so important.

~ ARYN *~*

"We need to talk," Dex tells me the moment we get to the hotel from the airport. I've already been here for half the day when their flight finally arrived.

"We don't have time for it."

"Bullshit," he counters. "We have plenty of time and this won't take long." He opens the door to his hotel room. Raine had some stuff to do and discuss with Mills so they've gone off to another room on the floor. Since Addison stayed home, this one is on Raine to handle and this is her first time handling a press tour for 69 Bottles. I have every confidence in her, so does everyone else that's here, but she's completely distracted. She'd said something in the car about how they should have gone back to Los Angeles so that she could discuss stuff with Addison and get things straight, but the Top in Dex took over and he handled her in a way that gave her no choice but to comply. Though one would say the situation would seem forced, but for me, I realized that his comfort and control over

Raine is a comfort to her. His encouragement and praise are a trait to be admired and I won't lie, the jealousy returned.

"We're here, so talk." I lean against the wall, crossing my arms over my chest.

"Stop posturing. You know as well as I do that we are not in here for me to attack you."

"No, you just want information so that you can feed it to Derek who can pass it along to Caden and I don't need you or Derek meddling in my business."

"Listen here, asshat." Dex turns on me. "I don't give a shit what you think, but you fucking know me better than that. I brought you in here because I am genuinely concerned about you. About what happened that night."

The sincerity in his eyes tells me he does mean it. "Since when do you give a shit about someone other than yourself?" I argue back at him.

"When have I ever not given a shit about you?" His voice is tight, he's pissed and he is fighting his anger and it fuels me just a little bit more. But he's right with what he said. Dex, despite his hard ass exterior and assholishness, has always been there for me, no matter what.

"There is nothing to talk about."

"Did he force you?"

My arms fall from my chest, "What? God, no. In fact it's quite the opposite, he rejected me."

That stops Dex cold. His anger subsides completely and his posture softens along with the hard stare in his eyes. "You wanted him?" His intention was clear in his eyes, strong and sure that he knows the answer to his own question but his words come out in more of an unsure whisper.

I shrug. "Does that bother you?"

He doesn't answer. He turns toward the window that overlooks Time Square. "No, I guess I just never thought that you were gay."

I huff. "I'm not gay."

He turns toward me. "Then what?"

"Curious might be a better word for it."

"How long have you been curious?" he asks.

"I'm not sure you want me to answer that question," I tell him and lean back against the wall. I've baited him and I know damn well what's going to come next.

"Me, isn't it? You want me?" His voice is confused, concerned and a hint of curiosity.

I give him a hard stare. "Hardly."

He rolls his eyes. "Denial does you no good." He turns back toward the window and adds, "Since when?"

I shrug, despite him having his back to me. "Probably around the third or fourth chick we shared together."

He turns back around, and I expect him to be angry, to come try and fight me, but he doesn't, he just looks at me calmly.

"Look, it's entirely irrelevant. I knew you didn't want me, that it would never go that way between us and I accepted that, Dex. It's not like I was in love with you or anything." I stop talking and he just stands there. His eyes bore into me and I know he wants me to finish, but I don't know how to tell him that I wanted to take things up a notch with him. That I wouldn't have minded turning the tables on the girls we were with. Giving them a little more of their fantasy. But it never went there. I never talked about it with him and more importantly, I never told him, until now.

"But what?" he finally asks.

"I just thought maybe it would be fun." I shrug, trying to portray to him that was honestly what I thought, which is true. "I don't even know if I could have done it to be honest with you, but, you were nice to look at. Especially if we had a rather uninteresting girl between us." I rub my palms on my thighs. "It was nothing more than a fantasy that I never acted on."

"That's good because I wouldn't have, not that. Oh for fuck's sake, I'm not into that. Not curious about it. Not now, not even back then."

My shoulders drop. "I know, which is why I never acted on it. But you have to admit, for as close as we are, it wouldn't be hard for someone's signals to cross and well, maybe they did with me a little bit. But Dex, I never would have done anything to you. I never did do anything to you. I threw the fantasy out the window for a couple of reasons, one of which being that I knew you weren't into it."

"What's another reason?"

"Because I didn't want to ruin the friendship we have. You know, the whole sex between friends thing."

Finally he nods. I know this conversation hasn't gone the way he probably planned on having it go, in fact, it wasn't what I wanted to talk about either, but it seems to have distracted him from Caden, which was my intention.

"You need to get ready to go-"

"What about Caden?" he cuts me off.

"What about him?" I snap.

"Did you text him?"

"No," I tell him. I didn't text him, I called him.

"Why the hell not?"

"What's the point?" I grumble. "He rejected me, remember?"

"I don't think that was his intention, Beck."

I shrug. "So what, it's what happened."

"So you were ready and willing to have sex with him and he rejected you?"

"Not exactly."

"Then what, exactly?"

"Why do you need all the fucking details, Dex? This isn't about you, this isn't about Derek, hell, this isn't even about Caden. This is about me and no one else. I was willing to give him what he wanted. He wanted me to do it, he ordered me to do it, and then he flipped a switch and rejected me because I was honest with him."

"About what?" Dex snaps.

"Don't get fucking pissy with me, asshat. You fucking dragged me in here to talk."

"What did you tell him?"

"That I'd never sucked a dick before."

"Oh." He stops and relaxes again.

"Are you happy now? You've gotten it all out of me."

"Not hardly. Why did you run away?"

"Fuck me, come on, man, that's really none of your fucking business."

He takes steps toward me. "Yes, it is. You abandoned me in Nashville, left me to bodyguards who are not paid to watch over me and Raine. What if something had happened to me or her while you were running away and wallowing in your personal pity party?"

"I fucking ran away because I was willing to give a man, who I barely fucking know, a goddamn blowjob because he ordered me to do it. Then he turned around and rejected me at the same time he was comforting me. He showed me the first inkling of fucking affection I've had in my entire life. It scared the living shit out of me, Dex. What the fuck else was I supposed to do? Not only was I ordered to give a man a blowjob, but I was more than willing to surrender to him, to do what he asked, despite the fact that I have never done anything like it before. So not only was I dealing with the fact that you all seemed to see it before I did, the fact that you all saw I was a submissive and not a Top, you all let it go, let me flounder, let me look weak in Caden's eyes, in everyone's eyes because here I was introducing myself as a Top and low and behold, I'm nothing but a goddamn submissive."

With that, I turn and leave the room, making a bad attempt at slamming an air controlled door on my way out.

THIRTY~SIX

Dex and I don't talk about Caden anymore after that. Despite his attempts throughout our busy week in New York. A look was all it took to shut him down. I got the impression that he squealed to Derek about what I'd told him and he was trying to come back at me with a counter argument from Caden. Frankly, I don't want to hear it.

I had hoped that the press tour and getting back to Los Angeles before taking off with Alyssa would be enough to put Caden out of my mind, but it didn't happen.

Despite all my best efforts, I couldn't get him out of my mind and there were three failed attempts with random barmaids that made me wonder what the fuck was wrong with me. Ironically enough, when their lips would land on mine as we fell into bed, all I could see was Caden. I wanted to be kissing him and that bothered me that much more.

When I got back to California, I was pulled into duty with Alyssa Serin and her tour. Casey and Troy kept me occupied with plans for the premiere circuit. We planned our routes, our escapes and lastly our timing on where we needed to be and when we needed to be there. Unfortunately, like with 69 Bottles, we don't have the ability to search out the venues beforehand and we certainly don't have the chance to practice for anything, but that's what makes us such a great team.

Fortunately for us, these events are under tight security anyway so what goes on in the buildings is hardly a concern for us. Our only goal is Alyssa and making sure she's protected and taken care of.

Alyssa's issues with her previous bodyguard are obvious to me when I meet her. She's a tiny, sexy thing. Only about five two or three with long blonde hair. She's gorgeous, but I knew that already. Actresses are notoriously gorgeous on the red carpet but hardly gorgeous outside of their 'stage'. Alyssa is an exception to that rule. I won't lie, I had a very hard time controlling myself and of course the raging hard-on she excited in me before I managed to push her off me. Which explains why her previous bodyguard was compromised and the suspicions behind his inability to remain objective are confirmed.

While normally I wouldn't hesitate to sleep with a gorgeous woman like her, I draw the line at my clients, especially on the first meeting. But since I left Nashville, I've come to realize that stopping her before hitting the bedroom would save her disappointment and my embarrassment.

Casey wasn't so easily deterred from her and while I can't confirm or deny them sleeping together, I'm at the point that I really don't want to know.

Casey's distaste for country singers became perfectly clear when one of Alyssa's friends was over at the house while we were discussing our escape plans for the Los Angeles premiere. She was far sexier than Alyssa is in my opinion and Casey made no secret of looking Avery Storm up and down on more than a few occasions despite his 'anti-country' campaign. I've never had the balls to ask him what his deal is with country singers but Avery seems to be pushing all his buttons.

Avery made no secret of checking Casey out either. I tried my damnedest to shrug it off and prayed that we wouldn't see much more of Avery while we were here in Los Angeles.

"Avery is coming with me tomorrow night," Alyssa tells me. "She's my date." Oh fucking fabulous.

"Does she have her detail?" I ask Alyssa, praying that I can use them to help keep Casey and Avery separated.

Alyssa scrunches up her face. "No," she says in her snotty way. "That is what I pay you for."

I nod. "Yes, ma'am."

Needless to say, I pulled Casey aside after that. Warned him to pay attention to Alyssa as she is our primary mark. He was pissed that I'd considered he was remotely interested in Avery. But he had very little conviction in his argument. Country singer, celebrity or not, Casey is a strong bodyguard and I have every faith in him. In fact, I trust my life to him and I know damn well that some hottie like Avery isn't going to get in his way.

~ CADEN *~*

"Son of a bitch," I say to the TV as I watch the red carpet premiere of Lost Hope in Los Angeles. "Motherfucker. That asshole knew all along." I shake my head as the movie's leading lady walks the red carpet and who is flanking her? "Aryn," I breathe before downing the rest of my scotch and grabbing my phone.

I press two buttons and call Jessie, my personal pilot. "Jessie, I need the plane as soon as possible."

"Yes, Sir. Flight plan?"

"New York City."

"On it. We need at least forty-five minutes."

"Fine, I'll be there in ninety."

I hang up the phone with Jessie and call Derek. "You cheeky bastard."

"Hello Caden," he says calmly into the phone. "To what do I owe-?"

"You knew about his assignment and you didn't tell me?" I interject.

Derek laughs into the phone. "How'd you figure it out?"

"Oh, I don't know, watching the Los Angeles red carpet on TV."

Derek laughs again. "I thought they were supposed to stay behind the scenes."

I roll my eyes. "I'm going to New York, you want to go?"

"I'd love to, but I'm stuck in Texas for at least the next week. Go, track him down, talk to him."

"That's not going to be easy. Besides..." I let the thought drop off. This is fucking stupid. Why am I firing up my plane to go to New York for something, someone, that doesn't want me?

"You're not alone, Caden. Trust me on this."

"How the hell would you know?"

He snorts into the phone. "I don't, but what I do know is that he's failed at least three times to bed anyone else since leaving Nashville. I also know that he's closed himself off and gotten defensive with Dex when it comes to discussing anything that has to do with the lifestyle and last, but certainly not least, neither one of you will ever know unless one of you grows a pair of fucking balls and makes the next move."

"I'm holding you to this."

"Fine, but remember you just don't know until you try and since you can't call him and he's doing everything he can to run away from it someone needs to confront the situation. Force him, order him if you have to, but damn it, talk to him."

"Yeah, alright," I tell him and hang up the phone before heading toward my bedroom, my suitcase and my closet.

THIRTY~SEVEN

The nicest thing about being who I am? Nobody cares when the stunt coordinator shows up, or a producer for that matter. I usually blend into the crowd and more importantly, I enter without drawing too much attention to myself. Sometimes, depending on the movie, I get inundated and when you're as attractive as I am, you draw attention to yourself. No, I'm not conceited, it's just a part of being in Hollywood and when you get labeled as such, it sticks with you.

Regardless, it didn't seem to matter this time because I'm not on the appearance list. Allowing me to enter the red carpet at a time of my choosing. In this case, about three cars after Alyssa arrives. Giving me the perfect opportunity to enter, see Aryn and yet keep my distance. Even if he is paying attention, the crowd won't be.

New York is the biggest premiere location on the US circuit, so that means that anyone who is anyone usually shows up for these things. Whether they intend to stay for the movie or not.

Stepping out of the car, I take in the sights, the sounds and most importantly, the reason I've come. He is precisely where I'd expected him to be. Near Alyssa, but a safe distance away from her and though I can see him from here, he'd be hard pressed to pick me out of the crowd surrounding me. Good.

I wave to some people, then talk to a couple of the reporters along the way, but I never lose sight of Aryn. Luckily for me, I was able to get to the reporters before they started calling my name. Though I don't expect Aryn to put two and two together if he would hear my name being called. It's once we're inside the theater that I can't control and I realize that maybe I should have come in sooner. Been inside hiding when he arrived. But I must say, watching him work makes me smile.

He's so engrossed in what is going on right near Alyssa that he's not paying attention to what's happening at this end of the carpet. Then he dips into the fans' line. This is a narrow part of the carpet where exclusive fans are given closer access and a chance at autographs as the actors and actresses file into the theater. I slide in behind one of the supporting actors from the movie and blend in with his little entourage as I too step into the same area.

Alyssa is doing what she does best, smiling and waving to the crowd. A few autographs signed, a few pictures taken and finally she slides into the theater and I breathe a sigh of relief.

I manage to make it into the theater after Alyssa went back into the press area before the movie starts. This is one event that I know Alyssa will stick around for. In fact, she has to. There is a massive question and answer session following the movie and she is required to be there.

I find my seat and talk to a couple of the people around me. Mostly extras and a few of the crew that I haven't seen since we finished filming. I stop short when Alyssa enters the theater to a roar of applause from the fans and claps from the crew near me. When I see Aryn, I take my seat, hiding among those that are standing and I watch him. I smile when he rubs the back of his neck and he shakes his head a little. I've seen him do that before. In the club, right before I've approached him. It's amazing what that heightened sense of awareness feels like when you least expect it. For Aryn, at this moment, I imagine that he's having a bad feeling coursing through him, like something bad is going to happen versus the fact that I'm staring him down.

Aryn and two other bodyguards spread out along the front of the theater. Aryn takes the theater entrance and the two other ones are standing in the isles as Alyssa takes a seat next to Travis Jackson, the movie's leading male actor and a very good friend of mine. Now that everyone is seated up front, the audience takes their seats and the introductions begin.

I couldn't take my eyes off Aryn the entire time. I've seen the movie close to a thousand times while we edited and finalized the film.

When the movie is over, the crowd erupts and my heart swells. Though I am only an associate producer on this film, one of the studios that I co-own filmed it. So my name is indirectly all over this movie and I'm pretty sure that Aryn has no clue.

Alyssa and Travis go through their question and answer session and Aryn goes back to being in full action mode, escorting Alyssa from the theater and onto their next event.

I had my assistant email me their tour schedule and while I want to stick around in New York, I don't.

After the premiere is over and I got what I came for, a glimpse at Aryn, I board my plane and head back to Nashville. The Nashville premiere isn't until Friday, but I know that they will be in Nashville Thursday night and they won't leave until Sunday when they take off for London.

~ ARYN *~*

Once we are back at the hotel, I can't settle myself down. I kept getting this weird, sinking feeling like something was going to happen today and it kept me on edge. I kept feeling like someone was watching me, despite the fact that I never saw anyone I recognized. I kept feeling like I did back in the club when I knew that Caden was watching me and I cannot for the life of me figure out why I felt that way. That movie was hardly anything I imagine him being interested in and why come all the way to New York when he's got a premiere in Nashville.

"Ugh!" I groan.

I've been dreading the Nashville stop on the tour since I ran away from there a couple weeks ago. I'm scared shitless that I will run into him.

I thought about going to the club tomorrow night, once we get to Nashville, since we have a night off. Alyssa has asked for privacy at the hotel and despite my objections, I'm going to give it to her. Anyway, I'd love to go to the club, but I'm afraid of running into him and if I'm going to run into him, more than likely it would be at the club.

Instead, I text Ash.

Aryn to Ashley: Coming to town tomorrow, dinner?

She doesn't answer me right away and then I realize that it's nearly midnight. I wouldn't answer either. Though Wednesdays are not a big day for the club, there is a good chance that she's there. I frown at my phone and throw it on the bed before I strip out of my clothes and head for the shower.

The minute my shirt comes off and my pants slide down, my cock grows hard and Caden comes to mind.

THIRTY~EIGHT

~ CADEN *~*

"He what?" I'm having a hard time hearing Ashley.

"I shouldn't be telling you this."

"Spill it, Ashley," I say into the phone. She called me at nearly one in the morning which means she was likely at the club tonight, but it is so odd for her to call me so late.

"Aryn texted me, asked me to dinner tomorrow night."

I slouch back into my chair. "He's coming to town?" I knew he would be, but I don't want to let Ashley know that I know. One thing about maintaining anonymity at the club is that there are only a few people there who know who I am or what I do.

"I guess so. He just texted me and said that he'd be in town tomorrow night and asked if I wanted to go to dinner. But, Caden?"

I let the fact that she is addressing me by my first name only slide off me. I need to hear more. "Yeah?"

"I can't go. Not unless he wants to eat at like four, I have club duty tomorrow and, well, I have to tell him no."

"So tell him no. What's the big deal?" I'm trying not to sound irritated at the fact that she even bothered to tell me if she hadn't planned on going.

"Well, I- I guess I don't know," she tells me softly. "I guess I thought you might like to know that he's going to be in town."

I knew that, but she doesn't know that. "I appreciate it. If he was asking you to dinner, do you think he'd go to the club afterward?"

"I don't know," she sighs. "I can try and probe him for you. But I, I told you because I thought you'd like to know, but I don't want to get in the middle of whatever it is that you guys have brewing." Her voice is unsure.

I lean forward in my chair and put my forehead in my free hand. "Don't worry about it."

"Why don't you just call him?" she asks me and it's a perfectly reasonable question.

"I can't."

"Why not?"

"Uhh, because when he called me a couple weeks ago, he blocked his number so I don't have it. I can't call him or text."

"Why didn't Derek or Dex give you his number?" She sounds agitated and I see the little crease between her eyebrows without actually seeing her.

"Because he never gave them permission to do so."

"Well, that's crap. I'll give it to you."

The lifeline I need is dangling before me. The chance to finally make contact with him again is right there for the taking. "I can't," I tell her.

"Why not?"

"You're sure being pushy here, little one."

"I'm sorry, Sir, I just, I don't understand what the big deal is. I knew him for less than three hours and he handed me his number."

"I don't know that I can answer that question for you, Ash, I wish I could. I will respect his privacy about not wanting to give me his number, but I need you to do something for me."

"Is this an order?"

"Does it have to be?" I sit up a little straighter.

"It depends on what it is, Sir."

I smile into the phone. "Text me tomorrow night if he shows up at the club?"

"That will have to be an order. You know Teddy and you know he won't let me use my phone at the podium."

"No, he won't. I'll text him and ask him to let me know."

"Erhm…"

"What?" I say.

"I don't know if he would do that either, you know that the club is private."

I smile involuntarily into the phone. "Oh, he wouldn't do so for anyone else, but for me, that's another story."

"Yes, Sir."

"Thank you, Ashley."

"Anytime." She pauses, "Sir?"

"Yes."

"Would you like some company tonight? I'm a little wired from the club."

I scrub my face with my hand. Every fiber of my being wants to tell her yes, but I know I shouldn't. Especially if what Derek told me about Aryn failing to bed anyone since leaving here is true. Though it wasn't for a lack of effort on Aryn's part, he failed more than he's succeeded and I'd almost feel guilty about having her over.

My response takes too long and Ashley jumps to conclusions. "I'm sorry, Sir. I shouldn't have, have a good night."

"Ash?"

"Yes."

"Come over."

"Yes, Sir," she says with enthusiasm and I hang up the phone.

Caden to Teddy: If Aryn shows up tomorrow night, text me.

Teddy to Caden: Why?

Caden to Teddy: Because I need to be somewhere else tomorrow night, but if he's there, I need to talk to him. But don't tell him I told you that.

Teddy to Caden: Will do.

Caden to Teddy: I asked Ash to do it... she refused. Just thought I'd let you know.

Teddy to Caden: Why'd she refuse?

Caden to Teddy: ;-) because she knew that no matter who gave the order, you wouldn't let her have her phone at the podium.

Teddy to Caden: Good girl. Thanks for letting me know and I'll let you know if he shows.

Caden to Teddy: Thanks, I owe you.

Teddy to Caden: What's the deal with you two anyway?

Caden to Teddy: Long story, but I've been trying for almost three weeks to reach him and he's unreachable, but I know he's coming back to town tomorrow.

My doorbell rings and I open it to find Ash, still in fetish gear, standing on the other side of the threshold. I open the door and she steps in, dipping under my arm holding the door and she drops her jacket. Her shoulders are fully exposed to me and she's wearing a black corset with a black tutu skirt and fishnets with hooker red heels. She steals my breath away, she's so gorgeous, but looking at her from behind, I realize my mistake. She isn't Aryn.

~ ARYN *~*

Ashley to Beck: Sorry, just saw your message. I have club duty tonight and have to be there by 6. I can meet you around 3, if you're free.

225

Beck to Ashley: I don't land until three. I have some stuff to do right after. Can you get out of club duty?

Ashley to Beck: I wish, but no. I'm already covering for the other girl. Come to the club?

Her question sends a thrill through me. Yes, I'd love to go to the club but I don't need to see him.

The thought sends a round of dread through me.

Just fucking text him, you idiot.

Beck to Ashley: What about Saturday night? In town till Sunday.

Ashley to Beck: Why not Friday?

Beck to Ashley: Can't, working.

Ashley to Beck: is Dex in town?

Beck to Ashley: no, in town on other business. I won't be free until probably after midnight Friday.

Ashley to Beck: Saturday will work.

Beck to Ashley: Great, I'll call you when I know what time I'm free.

Ashley to Beck: Perfect. Can't wait to see you.

Beck to Ashley: Ditto

~ CADEN *~*

Ashley to Caden: He's in town till Sunday - meeting him for dinner Saturday night. Join us?

Caden to Ashley: No, but thanks for letting me know.

Ashley to Caden: You talk to Teddy?

Caden to Ashley: Yup.

Ashley to Caden: Good. See you later.

Caden to Ashley: Sorry about last night.

Ashley to Caden: Don't be. I get it. :-D

Caden to Ashley: I'm glad someone does because I sure as fuck don't.

Ashley to Caden: you'll be fine. P.s. He didn't say one way or the other whether he was coming to club.

Ashley's last text gives me hope. A flat out denial means he wouldn't have gone, but since he's not decided, there is a small ounce of hope that he just might show up.

THIRTY~NINE

~ ARYN *~*

Tonight's premiere is especially crowded, which seems odd for an off the beaten path premiere spot. I realized while I stood there in New York watching the movie, or at least listening to it, that it took place here in Nashville. Alyssa looks great. Casey is back on track now that Avery is gone. Though he seemed happy to be away from her, it didn't stop him from looking at her every chance he got.

We've just arrived and Alyssa is doing her red carpet thing when the next limo pulls up, but we're moving on to the next reporter and I don't get to see who climbs out of the car. The security at the front of the carpet is more than sufficient that I turn toward the crowd, scanning for anything suspicious and all I really see are a bunch of screaming and overly excited girls waving and hoping for Travis to show up. I have to admit, I get the appeal with him. I get it with Tristan, Cami's husband, too, but I've known him for a while now so that appeal is gone for me.

"Caden!"

"Caden!"

"Caden, over here."

The name causes my body to shiver uncontrollably for a moment, but I don't pay any attention to it because the odds of it being him are slim. I turn toward Alyssa.

"Caden, so good to see you." Alyssa says as she walks toward a tall man dressed in a gorgeous tuxedo and the lights shift, giving me a clear view of the man she's embracing and my heart stops in my chest when my eyes land on none other than Master Caden.

My heart picks back up in double time and when I gasp for air, I realize I was holding my breath.

Our eyes meet and that familiar zing is there. I feel as though I could be lost in his eyes forever. Alyssa is doing everything she can to get his attention.

"You know Beck?" she finally asks him and the name stops him short and he looks at her.

"We've met. I'm friends with Dex." he says but there is a curious, knowing smile tugging at the corner of his lips. I find it in myself to take a deep breath and turn back toward the crowd, fighting the knowledge that he's looking at me while he continues chatting with Alyssa before they part ways moments later. When I turn back around, Casey and Troy are looking at me like I've lost my damn mind or like they need to know what the hell and how the hell I know this man. I shake my head and they both frown at me.

No need to go into the gory details.

I start thinking about the New York premiere. If he's here, at this premiere, is it possible that he was in New York? Nah, I would have seen him.

"Come on, man," Casey's voice says in my ear piece and I turn to my left, away from where Caden was, hoping I don't run into him. When I turn, he's standing a few feet away from me.

"Good to see you, Aryn," he says as I approach to walk past him.

"What are you doing here?" I try to sound angry about it, but of course I fail miserably. It's impossible to hide the fact that I am, surprisingly, happy to see him.

He smirks at me and pushes something into my pocket. "Check the program," he says before turning to walk along side me behind Alyssa and the other two. "We need to talk."

"Hardly. I don't think there is anything we need to discuss."

"On the contrary, I think we do."

"And I don't."

He drops his voice to a whisper near my ear, "Oh, sweet boy, I believe we do. Where are you staying?"

His pet name sends a new wave of desire through me and I fight to keep it in control. I fight the submissive desire to tell him what he wants to know. "You're a brilliant man, Caden, I imagine you already know the answer to that question and if you don't, I'm sure a few phone calls can get you your answers."

"Caden." Someone calls from my left and I am thankful for the distraction.

"I have to work," I grumble before increasing my pace back toward Alyssa and the guys.

"You alright?" I hear Casey in my ear.

I bring my hand to my mouth and reply into the mic, "Yeah, I'm fine."

I pray that it's enough. I shake my head and pull down on my suit jacket, straightening myself and putting my bodyguard mask back on while Alyssa finishes her press line.

Once we dip inside the fan area, Alyssa goes toward the crowd to sign autographs and take pictures. I relax a little bit because these fans are all screened before they're allowed inside. My only concern now is an overzealous fan who gets out of hand and this lot is a little more controlled than the one in New York.

"You're right, I can find you, but I'd much rather you told me yourself." Caden's voice is soft, coming from behind me but I don't turn to him when he steps up next to me.

"Are you stalking me now?"

"No, I'm just a man who doesn't take no for an answer and I need an explanation."

"For what?" I snap.

"Watch your tone," he snaps back at me and I immediately regret it. "For running out, for disappearing and more importantly, for why you simply left me a voicemail and didn't bother to allow me to ask you about your well being after that night."

"I didn't feel I owed you any explanation, you're not my Master. I don't answer to you, Caden," I whisper harshly in his ear.

"No, you don't. But it is about respect, Aryn, and while I truly respect your privacy, I'd like an explanation and here is hardly the place to talk about it. Now, tell me where you're staying and I will come by later tonight."

Unable to resist his demand, I tell him, "Loews Vanderbilt, eleven-fifteen."

I walk away, following Alyssa, Casey and Troy into the theater.

While Alyssa finishes up her final interview, I start to grow antsy and in desperate need of an escape from here. I've seen Caden moving around the different rooms after Alyssa. I finally manage to pull the program out of my pocket but it's not a program, it is just a computer printout from a popular entertainment site that lists the entire cast and most of the crew. The crew part is all I need.

Caden Matthew - Associate Executive Producer/Stunt Coordinator

"Well, fuck me," I breathe. So he was in New York.

Alyssa elected to go to the after party, which I had mixed feelings about going. I really wanted to get out of here, but I didn't want to go back to the hotel. Thankfully I didn't see Caden anywhere. Perhaps he went to the club or maybe he changed his mind about getting his answers.

I shiver. Concern, fear, excitement and anticipation are a nasty cocktail for someone already on edge, especially when I'm working. Somehow I manage and finally, around one in the morning, we return to the hotel.

I shower and down two bottles from the mini-bar before I am ready for bed. I'm about to strip down to my boxers when there is a knock at the door. My heart skips a beat in my chest and I look at the clock, it's nearly two. It has to be Casey.

I go to the door and turn the handle. "What's up, Cas-" I stop when I see Caden standing beyond the door. He's changed out of his tuxedo from the premiere into jeans and a dark blue button down shirt.

"Bad time?" he says with a smirk.

I shake my head slightly before opening the door wider, allowing him room to step inside. My gaze follows him as he walks into my suite. "Am I interrupting something?" he asks as he takes in the state of my turned down bed.

"Not particularly. Can I get you a drink?" I ask and I close the door.

"No thank you." A smile is playing at his lips and I get the impression that he's taking great joy in my offer. I was simply being hospitable.

I walk past him and to the mini-bar, pulling another mini bottle of whiskey from inside. As I open it, Caden's hands stop mine and my eyes meet his.

"Please don't. I'd like to have this conversation sober."

"I'm two in already," I tell him, hoping to push him out the door so we don't have to have this conversation.

"I know, it's alright, but I'd like to do this without anymore."

I pull my hands out of his. "One more will hardly do anything to me, except make me a little more loosely lipped." I finish twisting the cap and down the bottle. The look of disapproval in Caden's eyes makes me feel smaller than I did when he walked in the door. "Why is this so important to you?" I ask him as I breathe through the burn.

"Because, I get the impression you think I've done something to hurt you."

I snort. "Hardly."

He gives me a knowing look. "Then why not talk to me? Most people will only run away when they've been hurt."

"You rejected me? No big deal," I tell him and his eyebrows knit together.

"I rejected you, how?"

"You had me on my knees, ready and more than willing to suck you off and the minute I told you I'd never done anything like that before, you rejected me." I walk away from him, toward the bed, setting the bottle on the nightstand. The distance gives me confidence and I turn back toward him. "Not something that's ever happened before and I never talk to anyone after I've slept with them."

He takes a step closer to me, then another one, and while I know it's at a normal pace, it feels like slow motion. When he gets close to me, he leans in a little. His closeness sends my heart pumping and blood racing through my ears. I immediately regret the flannel bottoms I'm wearing when my cock grows hard at his closeness. "Bullshit," Caden states plainly.

That pisses me off. "Excuse me?"

"If that were the case, Aryn, you wouldn't be having dinner with Ashley tomorrow night."

His statement takes me by surprise. I back away, only to run into the bed and fall onto it. "So what, you're spying on me? Using Ashley to get information about me? If that's the case, Caden, why not get my fucking number from her? Why the stalking?"

Before I can finish my rant, Caden pushes on my shoulders, we fall back on the bed. His mouth is ridiculously close to mine. I want to push him off, but the fight is gone.

"No, I am not spying on you and I did not use Ash to get information. I'm stalking you, in a sense, because I needed to know why you ran away from me and as far as following you around, I saw you on TV during the Los Angeles premiere with Alyssa and I knew that you'd be here tonight. You being here was confirmed by Ashley when she called to tell me you'd asked her to dinner last night."

"Did you tell her to turn me down?"

"I'd never do that," he breathes, and his closeness causes my head to spin in a way I've never felt before. "She couldn't because she had club duty last night and your conversation with her was strictly her doing. She respects me enough as a Master at the club and someone she plays with on occasion to tell me what was going on with her. Just like she told Teddy. That's what she does. If you'd come to the club last night, we could have and would have talked there, but you didn't go."

"No, I went." He cocks his head at me. "I made it to the parking lot. I couldn't bring myself to go inside."

"Why not?"

I turn away from him, unable and unwilling to answer his question.

"Aryn." His voice has that command in it again and I turn back to look at him, his voice softens, "Why didn't you come inside?"

"I felt awkward without Derek or Dex there and, and I was afraid we'd end up like this."

"Like what?" he breathes.

I take his head in my hands and whisper, "This," and I press my lips to his.

He freezes momentarily before melting into my touch and my lips. My heart is racing in my chest, but I can no longer stop myself.

I pull back from his mouth. "I can't stop thinking about you and I'm tired of trying to tell myself that this isn't what I want or what I need," I breathe before pressing my lips to his again once more.

FORTY

~ ARYN *~*

He takes my hands in his and pins them down above my head before settling on top of me. My breathing is erratic and combined with his lips on mine, I'm sort of dizzy. Sensing my distress he pulls back.

"I never rejected you," he breathes and my heart skips a beat. "I just didn't want that to be your first time. I would never, could never, order you to do something like that without knowing you really wanted it."

"I did," I breathe, looking deep into his eyes. I see his sincerity.

He nods. "Then I'm deeply sorry you thought I was rejecting you, because I wanted you just as much as I do right now." His voice is soft, reassuring. There is no command, there is no order or dominance, simply just him and I lying on this bed.

"Then kiss me," I tell him and he doesn't hesitate pressing his lips back against mine and his tongue plays with my bottom lip before he nips it gently with his teeth, sending shivers down my spine and goosebumps across my flesh.

He slides his tongue along mine and there is an unfamiliar tingle that radiates all the way down to my toes. Kissing Caden is unlike kissing anyone else. It's heady, it's breathtaking and I never want him to stop.

He pulls back slightly but he takes the lead, kissing down my jaw line toward my ear, and my neck. When he gets there, he kisses me with gentle, open mouth kisses along my shoulder then over my pec, descending lower toward a nipple, toward my stomach, and further. I don't want him to stop.

He reaches the waistband of my pants and shifts to torture my sensitive nipples again.

"What do you want, Aryn?" he breathes as he looks deep into my eyes.

"You," I breathe back.

He smiles and I see the wheels turning. "On one condition."

I cock my head. "Anything," I answer without hesitation.

"You give me your phone number."

"Three two three, nine oh three five seven six eight…"

He scowls at me. "So you've changed your name to Jenny, have you?" His lips curl up in a smirk as he busted me on my fake phone number.

"In all the years I've handed out that number, no one has ever caught it," I tell him and he smiles a little wider.

"I've used the same line."

I can't help but laugh and he releases my arms to sit up, still straddling me.

"Your number, and you can have anything you want." There is a devilish little gleam in his eyes. He's having fun with this. He pulls his phone from his pocket and cocks his head at me.

I rattle off my number. My real number. He presses a button and it rings on his phone for half a tone before my phone lights up, and starts to play the ring tone I selected for Caden when I programmed his number after being forced to call him a couple weeks ago. He looks over at it and his eyes light up at the name that displays across the screen. His eyes come back to mine. "Master, huh?"

"I was having a particularly rough day," I mutter and he smiles wide.

"I like it."

"I don't know if I do," I mumble and he tosses his phone onto the table next to mine.

"Then let's forget about it, for tonight." His voice is soft as he leans down over me. "No Top, no bottom, just Aryn and Caden?"

I smile. "I like the sound of that."

He gives me a firm kiss and I'm right back where I was before I relented and gave him my phone number. Just as I'm about to lose my grip on my breathing, he pulls back. "Why did Alyssa call you Beck?" he asks me and it's a totally random question.

"Because that's the name I use when I'm working. Aryn was the name that Derek put on my club application and it just stuck."

"So that's not your name?"

I smirk. "Yes, Aryn is my name, Becker is my last name. It was shortened to Beck when I started working for Mills and Bold."

"I like it."

"I prefer it when you call me Aryn."

He looks pleased. "Good."

He places his hands on my stomach and slides them up my chest, over my shoulders, moving my arms upward until he has me pinned down again. "Now, where were we?" he asks, his voice is barely above a whisper.

"I believe you were kissing me."

He smirks, "I believe you're correct."

He moves in close, like he's going to kiss me, but he doesn't. He cocks his head to the side. His gentle breathing is calming as he looks at me. He's searching my eyes for something. I don't know what it is exactly he's looking for.

I really do want this to happen, surprisingly, but I don't know if that's what he's looking for or hoping to see in my eyes.

"What?" I finally breathe and he smiles at me.

"Just making sure."

"Of?" I press.

"That you want this."

"Let me up and I'll prove that I want this," I counter and he releases my arms.

Working out has its advantages when I manage to flip him over and onto his back. I stand up, facing him and I push down my flannel pants. "Is this proof enough?"

He smiles wide and shakes his head as he takes in the sight of my cock, hard as steel and ready for anything.

I see the challenge in his eyes. I kick off my pants before kneeling down to his shoes and slipping off one, then the other, followed by his socks. I slide my way up his body with my hands until I reach the fly of his jeans and I unbutton them. Before undoing the zipper, I can't help but run my hand over his prominent erection and his eyes roll up into his head and his breathing hitches at my touch. "How about now?" I breathe.

That smirk dances on his lips and he shakes his head again.

I've been with dozens of women before, but nothing I've done with them compares to what I'm feeling right now as I look at Caden laid out on my bed. There is an excitement to this that I haven't felt in a very long time, if ever. Much the way I used to feel around women, but he's different. Seeing him brings a longing that I didn't know I had, a feeling of desire that is immeasurable to anything else I've ever had before.

The excitement I feel when I realize that he is either giving me carte blanche to do as I wish, or he wants me to take him into my hand and mouth, sends my heart racing in my chest. Either way is perfectly fine with me. I grab the zipper of his jeans and lower it gently before sliding my fingers under his shirt, toward his chest. I rub the taut ridges of his abs and the smoothness of his skin as my hands slide further up his body, bringing his t-shirt with me. "I want this off," I mumble. My voice, though sure of its intentions betrays my nerves. He senses it. Regardless of whatever read he has on me at the moment, he can't resist sitting up. I help him remove his shirt.

Once he's free of it, he slides onto the bed further and I smile as he watches me climb back up his body. I slide my fingers inside the waistband of his jeans and smirk when he doesn't lift his hips. "I'm sure this will be way more fun if we're both naked."

He chuckles and lifts his hips, giving me access and the ability to pull his pants down his body and off his feet.

Taking in the full naked view of Caden is indescribable. He is sex on legs. Perfectly toned, sexy as fuck and seeing him like this makes me more eager than ever to do what I wanted to do that night.

I climb between his legs and I take my cock in my hand. I stroke it and the sensation on a very hard, ready to explode cock is almost too much. It causes my eyes to roll up briefly and his breathing spikes as he watches me stroke up and down a couple more times before I right myself enough to stop.

His cock is standing at full attention, twitching slightly as I lower myself closer to it. I inhale his musky scent and commit the smell to memory, not wanting to forget this night. The night I finally give into something that I have no business wanting or needing. Finally experiencing a fantasy that I've had for as long as I can remember.

Realizing that it's about to come true spurs me on and I take his cock in my hand. He flinches when I grip the base, but he settles when I stroke upward.

Stroking another man's cock isn't that different than stroking my own, only difference is the pleasure isn't radiating in my body, but in Caden's.

I watch Caden closely as he fights to keep his eyes open. I take satisfaction in that; allowing it to spur me on further. I lean in, pressing the head of his erection against my lips and I dart out my tongue, flicking it against the underside of his cock and catching that sweet, sensitive spot. Caden sucks in a sharp breath and groans softly. I flick it again and again before placing the swollen head along my tongue and into my mouth. I slide it along my tongue before wrapping my lips tightly around it. I moan as his scent assaults me further and I'm encouraged to continue when his hand slides into my hair. The gentle touch obliterates any and all self control I may have had and my mouth slides down further along his cock. Sucking him in and pressing him against the back of my throat. I leave him there while I stroke my hand up and down a couple of times while I attempt to swallow.

"Jesus," Caden breathes and I attempt to smile before pulling his shaft out of my mouth and back in, out and in. His hand remains in my hair, gripping gently. Holding me to him, but giving me free range to do as I wish to him and I can't stop.

I increase my pace, flicking, licking and sucking his cock like I need it to breathe. The grip in my hair tightens, hard and my eyes meet his. "You're amazing," he says, "But I don't want to come in your mouth."

I smile, releasing his cock from my mouth and hand.

"My turn," he smirks and I smile with a nod, then crawl up his body, licking and kissing my way up his chest until I find his lips.

My cock twitches against his and desire spikes to a new height knowing that we're so close to each other. Caden captures my moment of weakness and forces me onto my back before climbing on top of me. Before I know it, he has both our cocks gripped in one of his strong hands. I shiver in anticipation of what he's going to do next.

FORTY~ONE

~ CADEN *~*

My hand slides up our shafts as I stroke both of us to the point of madness.

I made him stop sucking me because I wasn't ready to come yet. I learned quickly the last time we were together that I had stamina and could possibly go again. However, in the past, a second orgasm has always eluded me. The last thing I wanted to have happen was to have him suck me only to fail at eliciting an orgasm. After I saw the look in his eyes when I touched him that night, and the pain that radiated within them, I knew my lack of orgasm might destroy him for a very long time and I couldn't have that.

That is something you don't come back from when you're unsure of who you are or what you want.

When he presses into my touch, it is clear to me that he needs approval, he needs to know what he's doing is the right thing. If I can't nurture him like that, then this will never work.

I want to take him, but I'm rethinking that. He's never done this and he needs some training before I can push into him.

"Where'd you go?" he asks, pulling me out of my thoughts.

I stroke up again on our cocks and he groans. It makes me smile.

"Nowhere, I'm right here."

He nods and I stroke us again before releasing both cocks and leaning down to press my lips to his and press my hips against his, trapping us together. I'm not usually one to bend over easily, but I think that's where this needs to go tonight. He needs training and one night, without any equipment to do so, won't work. But I am more than willing to see where this is going to go.

"I don't want to hurt you," he breathes.

I shake my head. "You won't. Now me on you is another story." His expression falls slightly and I feel it's necessary to explain myself. "Believe me, Aryn, I want you so bad, but it's not something you can just jump right into, you're going to need some training."

His face scrunches together.

"Not sub training." Though there is that aspect too, but we can discuss that later. I give him a little bit of space because what I'm saying is pushing him in the wrong direction and I don't want to lose this moment. "What I mean is that you can't just dive right into anal sex, my sweet boy." He glows a little at my nickname for him. "If I do, it is going to hurt like hell and I refuse to hurt you." He nods his understanding.

~ ARYN *~*

Caden leans down, claiming my lips for his once more. His hands roam up my body and I'm lost in the wave of sensation he is giving me as he flicks his hips against mine and I groan into his mouth. Since he hasn't pinned me down again, I take the chance to hold him a little tighter by sliding my fingers into his hair and holding him to me. He moans into my mouth and I push on him, indicating that I want to flip him back over and he adjusts for me so that I can.

Once he's beneath me, while our mouths are still locked together, I slide my legs between his, forcing him to open up for me and he does exactly that.

His cock rubs along mine and it sends a thrill through me.

I can't believe I'm about to do this. I'm going to be sliding inside of him.

The thought sends a wave of pleasure through me and it pools in the small of my back as I can no longer resist the idea of taking him.

I rear up and look at our cocks lying across his stomach and it's an insane sight to see.

Everything I've ever fantasized about when it came to Dex and I being together is coming true right here and now. I am very happy that it is Caden and not Dex or some other random man.

Caden strokes my cheek with his finger and my eyes go to his. "What's wrong?" he asks. His voice is soft, sincere and a little concerned.

I give him a small smile. "Nothing's wrong, it's just-" I sigh, reluctant to tell him what's on my mind but I get the impression that even though the top and bottom roles are off tonight, he will ask me to tell him in a way that will make it impossible for me to resist him. Despite the fact that no matter what I tell myself, I'm incapable of surrendering myself to him.

"You just? Please, Aryn, I'd like to know."

I nod softly. "I've always been curious, about being with a man, but," I pause and take a soothing breath before I continue, "Since I met you, I've fantasized about this and-"

"It's happening?"

I nod.

"Is that a bad thing?" he asks.

I smile and shake my head. "No, it's a great thing, it's just so-"

"Surreal?" he finishes and I nod. "We don't have to do anything tonight, Aryn."

I shake my head. "No, I do. I need to know."

He leans up on his elbows, his eyes never leave mine. "Know what?"

"If this is really what I want."

He gives me a sad smile. "You're unsure?"

I sigh. "No, I'm sure that I want this, here, tonight, but-" I hesitate and look away from him, hoping to break the trance he has me in right now but unfortunately my eyes fall to where we're coming together, which of course only spurs my fantasy and desperation to finish what we've started. "I'm scared that if we do this that it will be it. That you or I will get what we want and then," I shrug, "Nothing."

"I don't do one night stands, Aryn. I don't sleep with someone unless I know there is a chance that it will happen again. I wouldn't have gone to New York-"

I gasp. "You were there?" I breathe and he smiles with a nod. "I didn't want to believe it. I couldn't figure out why you would have a reason to be there, but, well, I guess I knew nothing about you, but regardless of that, it just didn't make sense to me."

"It's also the reason I pulled so many strings to show up after Alyssa tonight. I needed to see you, to talk to you."

"Yeah, I know, you needed to know why I ran away."

"Aryn." I look up into his eyes again. "I knew you ran away for a reason, but I couldn't fix that reason or explain anything if you wouldn't talk to me. It was more of an excuse to see you and if my theory was correct, I already knew why you ran and I was right. I'd deduced that you were scared more than anything."

"That's partially true," I tell him and I slide off him, sitting next to him and he sits up. "Though part of it had to do with what I'd done with Ashley and with you. It also had to do with the fact that I had no problem taking orders from you that night. And for someone who was struggling to admit that I'm not a Dominant, it was all just too much for me to take at that time."

"How do you feel about your submissive side now?"

I shrug. "I think I'm still trying to understand that side of me. Still trying to find it inside of me to hand over control to someone else, it's not easy."

"If it were easy for you, I'd be concerned. Not everyone is a natural submissive and those that are often face a time when they question their submission and you're no different. Before you showed up at Derek's, had you ever considered a Dom/sub relationship?" I shake my head. "I didn't think so."

"I didn't know much about it. Sure, when I'm with a woman I like to be in control, but looking back on that now, I think that my 'in control' was more to control the situation. If I was in control, I could essentially get off and walk away. When I let my guard down, like that night in your private room, everything kind of fell apart for me. It's the reason I never left my number, it's the reason I blocked my number from you. I was in control of that situation and now-" I pause.

Caden looks at me with encouraging eyes. "And now?"

"Now, I don't want that control anymore. I've realized that whatever is brewing between you and me is an inevitable truth that I can no longer deny and if I don't do something, I might regret it for the rest of my life."

Caden's smile is warm, genuine when he brings his hand up to cup my cheek. I can't help but lean into it. His touch obliterates any and all fear or concern I may have had about where this was going. "But, Caden?" He strokes his thumb along my cheek and my eyes meet his. "I don't think I can be your submissive."

~ CADEN *~*

Looking into Aryn's eyes tells me that he's scared. I knew he was scared all along and the fact that we've made it as far as we have, completely naked, is a true test of what this means to him and maybe means to me. "I think you're wrong about that.

But that is a decision you have to make. I cannot make it for you. But I will tell you that a Dom-sub relationship is all that I'm after. I don't do vanilla relationships." Even as I say the words, I'm not entirely convinced of their truth. Looking into Aryn's eyes, knowing that there is so much more under the surface, drives me to want to know more about the man who was straddling me just a few minutes ago.

My words settle over him and while I think that's what he wanted to hear, he can't hide the hint of disappointment playing with his features. "Then what are we doing here? Like this, right now?"

I give him a weak smile. "I needed you to know that this is what you want."

"That I want to be your submissive?"

"No, that you're willing to let go of your preconceived ideas about being with another man, that you're capable of and willing to surrender your body to another man. That you're willing to surrender it to me."

"But I'm not-"

I place my finger over his lips, silencing him. "You were sitting, on top of me, completely naked a few minutes ago and you were enjoying the view of our cocks lying beside each other and you tell me you're not willing to surrender? You're more than willing to surrender your body, but that is not all that I'm interested in, Aryn. I am interested in your mind, in your willingness to hand over the control, to allow me to take care of your body and your mind."

"That's all you want from me?" There is a hint of pain forming in his voice and I realize this quite possibly means more to him than it does to me. While I was willing to let myself give into him, give into his desire for tonight, I need more from him. I need his submission. I crave it from him and I can't begin to imagine it any other way, I'm not wired like that.

I nod in response to his question, unable to actually speak the response. The longer we sit here, the longer I look at him, the more I feel the need to give myself over to him in a way other than being his Master and that is unnerving to me. I've never felt like this before and it has me wanting to run from the room. The loss of control sends a chill down my spine.

I lower my hand from his cheek and the moment that contact is broken, he gets off the bed, away from me. "I think you should go," he mumbles.

"That's probably a good idea."

I climb off the bed as he pulls his pajama pants on and then he goes to his suitcase and pulls out a t-shirt. I'm disappointed when his body is covered from my view. I frown and pull my pants back on. The more clothing that I pull on, the worse I feel about what I'm about to do, but I can't let him see that. I can't let him see that I'm growing weak for him.

His pain and sadness is evident in his eyes as he escorts me to the door. I stop and look at him. "I'm sorry, Aryn," I tell him.

"So am I."

That's all he says and I haven't a clue what to say to him in return so I leave the room and he closes the door. The lock engages and the security bar slides over. I fall against the door. I've pushed away the one thing that has seen through my façade - the one thing that has brought me happiness for the first time in a very long time. But am I capable of letting go of my past, breaking the hold on my heart? Walking away from his door gives me my answer. No, I'm not ready to let her go.

I step into the elevator and as the doors close, I realize I've just made the biggest mistake of my life.

FORTY~TWO

** ARYN **

I set the sixth mini bottle of whiskey down on the table, or rather I slam it down after downing it.

That was not how I expected this night to end.

That was not how I wanted this night to end.

He walked out.

He left.

He left because he wants nothing but my submission. A submission I'm not capable of giving him.

He asked me a question, about before showing up at Derek's and whether or not I knew anything about Dom/sub relationships and I didn't. In fact, I took my desire to be a Dom from Dex. He pointed me in that direction and he did so for the right reasons. He honestly believed, like me, that I could be and wanted to be a Dominant. Which, until now, I wanted exactly that.

Maybe the lifestyle isn't for me.

Maybe I'm meant to be with someone who loves me for who I am and who doesn't want to change me.

My thoughts drift involuntarily to Ashley. She and I click, we get along well, but I can't give her what she needs or wants in a relationship. I can't picture her having a vanilla relationship with someone like me while still walking into the club. I know and understand that BDSM isn't always about the sex, but I certainly couldn't sit at home while she goes off with some other Top, with someone like Caden.

And just like that, my thoughts circle back to him. Things were going great. No, not great, they were going amazing. I was enjoying myself, enjoying what was happening between us just to have it shattered.

I fall into the chair and close my eyes, but the moment I do, all I can see is Caden standing before me with a sweet smile on his lips. I sit up, grabbing the seventh bottle of whiskey and open it. Bottoms up.

Knock, knock, knock.
I fight to hold my eyes open.
Knock, knock, knock.
"Come on, Beck, open the door."

I scrub my hands over my face. My head is pounding. My neck feels like it's been wrenched in a vice.

I stand up, knocking into the table and knocking over half a dozen empty whiskey bottles and a few full ones.

The knocking turns to pounding. "Yeah, I'm coming," I holler and stumble my way to the door, sliding the deadbolt and opening it.

"Dude, you know you're not supposed to drink on duty, you look like shit." Casey looks me up and down.

"Thanks, what's up?"

"We're taking Alyssa out. She wants to go shopping and she's meeting a friend for lunch," he tells me.

I scrub my face again. "Give me twenty."

"Nah, forget it, we got this. Go take some Tylenol or something."

"You sure?" I ask.

"Yeah, it's just lunch."

I nod. "Sorry, bro."

"Don't stress it. What happened last night?"

I shake my head, trying to remember what exactly happened and I can't recall much of anything. "I drank way too much."

"Obviously. We'll call if we need anything."

"I've got that dinner thing a little later."

Casey smiles. "Don't worry about it, we got this. Take the day, you've been working like a fool and Alyssa said she's having a few friends in her suite tonight. So we're all free."

I nod. "Thanks, Case."

"No problem."

I nod my head and he walks toward the elevator. I close the door before falling against it.

The events of last night slowly slide into my conscious and I immediately want to grab another drink.

I push away from the door and go back to the table. I pull a fresh bottle from the stash and down it. A little hair of the dog.

Then I turn back toward the bathroom, shedding my shirt and pajamas as I go.

Once under the hot spray of the water and with the whiskey starting to course through my veins, I start to feel a little bit better except for the damn kink in my neck, compliments of crashing in the chair. At one point I went for the bed, but all I could see was the mess on the duvet that Caden and I had made and I fell back into the chair with another shot of whiskey and that was pretty much the last thing I remember before Casey pounded on my door.

"Hey," I say to Ashley as she approaches the table. I stand up and kiss her on the cheek.

"You look like shit."

I roll my eyes. "Nice to see you too."

She smiles and shrugs as she takes her seat opposite me. "You didn't tell him where we were meeting, did you?"

She snorts. "No, I didn't. Though I wish I knew what the fuck was going on between the two of you."

I shrug and take a drink of water to avoid answering her question. She reads me in a heartbeat. "So that's how this is going to go? Listen, Aryn, whatever it is, you need to talk to someone about it."

"Hardly. There's nothing to talk about. We both want different things, so I guess we can just leave it at that." I say it with a sharper tone than I'd intended to have, but she doesn't call me on it.

~ CADEN *~*

Ash to Caden: I'm having dinner with him tonight.

That's the text message that greeted me when I got off a conference call with a new studio that is looking to contract me for a new movie that will start filming late this year or early next year. Though I am interested in the project, the timing is awful for me.

I sit at my computer and pull up the program I designed a few years ago for another project I did. The program was a nice tool to have when we were scouting because of where we were looking. It was a fast, rocky area in eastern Australia. The program allowed us to pinpoint the location of anyone on our crew. This made it easier to find someone should they have problems and it proved invaluable when there was an accident and we were able to track them down within fifty yards of their location.

I type in a number and wait.

Location Unknown

I scowl at the screen. "Impossible," I breathe.

Thinking that the power is off, I click a couple of boxes and search for a last known location but again it comes back as an unknown location.

"I know it was on last night, so how is there no last known location?"

I shake my head.

I have an alternative outlet. I text Ashley.

Caden to Ash: Where?

"You idiot," I grumble to myself and go back to my computer and type in another number and it pings back almost instantly. "Loews. The restaurant or his room?" I muse out loud.

I click a couple more buttons, zooming in on the map and pulling up the Loews in 3D format and I see the ping coming from the lower levels. I let out a rush of breath I didn't know I was holding in.

"What the hell are you doing?" I try talking myself out of what I'm doing. "He deserves your trust as he's done nothing to violate it and this is bordering on stupid stalker status, Caden." I click out of the program and shut down my computer.

~ ARYN *~*

"How did you know you wanted into the lifestyle?" I ask Ashley.

She shrugs. "I don't know, I think I always knew that there was something different, something that I seemed to be missing. Until I read a book that discussed it, that had characters in the lifestyle and while I didn't know at first if that was it, it sparked within me the idea that there just might be a reason why I felt the way I did."

"Once you started to put two and two together, did you fight yourself over it?"

She chuckles, "Yeah, I did. I think we all do. It's just natural to do so. You have to find yourself and figure out if it works for you. I struggled a lot with the idea that I would give up so much of myself, only to realize that any Top who forces you to give up any part of who you are, isn't worth their weight. It's about embracing who we are and nurturing what it is that we want to become."

"What happened when you finally realized it was what you wanted?"

She smiles. "I met Teddy. I talked to him and explained to him what I thought I wanted or needed and he helped me see the benefits of a lot of things that I needed along with a lot of the cons and why some of the things I thought were important were actually rather insignificant in the long run."

"What kinds of things?" I ask.

"You're awfully inquisitive tonight." She shrugs when I just nod dismissively. "It's different for everyone. But I realized that a lot of what was controlling me was the fear of the unknown. Like pain, being tied up, losing control over my environment, things like that. That's when I realized that the sub really has all the control. Nothing happens unless I want it to."

She pauses, allowing me a chance to soak up what she's saying and to take a drink of the water in front of me. I have to admit that many of her fears are my own, the biggest thing is finding it in me to be able to trust someone enough to surrender myself like that. I've lived too long trusting no one, the idea of being able to trust them that much is hard to process.

She swallows a large drink of water and continues. "It took me a long time to understand that the person who's really in control is not the Top but the bottom. Nothing happens unless the bottom is a willing participant and everything that happens is based on what the submissive needs and not what the dominant wants."

I scrub my hand through my hair. "It's all so confusing."

She smiles. "It can be, until you find what it is that you're after." She sets her silverware down and looks me square in the eye. "Why are you asking me about bottoms?"

I don't answer her, instead I look for anything to distract her from her question and I come up empty.

Reading my reticence, she says to me, "This has to do with Caden, doesn't it? He wants you as his submissive and you're unwilling, why?"

"I'm not a submissive," I snap.

She laughs, "Bullshit, Aryn." She takes a large sip of her wine while I stare blankly at her. After she swallows, she looks at me with a hard stare before she leans into me. "I knew the moment I met you that there wasn't a dominant bone in your body," she whispers. "You're alpha by nature, but hardly the dominant type."

"How in the hell do you know?" I snap.

"Don't get testy with me, Aryn, I'm your friend, if nothing else. I know because while you like the idea of dishing out pain and punishment, you haven't got a clue the level of caring and respect that goes into being a Top. If you did, you'd have never run out of that room, you'd never have ignored Caden's attempts to check on how you were doing following what happened. Despite what you may think, he wasn't doing it to be a dick, he was doing it because he cares. Where you, on the other hand, don't give a shit about anyone else. You don't care that Caden was going out of his mind, despite what I or anyone else may have been telling him. Until he heard it from your mouth, he was never going to give up. Not until he knew that you were alright."

She pulls her napkin from her lap and sets it on her half eaten plate before standing up. She throws a hundred dollar bill on the table. "That should cover most of it."

I grab her wrist before she can walk away. "Why are you running away from me?"

"Because, whatever it is that Caden wants from you and you're unwilling to give him is something you should be discussing with him. Not with me. I am more than willing to help you better understand this lifestyle, but first, you need to decide if this is a lifestyle you want to have, then you need to decide which role you wish to take on. If being a Top is really what you want to be, than be one, but if being a bottom is what you want or what you need, then you be exactly that. There is no bouncing back and forth until you're capable of mastering both sides and the way you're handling all this, I am leaning toward this lifestyle not being for you. And that's fine, but until you make that choice, I can't help you."

She pulls her arm free of my grip.

"Good night, Aryn," she says before leaving me staring after her like a fucking child who's left the refrigerator door open.

FORTY~THREE

~ CADEN *~*

"You did what?" I snap at Ashley as she paces away from me in my private room at The Box.

"I'm sorry. He pissed me off, so I just kind of lost it on him."

"Damn it, Ashley, you were probably the one person he trusted to talk to. And now?"

"Oh for Pete's sake, Caden, I'll apologize to him."

I charge up behind her, grab her arm and spin her around. "What did you call me?"

Her face falls and fear blooms in her eyes. It's a healthy fear that she knows what she did wrong. "I'm sorry, Sir. But this is not my fault, and yes, I will apologize to him, I'll make it right, if I'm doing it for the right reasons. I'm going to piss you off further by saying this, but I am not your lackey. If you want to know about him, about what questions he has, what problems he is having, you talk to him," she snaps and rips her arm from my grip.

"I'm sorry," I apologize to her. "You're right, this isn't your responsibility. I shouldn't have put you in this position."

"No, you shouldn't have. You're inadvertently using my submission against me. Using me to get information from a friend of mine or someone who I'd like to be friends with. It's not fair."

She crosses her arms over her chest. "You're absolutely right, Ash, and I'm sorry."

"What's the deal with you and him? What is it that you want from him that he's so scared to hand over?"

I sigh. "I want what I want from anyone I'm with."

Her eyes widen. "Their submission and?" she prompts.

"And nothing."

She huffs. "That right there is your problem, Sir. You can't ask someone to fully submit to you and not expect feelings and attachments. It doesn't work like that."

"You handle it just fine," I counter.

"No, Sir, I don't. But the difference between you and I is I am not your submissive. I submit to you in the dungeon because it's fun and because Teddy likes you. He's willing to allow you to Top me. And if you didn't want to have me that way, I'd find someone else."

"Is that so easy for you to do?"

She shrugs her shoulders. "With you, yes. You were very clear when we started talking that you wanted nothing more than a submissive who was willing to bottom for you. There were no strings, no attachments and if you think about it, of all the times we've scened together, you've slept with me three times and that was only after I practically begged you to do so. With the exception of when Aryn was in here."

The mention of his name has me backing away from her, putting some distance between us, and I end up turning toward the bed. All I can see is Aryn tied to it. I close my eyes.

"The difference with that night versus the others was that I knew it wasn't about me. I knew it was about the two of you. I knew that one of you needed a buffer and I was in the right place at the right time. A lesser person might feel used by that." Her tone is getting snarky and it's making my palms twitch, but they're itching to punish out of anger and that is one thing I would never do. Not to Ashley, or anyone for that matter.

"Do you?" I ask softly.

"Do I, what?"

"Just because I've given you some attitude, I'd watch yourself, girl. You're pushing the limits of my control."

"Do I feel used? No. I got off, you both did, it was fun, but I don't know if it's an experience I want to have again, at least not under those circumstances. I'd much rather have a more hands-on approach."

"You're not making me feel any better."

"I'm not here to stroke your ego."

I turn to her and she steps back from me when she takes in my expression. "That's it. Get out. Whatever your problem is tonight, it's not me or my fault. I suggest you go home."

"I'm scening tonight."

"You most certainly are not," I snap. "Go home. I'll discuss with Teddy what your punishment shall be once I've had a chance to calm down."

"But-"

"But what?" I snap back.

"Nothing," she bites back and heads for the door. Before opening it, she turns back to me. "If you want him, go fucking get him. If all you want is his submission, you're not going to get it. In case you haven't noticed, you mean far more to him than he does to you and that will never get you anywhere."

She opens the door, slamming it shut on her way out.

I clench and unclench my fists a few times before I go after her.

When I enter the dungeon, I'm surprised to see her standing there talking to Will. I go up behind them.

"Hello Master Caden," Will says with enthusiasm which tells me that Ash hadn't told Will she was supposed to leave.

"Where's Teddy?"

"Right here, what's up?" Teddy says from my right. I turn my head toward him and he has drinks in his hands.

"Ash is grounded. She is to go home immediately and you and I need to discuss a proper punishment."

"Ashley," Teddy barks and she wilts before Teddy as she turns toward him. "Care to explain to me why Master Caden feels it necessary to punish you?"

She doesn't respond. She simply lowers her head in supplication and it takes a little bit of my anger away, seeing her like this, but it doesn't mean she's going to get punished tonight. "Ashley, I asked you a question."

"I'm sorry, Sir, but my mouth has gotten me into a lot of trouble tonight, and therefore I think it best if I just say nothing at all."

Teddy snorts, "I can hear that. Go home."

"I'm supposed to scene tonight with-"

"It's cancelled effective now. Whatever you did to piss off Master Caden was obviously enough to send you home for the night. You can come back tomorrow night." Teddy looks to me to confirm and I nod slightly. "We will handle your punishment then."

She doesn't answer him right away. She is hot tempered tonight and I don't understand what her problem is and unfortunately I won't be able to find out until tomorrow night.

"Do you understand?" Teddy's voice is tense.

"Yes, Sir," Ashley finally murmurs.

"I can't hear you," Teddy says and she raises her head. Her tear streaked cheeks are almost my undoing. While I enjoy tears with physical pain, emotional tears are harder to process.

"Yes, Sir," she says a little louder and Teddy seems satisfied. "Go home," he says again, this time it is more of an order. An order I know that she can't resist, which means she'll be a good girl and go home.

She turns on her heel and heads through the velvet curtains.

"Will, go help Emma at the bar. I need to talk to Master Caden."

"Yes, Master," Will says quickly and somberly. He starts to head toward the bar but Teddy grabs his arm, then the back of his neck, and he tilts his mouth up and crushes his lips to Will's. Will visibly melts.

"Good boy," Teddy praises when he releases Will from his grip and he sends him on his way.

No need to bring up the fact that watching that only makes me think of Aryn and what happened between us last night.

"Your room?"

I nod and lead Teddy down the hall toward my room.

FORTY~FOUR

"Are you sure that you being pissed off at Ashley has nothing to do with Aryn?" Teddy asks me and the question was expected.

"No, it doesn't. She's right, I shouldn't have put her into the position that she was in, but in the same aspect of that, I didn't ask her to provide me with information on Aryn, she volunteered it. Until tonight when I asked her about her dinner with Aryn. Regardless of that, I didn't deserve her attitude or disrespect."

"No, you certainly didn't deserve that and for that I will allow you to punish her."

"You know I don't relent on punishments, but under the circumstances, something is either bothering her or the position I put her in has put her into the mood she's in. I don't know that a physical punishment is necessary."

"I disagree with you there. She still needs to show some respect and whether it was you or another Top in the club, the result would be the same. She had no right to have an attitude with you. She had no right to disrespect you."

"I think she owes me an apology and an explanation. How about I decide what her punishment should be after I have that from her. Or a delayed punishment, allow her the chance to apologize but if it happens-"

"No, either you punish her tomorrow night or not at all. You can't hold it over her head. I'd punish her myself but I wasn't in the room when it happened and it's not my position to do so. I'm failing to understand why you're so soft about this. Is Aryn really getting to you?"

I look at Teddy. He's been my friend for years and he knows more about me than maybe even Derek does. "He doesn't think he's submissive."

Teddy snorts. "Don't they all think that?" I nod. "So he, what? He wants more?"

I put my hands in my pockets and start to pace the room. "I think so, I don't know."

"What do you want?"

"I want what I always want. A sub."

"But if there are feelings there, why's wrong with it being more? You know as well as I do that it's impossible to have one without the other. Unless you're looking for someone to play with on occasion, someone like Ashley. But if you want more than that, then you have to expect feelings to get involved."

I shrug.

"Does this have anything to do with-"

"Don't say her name," I murmur as my chest tightens.

"Well, does it?"

I look at him, anger in my eyes. "No."

"And yet I don't believe you. How long has it been? Ten years? Come on, Caden, you gotta let it go. You can't hold on to her like this. It's not healthy for you."

"That's easy for you to say."

Teddy stands up. I'm a tall man, but Teddy makes me feel small. "No, it's not easy for me to say it. She was my sister."

"And you don't miss her?"

"Every damn day, but I don't let my missing her get in the way of my everyday life. I don't let her get in the way of moving on with my life. She's gone, it sucks, it hurts, but you've got to let it go. Do you honestly think she's happy watching you give up on happiness because you're still holding on to her?"

"She was everything to me."

"I understand that, but ten years is a long time. Caden, she's not going to be happy if you spend the rest of your life miserable because you're still hanging on to her. You deserve better than that. She deserves better than that. It's time to let her go." He puts his hand on my shoulder and squeezes it. "I certainly won't think anything less of you if you move on. You're still my brother, you always have been and you always will be."

I nod.

All my anger over Ashley subsides and my heart hurts. I rub at my chest. "I don't know if I can."

Teddy smiles. "How do you know you can't if you don't try?"

~ ARYN *~*

Ashley to Beck: I'm sorry about last night. I had no right going off on you and I am sorry that I walked out on our dinner.

Beck to Ashley: What did I say?

Ashley to Beck: you didn't say anything. I was just in a foul mood.

Beck to Ashley: Apology accepted. Gotta run, taking off. I'll get in touch when I get back to LA.

Ashley to Beck: How long will that be?

Beck to Ashley: A week or so. Headed to London now.

Ashley to Beck: Oh Wow! So jealous. Have fun.

** CADEN **

"I don't know what to do." I wipe away a tear from my eye as I stare down at the ground. "I've tried to let you go, tried to move on, but I've never been able to and I don't know if I can."

"God, I wish I could talk to you one more time. Kiss you, hug you, hold you, have you tell me that it's all okay."

"He's a great guy, Shell. I really want to get to know him better and I don't know what to do to make it right again. I've pushed him away and he deserves so much better than that."

I kneel down and lay a red rose across the grass in front of the headstone that reads:

Michelle Matthews, daughter, sister, wife, mother

I run my hand over her name as another tear streaks down my cheek.

"Teddy says that I won't know if I don't try but I don't know if I can try."

Just as I say that, a robin lands on the top of Shelly's grave. I take it as the sign I needed and it takes my breath away. The bird looks at me and it appears to be nodding her head before flying off, but the final clincher is when she meets up with another bird midflight and they fly out of sight.

FORTY~FIVE

~ CADEN *~*

Before walking into the club, I do everything I can to clear my head.

I shouldn't have gone to see Shelly today, but I couldn't resist. I needed to talk to her and that is the only place I feel like I can connect with her.

Ashley deserves my best, especially after I gave her my worst the other night and I need her to know that I've forgiven her. Teddy insists on the punishment and because of that, I am in a much better place. She does deserve to be punished for acting out, but I hope, before I can get to that point, that I get the answers I need from her first. Like what the deal is.

I climb out of my car with my bag and follow another couple into the club. Teddy said that he'd have Will replace Ash at the podium and it's Sunday so the club should be relatively quiet.

I pass through the doors and everything from the outside world is wiped away. As predicted, the lobby is empty and Will is standing at the podium.

"Good evening, Master Caden."

"Hello Will. Is she in your room?"

"Yes, Sir. She was sent there by Teddy."

"Thank you." He gives me a sad smile. "Something to say?"

His eyes dart up to mine. "No, Sir."

"It's alright, Will. You can tell me."

"She's petrified."

Good. "I'll take care of her, I promise."

"She's really sorry for what she did," he murmurs.

"I hope so." I wink at him and he smiles at me as I duck between the curtains and into the club.

There are only two couples on the apparatuses and another Top is setting up another station. I find Teddy sitting at the bar.

"You look like shit."

"Thanks so much," I grumble.

"You alright?" Teddy asks.

I nod briefly and set my bag down on the floor before grabbing a stool next to Teddy. "I went to see her today."

"That probably wasn't a very good move," he replies.

"Believe me, it was."

He turns on his stool to look at me. "Why is that?"

"Because I got the answer I needed."

He looks at me like I've grown twelve heads. "And what was the question?"

"Whether or not I can let go," I tell him and his eyes widen.

"If you tell me she told you no I might just have to dig her up to have a talk." The protective brother I've always known surfaces with a vengeance and I smile.

"The opposite, actually." He raises an eyebrow at me, egging me on. "A robin."

"And what did this robin do?"

"Left me for another bird."

He snorts once, then again and then bursts into a roar of laughter. I can't help but join in with him.

Once we settle down I ask him, "Is she in your room?"

"She is, scared as ever."

"Good. I'm going to go talk to her."

"What's her punishment?"

"Twelve, no warm-ups."

He nods. "Make it six or give her a warm-up."

I smile. "I might not make it any at all."

He chuckles and hands me the key to his room. I stand up and grab his shoulder in a reassuring gesture before grabbing my bag and heading down the hallway to his room.

I take a deep breath before entering. The laughing session with Teddy put me in a much better mood than I'd expected to be in, reaffirming what I am about to do is the best for Ashley and not for my personal gratification.

I unlock the door and step inside.

She's topless, wearing a pair of black boy shorts and kneeling in the corner with her head down. I smile.

I walk over and put my bag down on the bed and she jumps a little. I walk over and place my hand against the top of her head, caressing it slightly.

"Thank you, pet."

"You're welcome, Sir," she responds with a whisper.

"Stand up," I tell her in a commanding tone and she doesn't hesitate but she keeps facing away from me with her head down. "Relax," I tell her and she softens at my request. "Turn around, please." She complies. I go into my bag and pull out one of my t-shirts that I'd thrown in there. I needed it in there so that we could talk, undistracted. Ashley truly is a beauty and I get distracted by her nakedness.

I hand her the t-shirt. "Put it on, please."

Her head comes up and her red rimmed eyes stare back at me. I give her a reassuring smile. "We need to talk before I take you out there for your punishment."

She nods and unfolds the t-shirt before pulling it over her head. She drowns in it and I take comfort in that. "Sit," I tell her and she climbs on the bed, crossing her legs and placing her hands in her lap. She lowers her head. "I'd like an explanation for your outburst at me yesterday."

She doesn't answer and it only stands to irritate me further but I take a deep breath. "You're already in trouble with me,

Ash. I simply need to understand what caused the outburst, why you were so cross with him and then with me."

"I'm sorry, Sir."

"That's not what I want to hear right now, though I appreciate the apology."

"I'm sorry, Sir, but I'm afraid that my mouth may only get me into more trouble if I talk, so I'd really prefer not to, Sir."

"I assure you, from now until we leave this room, your mouth will earn you no further punishment from me. I won't even tell Teddy. I really just need to know what's going on."

Her head comes up and her eyes meet mine. "I was pissed off, still am, at what you did to Aryn."

"What exactly did I do to Aryn?"

"You rejected him, again."

Her words hit me hard, knocking the air from my lungs. I never thought about it that way, but it doesn't take a rocket scientist to understand what she's referring to and I can understand why she would think that about what happened in his hotel room. "That isn't what happened."

"But it did, Sir. You basically told him that all you were interested in was a D/s relationship and nothing more. By doing that, you rejected him. Failed to listen to him. You simply stated what it was that you wanted and that was it. No negotiation, no compromise, no nothing. You rejected him, again."

"Did he tell you all this?"

"No, Sir."

"Then why do you think that's what happened?"

"Because he told me enough to make that decision. I snapped at Aryn because I was pissed off at you for what you'd done, but I was also angry at him too."

"Why is that?" I ask.

"Because he, like you did to him, rejected you. Rejected any idea of what you wanted and continued to believe that his role in this lifestyle was as a Top. He is certainly capable of being a

Top, though he's got a lot to learn about it. His selfishness will get him nowhere."

"Perhaps he wasn't the only one being selfish?"

Her eyes widen at my pointed look in her direction. "What does that mean exactly?" Her snarky tone has returned as I expected it to, but I gave her carte blanche on this discussion so I let it slide.

"Why does what happens between Aryn and I matter to you anyway?"

"Are you serious?" she counters and I nod. "What difference does it make?" Her voice drops to a whisper, a hurt whisper.

"It makes all the difference in the world, pet." I tacked on 'pet' so she could remember her role here before she slides too far off the submissive scale.

"I don't think it's relevant to this conversation," she mumbles so low that I have a hard time hearing her.

"On the contrary, I think it does. I think that your frustration and outburst were driven by something. Something I haven't uncovered and I'd truly like to know where it's coming from."

"I was here first," she says with a rush.

"Let's try that again, shall we, pet?"

She looks up at me, her expression chock-full of defiance and I'm eager to hear what is about to come out of her mouth. "I. Was. Here. First."

I take a step back at her tone.

"I had you first, I saw him first, I-"

My expression stops her cold. "Actually, I met him about a week before you did, not that it's any of your business. And as far as you being here, with me first, the ground rules were clear before we started our exchange. I promised to help further your training beyond what Teddy could do. I promised to take care of you while doing so, and I also promised no strings. All of which you agreed to. Are you taking that agreement back?"

"No," she snaps.

"Then what is the problem?"

She turns red and lowers her head; embarrassment is evident as the redness spreads onto her chest. "You didn't honestly think that after six months of playing together I wouldn't develop feelings for you."

"No, hoped was a better word for it, but you pick now to bring it up and throw it back in my face. That's hardly fair, Ashley."

"Because I knew that if I brought it up before either I'd get my heart broken when you rejected the idea or you'd stop playing with me and since you're so hung up on Aryn, I figure that both of those things are about to come true anyway, so there is no point in denying them anymore. I am sorry that I grew feelings for you and I'm sorry that you can't figure out what it is that you want. But I have to do what I have to do to protect myself. When I saw the sparks flying between you and Aryn, I knew where I stood and of course I started to question where I stand in your eyes. After what happened yesterday, I have that answer and it's a painful pill to swallow."

"I had no idea," I breathe.

"That's because you're too dense. Too caught up in your self pity to see what's happening in front of you. If you'd get your head out of your ass, you'd see what you have growing with Aryn is something that I can't give you. That I don't see when I look at you. Because you have that look, that deer in the headlights, head over heels look in your eyes whenever you see him and when I realized you'd rejected him for a second time, I got angry. It was easy to push that anger at Aryn because he was throwing away an amazing thing and that he too is just as stubborn as you are. Then when I saw the same thing when I got here, I just lost it. As much as the idea of you with him and not with me hurts me, the thought of the two of you not being together kills my faith in love, in finding love, and finding my one and only. Despite the feelings I have for you, Caden, I know that while we could be good together, we're not right for each other and I'm okay with that. But I'll be dammed if I am going to let you push Aryn away like that." She takes a deep breath. "And I'll be damned if you let him slip through your fingers."

Her words slide over me like a dark black sludge. Once she's silent, and the sludge feeling abates, everything becomes clear to me.

The robin gave me the strength I needed to attempt letting Shelly go and moving on with my life and now Ashley gives me a two by four to the head about what I'd been missing all along.

"Conversation is over." My commanding voice is back. "Kneel, now," I order and her face falls but she complies. I walk over to her and place my hand in her hair and she leans into my touch. "Thank you, pet. For your honesty, for seeing what I've failed to see and more importantly, for making me see what it is that I've been missing all along."

"You're welcome, Sir." Her voice is a little lighter and a little less defiant. I like this side of her. She's never been big on the brat side of things, but this is definitely something that would be fun to explore with her. "Sir?"

"Yes?"

"Am I still going to be punished?"

"Yes," I tell her.

"Yes, Sir," she says quietly.

"Stay here, I will be back."

"Yes, Sir."

I pull my bag off the bed and leave the room, closing the door behind me. I head toward the dungeon where I find Teddy and Will sitting on one of the couches near the entrance and I go sit next to them. "Punishment is off," I tell Teddy who looks disappointed.

"Will, can you go over to the bar while I talk to Master Caden?"

"Yes, Daddy."

Will winks at me as he passes me on his way to the bar.

"That's not fair," Teddy says.

"It is. I'm punishing her enough without physically doing so."

"How so?"

"She has feelings for me. Her outburst was a direct connection to her being hurt by me, regardless of whether or not I knew her feelings. But I can't help asking, did you know about this?"

"No, absolutely not. Which is entirely my fault. I should have kept better tabs on it, talked to her about it," he says in a way that I know he's beating himself up internally and I don't need him to be doing that either.

"The point is, she was mad at me for not only hurting her, but also because she is seeing everything I'm not when it comes to Aryn and I cannot be mad at her for that. Ultimately, she understands that I don't reciprocate her feelings and she knows where my heart has wandered off to and she respects it. Though she'll accept it a little more once I get my head out of my ass. That's a direct quote by the way."

"I'll kill her."

I laugh, "No, don't. I gave her free reign on the conversation and once I knew the reason behind why she snapped yesterday, I put her back on her knees and told her I'd be back. When she asked if she was going to be punished, I told her she would be, so she is back there stewing on what's going to happen."

He snorts, "She was a mess before."

"I'm sure it's worse now. But at this point I'm incapable of punishing her for her honesty."

He nods his understanding of what I've said. "I'll leave her in there for a few more minutes, then collect her."

"Good," I say to Teddy.

"So, what are you going to do now?"

"Book a flight to Australia."

FORTY~SIX

~ ARYN *~*

I've managed to survive until Sydney. We're nearly done with Alyssa's premiere tour and all the press that accompanies it.

I've also managed to survive without Caden showing up or at the very least without getting the feeling that he's here and I have to admit that I'm a little disappointed.

Ashley got punished by Caden for something that happened and she wouldn't elaborate. I was disappointed she didn't spill the details of why. What she did tell me was that she wasn't exactly the model submissive and she deserved what she got. I wanted to press her for more, but when I tried, she shot me down. Why she told me in the first place is beyond me.

Regardless, Ashley and I haven't talked much. Whether she's respecting me until I return back to the States or whatever happened to us has done irreparable damage to our relationship is to be determined.

I've spent a lot of my free time with alcohol bottles in my hand. It's been the only way once the lonely nights set in that I can keep Caden out of my mind. When I'm not drinking away the memory of him, I can't help but think maybe he's right.

Maybe a D/s relationship with him is what I need because I cannot get him out of my mind. You would think if I truly had no desire to be with him that I would have been able to move on from it, but instead I find myself more agitated than I should be and above all, lonely.

Loneliness is a part of the job. It's also a part of who I've always been, but for some reason it's almost impossible to deal with it anymore.

I see relationships every day. I see men and women on the streets, at the premieres, and I've seen my fair share of two men together since going on this tour and while they've always been there, I've never paid them much attention before and now it seems like every time I turn around, another gay couple pops up in front of me. Each one twisting the ache in my chest a little more.

The saying goes, "absence makes the heart grow fonder" and in this case, it seems to be the truth.

I look at my phone and there isn't a text, a missed call, nothing from him and I wonder if I've missed my chance. Maybe his punishment of Ashley was a step in another direction for Caden. Maybe she texted me about the punishment to prove a point, to show me that Caden no longer wants me the way I thought he did.

Dex to Beck: When are you coming home?

Beck to Dex: We fly out in the morning. Be home around six or so. Once Alyssa is home, I'll be headed home.

Dex to Beck: We're going to Nashville, you don't need to go, just thought I would let you know.

Beck to Dex: When?

Dex to Beck: day after tomorrow.

Beck to Dex: I have no business there.

Dex to Beck: Why do you say that?

Beck to Dex: Because I'm pretty sure I'm no longer welcome at The Box.

Dex to Beck: Hardly. Did they revoke your membership?

Beck to Dex: Nope, but I'm pretty sure that I don't belong there.

Dex to Beck: This is hardly the conversation for texting.

I barely finish reading the text when my Skype lights up. Thank god for hotel Wi-Fi.

"Yeah," I say once his ugly-ass mug appears on my screen.

"What makes you think you're not welcome at the club or that you don't belong there?" Dex asks.

"It's a long ass story."

"It's what, ten in the morning there, I've got time. Talk," Dex says in a commanding tone and I scowl at the screen.

"I don't take orders from you."

"Who would you rather be taking orders from?"

"For the hundredth time, I'm not a damn sub," I snap.

"Hardly."

"Why the fuck does everyone keep saying that?"

"Because we all see what you're so unwilling to see. Listen to me. Just because you don't think that you are doesn't mean that you aren't. So what if you're a submissive, Beck. No one is going to judge you for that. No one, especially not me or Raine, is going to think any different about you because you decide to submit to someone. It's just a part of who you are."

"So what? Just because it may be a part of who I am doesn't mean I have to do it."

He leans toward the screen, putting his chin in his hand. "No one said you had to, but how can you shoot something down when you haven't got a clue what it means?"

"I can't let go like that."

"You've never tried," he counters.

"Maybe I don't want to," I tell him dismissively.

"Maybe you don't want to or maybe you don't want to submit to Caden?"

My eyes find his on the screen. "He doesn't want me."

"I wouldn't be so sure about that."

"Oh believe me, I have more information on that fact than you do," I tell him.

"Now you're going to have to explain yourself."

"No."

"Aryn, stop. Your defiance is getting you nowhere. How can you expect to work through all of this if you keep dismissing everything or you flat out refuse to talk to anyone about it?"

"There isn't anything to talk about, Dex. He had his chance and he walked out of the room," I tell him.

"Before or after you walked out on him?"

"How can you be so calm about this? About the fact that we are talking about me being with a man?"

"Because I don't give a shit who or what you're into. I won't think any less of you if you're with a man or a woman. You like who you like, love who you love. Aryn, I am not the person to judge you for that. Regardless of who it is, even if you submitted to a woman, I wouldn't give a shit. What I think you need to worry about more, is what it is you hope to gain out of a relationship."

"That's pointless because I honestly don't know. I thought I wanted Caden, but it is obvious he only wants a submissive, he doesn't want anything more than that," I explain.

"What is it that you want?"

"I don't know. I guess I didn't know I wanted to be with anyone until I met Caden at Derek's house. Ever since then I've been doing my damndest to fight that I am overly attracted to him. I want to be with him. So not only am I attempting to come to grips with the fact I want to be with a man, but I have to deal with the fact that I want to be with a man who doesn't want me in return. To top all of that off, he doesn't want to be with me as anything more than his submissive. Someone that he can control, someone that he can mold to his desires. And lastly, tie that to the fact that I went into this whole thing thinking I was a dominant and I've had it so eloquently pointed out to me that I am incapable of doing that. So rather than do that, or attempt to be a Top and fail at it, I'm just going to be me. If I can find someone that I can stand to be around longer than it takes to get off, then maybe I can find another one."

"I married the first one that I could stand longer than getting off," he tells me. He has a smile playing at his lips. "And let me tell you, I've never been happier than I am with her."

"But you have everything you could possibly want with her. The first person I actually managed to give my real number to is another submissive at the club and she bit my head off the last time I saw her. If I'm not the dominant type, how can I give her everything she needs?"

"What about Caden?"

"What about him? He doesn't want anything beyond a Dom/sub."

"And again, we're back at this? How do you know that's all he wants?" he asks.

"Because that is what he said to me, right before he put his clothes back on and walked out of my hotel room."

"You slept with him?" He can't hide the surprise, but he's not disappointed.

"No. We didn't make it that far." I don't add that up until that moment, everything between us that night was perfect. It was fun, it was full of banter and complete bliss. "He coerced me into giving up my phone number, but he's yet to use it since then."

"Maybe he's waiting for you to reach out to him," Dex counters.

"Maybe, but I know what he wants and I can't do that."

"Again, how do you know if you can or can't if you don't try. Look, do you want to be in the lifestyle?" I nod. "Do you want to learn about the lifestyle? Understand it, learn what it means to be a Dominant, learn about what it takes to be a good Top?"

"Yes," I say.

"Then what is stopping you from submitting to him? The only way you can learn, understand and have a complete wealth of knowledge in this lifestyle is to surrender yourself to someone else. Let them guide you and you may find that being on top isn't right for you. You may find out you prefer being on the bottom and there is nothing wrong with that. Hell, even Raine thought she wanted to be a Top and I think some of her bratty tendencies come from that desire within her, but it's also what keeps our relationship fun and it sure as shit keeps me on my toes when it comes to her. But in the midst of all that, she's found a happiness that she can't explain by submitting to me, by handing everything over to me. And that happiness did not come overnight. It took a long time for her to find it, but the bottom line, she was willing to try."

Dex's words hit me hard.

"You're right."

"Of course I am."

"Oh shut up," I grumble. "I gotta go. I'll see you tomorrow."

FORTY~SEVEN

"Ready?" I ask Alyssa and the security team as we approach the red carpet for our final premiere on this tour. Thank god, it's almost over.

"This should be short," Alyssa says. "We did most of the press stuff yesterday. What's here is just going to be photographers sans reporters."

I nod and Alyssa smiles at me. She's a nice girl and I have to admit that this trip has been less torturous than I'd expected it to be. She's young, but well rounded. Partying isn't at the top of her list.

"One more," I say to her and she nods before looking out the window.

"I will be so glad to get home," she groans. "This has been torture."

I smile, but not at anyone in particular. The limo moves again and Alyssa yawns.

All the time zone hopping is starting to take its toll on all of us, and I'm glad Alyssa doesn't want to go out tonight. I'm not sure any of the team would be up to it either. We stop again and Casey opens her door while I slide out the other one. Troy exits the front. The crowd is pumped, but smaller than anything we've had so far. Sydney is a pretty small market when compared to the other places we've been and I've wondered more than a few times why we're here. But that certainly wasn't my call.

Alyssa waves, smiles, waves some more and we move onto the aisleway. My eyes don't stop scanning our surroundings. It's a product of who I am, how I'm built and how I've been trained.

That familiar tingle returns, raising the hairs on the back of my neck and I start to scan the carpet looking for Caden. I don't see him but the next car arrives.

Because of the smaller venue, Alyssa and Travis are the only celebs here and that's all the crowd cares about.

Alyssa slows her pace for Travis to catch up to her and when he does, they pose together for the paparazzi and then the fans on the other side of the line.

That tingling feeling hasn't subsided but I don't see Caden anywhere. My defenses start to rise, worried that something is going to happen and my senses sharpen.

Alyssa moves away from Travis and finishes up her stint in the press line and enters the fan area. The area where attendees line up for entrance into the theater is where Alyssa will meet fans, sign autographs and take a few pictures. This is where things often get hairy, but at the same time, they're prescreened for weapons before being allowed in line so nothing too hairy.

Alyssa does her thing and I can't shake the bad feeling rising in my gut. I signal Casey. He immediately turns around and scans the crowd with me, looking for anything out of place. My heart starts pounding in my chest, but before I get too worked up, Alyssa backs away from the line and heads toward the doors of the theater.

Once inside, the feeling intensifies but there are not very many people in here so it's easier to scan. I recognize a few of the faces but they're people with the studio so I don't consider them a threat.

I stand back, watching the people milling about, and Travis's entourage enters the theater. Travis approaches Alyssa and they start heading toward the interview area where they're scheduled to be until the movie starts. Australia is doing things a little differently. They're having a press conference rather than individual interviews.

"Beck," Casey calls from behind me. "We're heading into interviews."

"You got this, right?"

"What you are you going to do?" he says into my earpiece.

"Check the theater, keep an eye on things out here."

"Yeah? Alright, we got this."

"Thanks, man."

Casey proceeds to follow Troy and Alyssa into the room where Alyssa will have her final interview while they fill the theater with the fans outside. Once it's full, she'll enter and yada, yada, yada.

The hair on the back of my neck stands on end again when I sense someone approaching, but I don't feel threatened. That's when someone comes to stand beside me. "You do realize that stalking is a very unfavorable characteristic," I grumble.

"How'd you know I was here?" he asks.

"The same way I always do and you have my number now, all you had to do was call, text, anything other than fly halfway across the globe."

"I'm here on business," he says as the doors close on the interview room and I turn to give Caden my attention.

"I hardly doubt that. There is hardly anyone here from the crew. Hell, the director isn't even here, so tell me, Caden, why exactly are you here?"

I lean toward him. "You have my cell phone number now, stalking is hardly necessary."

"I came for business," he counters.

I roll my eyes and he scowls at me. "A phone call or even a text message would have sufficed considering I haven't heard from you in over a week."

"It took me that long to figure a few things out," he tells me.

"So what, you figured you could just show up here, we'd talk and everything would go back to the way it was? I'm not wired that way."

"I came here because I had business to attend to. In fact, I've been here for a few days already. Regardless, I'm not entirely sure I owe you an explanation."

I give him a hard stare. "So why show up here?"

"Maybe I wanted to see you."

"I fly home tomorrow, that would have been a cheaper trip."

"Sure, if I knew where to find you once you got home."

"Again with the stalker behavior and again, a phone call or a text would have sufficed. Who knows, it may have given you the information you were seeking."

He snorts, "I doubt you'd give me your address."

"You never know, unless you ask."

"Fair enough," he says with confidence.

"We leave early tomorrow morning," I tell him.

"I know, so do I. Would you like to go out tonight, when you're done here?"

"Caden, I'm not sure that's a good idea. You've made yourself clear about what you want and when I can find it in myself to consider that offer, I will let you know what I decide. Going out just might screw with me a little more and frankly, I'm fucked up enough as it is. Now, before I lose my job, I need to get back to work."

~ CADEN *~*

Aryn's words give me hope that my trip here isn't in vain.

He walks away and I can't take my eyes off of him.

He's right, of course. I've asked him for something, asked him to be something, that I'm not even convinced he is. But he obviously has a better grasp on himself than I thought. I could have called, I could have texted, but I couldn't, I needed to see him. I needed to know that what I'm fighting myself for is really what I want.

When I saw him out on the carpet, I felt a twinge of regret for telling him that all I wanted was a submissive because seeing him again eradicates all I thought I wanted. All that I thought I needed. But I don't know how to do vanilla, I'm not capable of it, not after all this time.

I rub my hand over my chest as I remember Shelly. Her death led me to the lifestyle. I was looking for something fun and unattached. Something I could take care of without having the emotional attachment and until Aryn walked into Derek's and then into that club, I'd had it. I'd had everything I wanted. Now I realize that I need more, I want more and I will stop at nothing to get what it is that I need.

I grab my phone and press a button. "I'm ready," I say and hang up.

Looking at my phone, Aryn's words come over me. "You could have just texted or called."

I pull his number up and press the chat bubble and type out a message to him and press send before heading toward the door to leave.

~ **ARYN** *~*

My phone vibrates, and thinking that it's Casey or Troy, I reach for it as I stand guard at the front of the theater as the fans come in.

"Sometimes what we want was standing in front of us the whole time. Sometimes, what we need gets pushed away when it was unintentional."

I dart down the hallway, through the theater doors and into the lobby. My eyes scan the room frantically looking for him and when I don't see him, disappointment and dread wash over me. Then I look toward the glass of the side door and I see him walking toward a car that's just pulled up.

My heart pounds in my chest. A decision has to be made, right here, right now. Go after him or stay here.

I dart toward the door as I slip into that slow motion movie mode where no matter how fast I run, it seems to take forever before I'm pushing through the door.

"Are you telling me you're sorry?" I shout and he stops in his tracks.

After a few frantic heartbeats he turns toward me. "I'm telling you that what I want has been staring back at me and I refused to see it until now. That what I need, needs to make up his mind about what he needs and that I'm willing to wait until he does." His lips spread into a smile and I walk toward him.

When I'm standing in front of him, there is only softness in his eyes, no dominance, no Master, just Caden. "I know what I want," I breathe. "But I need some time to figure out what I need."

He brings his hand up to cup my cheek and on instinct, I lean into it and he smiles again. "I have time, my sweet boy."

I smile and press his hand to my cheek before kissing his palm. "Thank you," I tell him and he takes his hand back and climbs into the town car that's waiting for him.

Watching the car drive away is my undoing.

As the car turns out of sight I know that giving Caden what he wants is far less painful than watching him walk away from me again.

FORTY~EIGHT

"What's the deal with you and that dude?" Casey asks me as we leave Alyssa's house in Los Angeles the next day.

"What guy?"

"You're an idiot. That guy, he was in Nashville and then he shows up in Australia and you get all dopey. Are you gay?"

"Would it matter if I was?" I ask.

"No, except you're as much of a womanizer as Dex is and unless you have some shit fucked up in your head like Calvin does, I don't picture you suddenly turning gay."

"What's wrong with Calvin's head?"

Casey rolls his eyes. "You focus on that?" I shrug. "Nothing."

I scowl at him but I don't press him for more information. He won't tell me. He lives with Calvin and Eric so I can only imagine the shit he knows, but he won't tell me anything. If it was important for me to know, I'd have heard already.

"You going home?" Casey asks me.

"No, I have to swing by Dex's place, then I'll be heading home."

Casey nods. "Thanks, man."

"For what?"

"Letting me tag along on this trip. I had fun."

I smile. "You're welcome. You did great, Troy too."

"Thanks, bro." I shake Casey's hand. "See you later?"

"I'll be here." I smile and we both climb into our cars. He backs out and takes off before I do and I follow him out, turning left instead of right as I head toward Dex's house.

I ring the doorbell twice before Raine finally comes to the door.

"Well, hello you. Welcome home."

I look her over. She's dressed in a robe with bare feet. "Am I interrupting anything?" I smirk.

She laughs, "No, come on in." She holds the door open for me and I step up the three steps into the living room to find Dex sitting on the couch. He's paused something on the TV and I notice a cushion on the floor at his feet. I don't think much of it.

"What going on, man?" Dex gets up and shakes my hand while Raine goes to kneel on the cushion.

"Uh, not much. Just tired."

"No doubt, want a beer?" he asks.

"Love one."

Dex turns to Raine who hops up without hesitation and a smile on her face as she goes into the kitchen. "I should have called first," I tell him.

"We have no secrets with you. Though she'll keep the robe on," he laughs. "Come, sit down."

"I'm not staying long. I just came by to say hi." Raine hands me a beer and then hands one to Dex.

"Thanks, pet," he says and she beams with pride before returning to her cushion. Dex gestures toward the other couch and I take a seat as I take a long swig of the beer in my hand.

"When are you guys leaving for Nashville?"

"In the morning, flight's at eleven. Why?"

"How are you flying?"

"We chartered a plane. Didn't want to do the whole commercial thing. Why?"

"Got room for one more?"

"Absolutely," he says with enthusiasm. "What's made you change your mind?"

"I got a visit from someone in Australia," I say cryptically.

"He flew all the way to Australia?" Raine chimes in and I chuckle.

"Yeah, he went to New York too, though I didn't know it at the time. He showed up in Nashville, for obvious reasons."

"How'd he know how to find you?" Dex asks me. "Those trips are kept under lock and key."

"It's pretty simple when you hold one of the keys."

Dex's eyes go wide briefly so I explain, "In the interest of anonymity, let's just say I've figured out where his money comes from."

"Hollywood?" he asks and I just raise an eyebrow as I take another sip of my beer. "Didn't see that coming. But I guess I shouldn't be surprised. He never seems to be working. So I can see why that would make sense. Derek is always working."

"Speaking of which, I'll handle my own accommodations in Nashville, just need to get there."

"Why not stay at Derek's?"

I smirk. "Because he gossips worse than an old lady. I don't need Caden knowing I'm in town."

Dex shakes his head. "I don't understand what's going on between the two of you, but secrecy is never a good thing."

"Not much will be a secret much longer."

"Oh?" Raine perks up from her perch next to Dex.

I launch into full detail of my plan and when I'm done, Raine is bouncing up and down with excitement. With my plan in place, I leave them to go home.

Once home, I send a text.

Beck to Ash: Just got home, I need your help with something.

Ash to Beck: you name it.

Beck to Ash: This stays between us, you cannot tell Caden.
Ash to Beck: I'm all ears.

I only tell her what I need her to do. She is my best bet at getting Caden to where I need him to be without involving Derek. Derek would do it, but I'd have to explain everything to him and I don't trust him to not tell Caden, or anyone else at the club for that matter.

Ashley's instructions are simple but I don't offer her much explanation and while she presses me for details, I refuse to tell her by letting her know that when it's done, I'll tell her everything.

FORTY~NINE

~ CADEN *~*

Ash to Caden: Are you coming to the club Saturday?

Caden to Ash: I hadn't planned on it.

Ash to Caden: I haven't had a chance to see you since that night, I'd like to talk, to apologize to you.

Caden to Ash: No need to do it at the club.

Ash to Caden: Actually, Teddy told me I had to do it in person.

Caden to Ash: I'll talk to him.

Ash to Caden: No, it's alright. I really would just like to apologize.

Caden to Ash: Are you working the door?

Ash to Caden: No, we have that new girl. Um, I'm wondering if…if you'd scene with me?

I stare at my phone. After everything she told me, she still wants to scene with me? I find it odd. Who's the bigger glutton for punishment, her or me?

Derek to Caden: Coming to town Friday. Dinner Friday night?

Convenient.

Caden to Derek: Sure, what time? Where?
Derek to Caden: The house, around seven, but come whenever.
Caden to Derek: Sounds good, you guys going to the club after?
Derek to Caden: No, Saturday night though. Dex and Raine are coming to town.

Those two names perk up my attention because with Dex comes Aryn.

Caden to Derek: Aryn coming?
Derek to Caden: No man, sorry. He just got back from his premiere tour. Dex said he'd come along next time.

I frown at my phone. My brief ounce of hope shatters. I guess I really had no right to think that he'd come along. I didn't know Derek was coming to town and now Ashley's questions about the club and scening with her are a little more intriguing.

Caden to Ash: I'll think about the scene, but I'll come to the club.
Ash to Caden: Good and okay. I'll come prepared.

I arrive at Derek and Cotah's just a few minutes after six. One of Derek's staff lets me in and I head for the living room.

When I step into the living room, Dex, Cotah, Raine and Derek are talking and having drinks. The girls are at their mens' feet and a twinge of disappointment rocks through me. I'd secretly hoped that Aryn would change his mind and come, though I had no right to think of him sitting at my feet.

We exchange pleasantries and Cotah runs off to get me a drink.

The conversation flows easily. Eventually Derek asks me about business.

"What do you do?" Dex asks me and I look from him to Derek and back to him.

"Aryn didn't tell you?" I cock my head.

Dex's eye meet mine. "No, why would he?"

I shrug and take a drink. "I work in Hollywood. I'm a producer and when I'm not producing, I'm a stunt coordinator."

"Wow, no kidding?" Raine says with enthusiasm.

"Raine," Dex admonishes her.

I smile. "It's alright. It can be pretty cool, but it's also a lot of work. Do you work?" I ask her.

She looks to Dex for approval and I admire her for it. He nods. "I do," she says.

"And what do you do?" I ask her.

She lights up. "I'm a PR Rep, I work for Bold and I'm the assistant to 69 Bottles' rep, Addison."

"I take it you love your job?" I chuckle.

"Absolutely. Considering that a year ago I was an executive assistant to the company's owner."

"Cami," Derek says. "She works for Bold."

I snort. "Is there anyone in this room who doesn't have something to do with Bold?"

Cotah sheepishly raises her hand.

"Well, Derek does, so indirectly so do you." I laugh a little.

"That's true," Cotah says.

Our conversation is halted further when dinner is announced. The girls rush ahead, which doesn't surprise me, and Derek heads to his office for something. I grab Dex by the arm. "Is there a reason Aryn didn't come with you guys?"

"He was tired. He'd been home barely twelve hours before we took off. He needed time to do laundry and things like that. Why?"

I nod and give him a small smile. "I was just hoping that he'd be here."

"Maybe you should try calling him," Dex says. "Talk to him."

"I told him that I would give him space."

He gives me a sad smile. "Aryn's complicated, but he'll come around. If you don't want to call him, at least text him, let him know you're thinking about him or something. Let him know you're there for him. That's what he needs more than anything right now."

I nod and follow Dex into the dining room. He gives me a knowing smile before taking his seat. The subject isn't broached anymore and while I'm thankful for what he said to me, it doesn't ease the loneliness I feel at the dinner table.

Seeing the two couple so happy makes me feel like a fifth wheel.

I do my best to ignore it. Aryn not being here and this loneliness is making me feel uncomfortable and weak. I don't pine over people, it's not who I am. In fact, it's stupid of me.

Everything that I've done since Aryn walked out of my private room at the club is uncharacteristic of me. Yes, I always get what I want, but running around the world is insane.

I do my best not to let my downward spiral effect the rest of the night.

It's around one when I leave Derek's, but it's only ten in Los Angeles.

Caden to Aryn: Just wanted to tell you, I wish you were here.

I don't get a response and I'm disappointed.

FIFTY

~ ARYN *~*

Caden to Aryn: Just wanted to tell you, I wish you were here.

"I am here," I say for the thousandth time since this morning when I look at my phone again.

The later in the day it gets, the harder it is to sit still. I've been pacing back and forth in my room for so long I'm going to wear out the carpet.

I've never been good with sitting idle but it's all I can do right now. I've already eaten, but if I have to stay in this room any longer I'm going to crack into the mini bar and that won't do anyone any good.

I came out here for a reason. It's time to get what I want, even if I go insane in the process.

Dex to Beck: We're on our way.

"Thank god." One text down, which means it's time for me to get moving.

I grab my jacket and my keys. I'd called for my car about an hour ago, I wanted it to be ready when Dex's text came through. I step out of my room and let the door close behind me as I walk toward the elevator.

I can't stop pacing while I wait for the elevator. I check my phone, you know, in case I didn't hear it in the absolute silence of my hotel room and of course, nothing.

The elevator chimes and it makes me jump, but when the doors open, I step inside, press the ground floor button and descend to my car and what comes next.

~ CADEN *~*

"Good evening, Master Caden."

"Good evening, Cali," I tell Ashley's replacement at the podium, though I find it odd that Teddy is standing behind her. He's usually only here when Will or Ashley have the podium, but we grab each other's wrists and hug anyway.

"You and Ashley playing tonight?"

I lift my shoulder, adjusting the bag hanging from it. "She asked."

"Since when do you let anyone top from the bottom?" Teddy counters.

I snort. "I don't, but I guess I kind of feel like I owe it to her after I left her that night. But I haven't promised her anything either."

"Good," Teddy says with confidence.

I just smirk and shake my head. "Is she here yet?" I ask.

"No, should she be?"

Huh, that's odd. She's almost always here early. "Well, okay then. I guess I'll see you inside?"

"Absolutely," he says.

I get the impression that he's up to something and not seeing Will with him only raises my suspicions.

I step through the curtain into the main room of the club and spot several people I know, though not many I want to talk to, at least not right now. I spot poor Will, blindfolded and cuffed to the bar. I smile and shake my head. That boy certainly knows how to push buttons with Teddy and it makes him happy.

When the two of them hooked up inside the club I had my doubts. Only because Teddy is three times the size of Will, and they seemed to make such an odd couple. There is something in their dynamic that works well for both of them and I can't knock that.

Ever since the first time I met Teddy back in high school, I knew he was gay, but I never imagined this side of him. He's the one who introduced me to the lifestyle and got me hooked on it. I guess I have him to thank. When Shelly died, I was so lost, so confused, and unsure of myself. He brought me here under the pretense of letting it all go. And I had to agree with him. I truly believed being a submissive was who I was but as time went on, I found strength in my submission and wanted to turn the tables. Granted my submission only lasted for a few months, but it was enough to teach me more, and more than anything, it was enough for me to realize that being on Top was where I belonged.

Being a submissive also gave me more confidence in myself. It pushed limits I didn't know I had, which was what it was supposed to do. Finding that confidence gave me what I needed to succeed in Hollywood. Sure, I was already there, just not the aggressive type when it came to getting what I wanted. I learned that sometimes you have to stand up for what you believe in, in order to get what you want.

That was the start of my career and the life I've lived since then. I wouldn't trade it for the world.

I finally manage to break my train of thought and I head toward my private room to drop off my bag. No sense in setting up anything because I'm quickly losing the desire to play with

Ash tonight. Being here, seeing Will tied to the bar, reminds me of Aryn and my desire for him grows that much more.

When I emerge from my private room, Derek, Cotah, Dex and Raine are standing around chatting with their backs to me at the bar. I can't see who they're talking to so I step around them to find Ashley.

"Good evening, Sir." She lowers her eyes as she acknowledges me.

"Good evening, Ash, Raine and Cotah."

The girls acknowledge me with small smiles.

"What's the plan tonight?" I ask Derek.

"Girls, why don't you go grab us some drinks?" Derek says to Cotah and Raine.

The three girls acknowledge us with our respective titles and go toward the bar together.

"We'd planned on working on Raine tonight," Dex says. "She's curious about the single tail and I'm not proficient enough."

I shiver. "One of my personal favorites. Let me know if you need some help," I tell Dex and Derek. Though Derek is pretty good with it himself, he learned a lot of what he knows from me.

"I think we'll be alright, but I'm glad you're here. Are you and Ash playing tonight?" Derek asks me.

"I haven't decided. I'm not sure I feel comfortable with it," I tell him and he gives me a puzzled look, wanting me to explain further. "We can talk about it another time."

"Does it have anything to do with Aryn?" Derek asks me and his question and Aryn's name brings my eyes to his quicker than I'd wanted them to.

"Yeah, I think it does. I'm not sure what it is exactly. It just doesn't feel right."

"Does Ash know that?" Dex asks me.

I shrug. "I'm not entirely sure. I haven't said much to her about it, but you also need to remember that Ash and I are strictly play partners. It doesn't go beyond that."

"Are you sure she knows that?" Derek counters.

I shake my head, unsure. "Except she's all but castrated me in regards to Aryn. The fact that she asked me here tonight surprises me."

"What do you mean?" Derek asks.

"It was right after Aryn was in town with his client. She'd come to the club but she was full of attitude and when I went to punish her about it, I gave her carte blanche to spill what her problem was and when she did she woke me up to some things I wasn't capable of seeing for myself. It put me on edge with her and her intentions."

"She fell in love with you?" Dex asks.

"I assume that's what she was getting at, I didn't see it. I made my intentions clear to her before we started playing. I'd agreed to help Teddy with her training. There is only so much a gay man can do for her and she doesn't have a Top, but that was more than six months ago and she's the only one I scene with regularly, but only ever at the club. So when she spelled out what was bothering her, it all started to make sense."

We fall silent when the girls return with our drinks. Ash hands me a bottle of water and I take a long pull on it when Teddy approaches us.

"I see your boy is in trouble again," Derek says to him.

Teddy rolls his eyes and shakes his head. "That mouth of his is gonna get his ass lit up tonight."

I snort. "And you're going to love every minute of it."

"Damn straight." He smiles wide.

"Ash, will you take Cotah and retrieve my boy from the bar and bring him to me?"

"Master, may I help?" Raine asks Dex.

"Is this really a three girl project?" I counter.

"No, Sir," Raine says to me sheepishly.

"I don't mind," Teddy says with a strange smirk. "He won't know what to think."

"Can I, Master?" Raine asks Dex again.

"You may," he tells her with a smile and the three women head back to the bar for Will.

"I've never seen a bond like the three of them have with Will." Teddy says. "He's always in trouble and they always want to rescue him."

We laugh at Teddy who watches the girls as they uncuff Will from the bar and take off his blindfold.

"Sir?"

My heart freezes in my chest before picking up in double time and I see Dex's lips twitch into a smile and Derek's eyes widen. My eyes roll over to Teddy who has a Cheshire grin on his face.

The voice is familiar, and it makes my heart skip beats and steals my breath away. I'm scared to hope over what this means.

Finally my brain and muscles get in sync with each other and I turn around.

FIFTY~ONE

** CADEN **

I hiss through my teeth when I come face to face with Aryn. His eyes meet mine momentarily before he lowers his head.

I'm disappointed that he's cut off my view of his eyes and my chance to read him. His downward glance gives me a chance to look over what he's wearing, or not wearing as the case may be.

He's shirtless. His muscles are defined but soft and not at all tense. His arms are clasped behind his back, his legs are clad in tight leather pants and then I spot his feet. He's barefoot. It's usually only the submissives who go barefoot in the club.

"What are you doing here?" I breathe.

He lowers himself to the floor. First to one knee, then both and he bends so that he is sitting back on his feet and I can no longer breathe.

Seeing Aryn, on his knees, his head lowered, contrite and defeated, sends my blood racing through my ears. I manage to make my legs work and I lower myself. I crouch so I can hear his answers over the noise of the dungeon.

"Answer me, boy. What are you doing here?"

"I've come to you, Sir. To offer myself to you. To give you my mind and my body to cherish. I've come to surrender to you, Sir. To give you what you seek. A submissive at your feet, a lover for your bed. I cannot promise I will be any good at this, Sir, but I will do everything in my power to listen, to learn and to be everything you wish me to be while I am everything I want to be. To please you, to serve you and be cherished by you, my Sir."

My heart is pounding in my chest. My lungs fight for air.

I bring my hand up to his chin and lift his face. I need to see his eyes, to see he means this. That this is really what he wants.

"Are you sure, my dear sweet boy?"

"I've never been more sure of anything in my life, Sir."

When I met this man, I knew there was something special about him, something that I had to have, but I never realized that he would need me as much as I need him.

"I prefer to be called Master," I tell him.

"Yes, Master."

My heart swells with pride and I realize the dungeon has fallen silent around us.

"I promise to nurture you, to cherish you, to train you and to push you to reach your goals. I promise to protect you and to honor you both as my submissive and as my lover."

I can see the emotion welling in Aryn's eyes, but it's not out of fear. It's out of desire. Aryn's desire for me and my devotion to him.

"Stand, my sweet boy. I want you to stand for me now," I order and he complies, rising to his knees and finally his feet. With my hand still on his chin, I slide it around to cup his cheek.

He settles into my palm, the pain of his past reflects in his eyes as he closes them, savoring my touch. With my free hand, I cup his other cheek and pull him toward me.

"I've waited for you for a long time," I breathe as I press my lips against his. Our tongues slide along each other and I know I've found my home. My submissive, my sweet boy. Now to train him, command him and keep him.

COMING SOON

Caden's Command: Finding Submission #2 - A Bold Security Novel!!

Make sure to follow Zoey on Facebook for all the latest information regarding this upcoming release, including Pre-Order!

Releasing Early Spring 2016!!